I0544866

FORKY'S HOUSE

BY PETER MARK MAY

Peter stood in the doorway watching as Tracey crept closer to the red screen in the corner, like she had heard something behind it, that he had not. His boots hesitated at the threshold of the red room, only half an inch away from the thin red carpet. He did not know why his whole body told him not to go inside. Perhaps coming from a small village in Poland he was more superstitious than the city-living woman. Then it suddenly dawned on him, like a double slap on each cheek of his face, how could the red room be so well lit?

The corridors and stairs coming down had been pitch black, and they needed light to see. The red room was clear and well lit. His eyes flicked to the candles on the table, all three burning brightly like the red had picked up on his thoughts and projected an explanation. Yet even with those, and the lit ones on the desk, the room should not be so bright. There were no electric lights on the ceilings or walls.

And if the candles were lit, who had lit them?

His eyes opened wide as Tracey moved closer to the red screen, her painted nails reaching out to pull it aside.

No, there must be someone inside the room.

Peter ran into the room, hearing the strange mutterings as he raced forwards to get his body between the estate agent and the screen. He managed to shove her back roughly against the other door, but his failing right arm knocked the red screen over, sliding painfully down his right side and leg to the floor.

Something cowering in the shadows leapt up at him to bite hard with grinding teeth, down on his right wrist.

This book is dedicated to Rachelle Bronson

CHAPTER ONE

The house was unexpected.

It sat slap bang in the middle of one of the busiest, most cosmopolitan cities in the world, and hardly anyone noticed it was there. One of London's central hub roads flowed past its' boundaries like a shoal of steely fish in a swollen river. Walls of dull-yellow, old brick, overhung by a dense double line of veteran sycamore trees kept it hidden from the prying eyes of the modern world. Google maps just passed it by, recording only the twelve-foot-high walls and the lines of trees that cast shadows, even on the sunniest of summer days.

A cemetery guarded the western and northern sides. The gate in the west wall had been bricked up since before the Second World War, and the cemetery wall extended by the local council to keep unwanted visitors out. The house sat at the corner of a crossroad of two extremely busy bus routes, so had no neighbours on its southern and eastern sides, only cold pavement and hot tarmac. Yet the house had been largely empty since the turn of the twentieth century. No families stayed there long. Tramps, squatters, burglars and idle youths had found their way into the overgrown gardens from time to time, but none had stayed around, except those who stayed forever.

The ownership of the house had passed down through the two hundred and sixty years since it was built, remaining in a family of wealth and tradition. None ever took a fancy to its strange design or morbid interiors. It had been an albatross around each generation's neck. No decorating or trimming of the trees was allowed, as set down in the covenant of its builder, whose bones had long since turned to dust. Yet a vast sum of one hundred thousand pounds had been set aside in a legally watertight bequeathment to the family. It could never be sold, or leave the family's ownership, only rented or leased for a period or no more than twelve months at a time.

So it remained, dark and brooding, hidden in plain view, waiting.

Yet it had temporary residents from time to time over the years. The house seemed to attract the imaginative, darkly talented, or the sorrowful, twisted men and woman the creative arts seemed to attract. Poets wrote soulful laments there about loves lost and childhood angst. It was rumoured that Byron himself had rented the house for a month, yet no records show of such a stay. Artists, painters, sculptors of the surreal, all loved the quirky awkwardness of its layout. Paintings of the house were images of greys and dark greens, with morbid umbra tones that never cast the house in a sunny light.

Actors, socialites, and men with minds of dark design, found it a safe abode but never outstayed their welcome. The house let very little light in, and the darkness in the hearts that resided there stayed festering under the enveloping canopy of the trees, surrounding it with a claustrophobic embrace.

The house was well tendered by contractors, kept up to date with the ever changing needs of the modern world. Gas had followed candles, then cables of electricity, and much later still central heating. All were in keeping with the decor, yet did little to warm the house, that seemed to bask in its own shadows.

Even though its own bank account kept the house in good order, no one had lived there since the sixties. A rock-and-roll guitarist/singer called Billy Ryan was the last. He somehow died in the fountain by the front doors with half a kilo of industrial cleaner sniffed up his right nostril, and a plastic daffodil sticking out from his trouser-less backside.

The house was known locally as the *Haunted House* by everyone under the age of fifty. For older residents, who remembered more of its sordid past, it brought up hushed whispers in the local pubs and the crossing of bosoms by more religious spinsters of the parish. They gave it another name. During the war, it had been turned into a small military hospital to take some of the many wounded, as an overflow to a Doodlebug hit local hospital. It was there in 1942 a French Doctor Pierre Forque, one night in a shell-shock bout of madness– due to the constant local bombings–took his surgeon's knife and slit the throats of fifteen patients while they slept in their beds, before an alert orderly wrestled him to the ground. Lying overpowered on the blood covered ward floor, he screamed *blue-murder* until he ruptured a lung, dying of internal bleeding half n' hour later. In an action so morbidly droll, with a curious twist of irony and fate, its original name was lost to living memory.

After that, it was simply referred to, erroneously, as *Forky's House*.

CHAPTER TWO

Tracey Sunderland wasn't a happy woman.

She had been with Sims, Maynard, and Lee, Estate Agents to the area, for over five years, and had worked herself up to being one of the best sellers in the business. That was until her boss Richard Lee had dumped *Forky's House* on her desk the day before, telling her to go find some clients to rent or lease the place.

Normally Tracey would be up for any challenge her bosses threw at her. But this one was the poisoned chalice of *no hope in hell* of getting a client for the haunted house. She wasn't happy having to park nearly three streets away from the red route front of the building. The house, in her mind, should be torn down and turned into luxury flats, *now those she could sell like hotcakes.*

She looked up at the mainly blue sky and could still see half the moon visible in the daytime. It always seemed an odd thing to see the moon when it wasn't night-time, but it wasn't a rarity at all.

Tracey's high-heeled shoes were not used to pounding the pavements of this part of London. She winced as her heels pinched her, knowing she would have two blisters before the day was out. She was a natural blonde, and forty-six, but had the body of a woman half her age. She could still slip into her tight blouses and skirts from a decade back if so required. She loved her job, the money it brought in, and her two hundred pairs of shoes back at home, where she lived with her cat Tom-Tom. She was ten years divorced, but happy about it. Her red-soled *Christian Louboutin* and her *Jimmy Choos* brought her more pleasure than her ex-husband ever had.

Her red soled shoes skipped over the road she'd just crossed to reach the busy crossroads. Two lanes of traffic rattled past in both directions, hundreds of cars in an hour, thousands during a busy working day. She could see the figure of Peter Podolski the Polish caretaker, waiting in his blue jean boiler suit by the entrance to the house. He was staring across the busy crossroads towards the tube station. Tracey followed his eye line. She snorted, seeing he was eyeing up a group of giggling schoolgirls, with mere belts for skirts. In her day, at the all-girls school she'd attended, you had to wear a proper uniform, with unflattering navy blue knickers for PE. The most daring thing she and her classmates got up to uniform-wise was to have their ties tied high, about three inches in length.

The schoolgirls turned to go inside a glass fronted fast food shop across the road. Peter turned then, seeing Tracey huffing and puffing her way up the sunlit pavement towards her. He smiled without showing any teeth, then, seeing the business face she had on, began to unlock the sturdy high gates, which were the only entrance to the house.

"They really think you can get anyone to rent this place?" Peter had to lean into the tall wooden gate, before shoulder barging it three times to make it judder inwards enough for them to enter.

"That's not really your concern is it," Tracey said, pushing past the tall man, as he held the gate open for her.

"I suppose not." He shrugged his thin set of shoulders. "I *only* keep the place running. If new tenants are found, I would have to increase my hours here to make the place...*liveable?*"

"I'm sure *when* I find a new tenant, you will be plenty busy enough getting the place habitable again." Tracey stepped over a fallen branch from the trees that crowded around the old house, like kids huddling around a fight in the playground. Even though it was a sunny spring morning, the cobbled drive and grounds seemed festooned with old brown leaves, shed the autumn before. They were brittle, cracking into many pieces underfoot as she strode down the drive.

With purpose in her short, but shapely legs, she walked past the fountain where the rock star had died. It was half covered in ivy, trailing down from a sycamore tree that had rooted on the very edge of the cobbled drive over thirty years ago. She pulled a notepad from her large brown leather bag to make sure clearing the ivy away from the fountain was top of Peter's to-do list.

She scribbled as she walked around to the front entrance steps. Her thin left heel caught in the cobbles for a second, causing her ankle and leg to wobble. She recovered quickly, hurrying even quicker towards the large front double doors. She glanced back at the Polish handyman, but if he'd seen her near stumble, his face showed no signs.

Tracey delved even deeper into her *Hermes* bag to fish out the *Yale* and *Chubb* keys to open the door. Peter had fitted the new locks three years ago after some teens thought the house might make a great place for an illegal rave. The police caught them fleeing the place just after midnight, yet it wasn't the Met Police that had unnerved them. There had been an argument between two girls over a boy. One girl had run off into the warren-like house, trying doors at random, just to find a solitary place to cry her eyes out. After an hour, three of her friends went to look for her. They found her eventually–well her head at least, where it sat in a lake of her blood, her body nowhere to be seen.

The police, directed by the frightened ravers, searched the house from top to bottom but could find no trace of the girl, or even a single drop of blood anywhere else. When the girl did not return home, they searched the house a week later. Then once again a month after that, but they found nothing on both occasions. That did little to get the place leased out either.

Chubb first, then *Yale*, the thick heavy oak doors to the house were finally open. Tracey shoved at the right-hand side of the double doors, her palms on the rough weather beaten wood.

"Ow, shit," she swore, pulling her right hand back to reveal a two-inch long splinter sticking out from the fleshy pad under her thumb. Tracey stepped back to grab the splinter between the nails of her left thumb and forefinger, to draw it out with a long hiss through her teeth.

"Here, let me," Peter said, rushing up the steps to push the four-inch thick door inwards for her.

Tracey sucked at her injured palm, nodded her thanks and then followed him inside.

The main entrance hall was always a surprise to her, as she could never clearly recall its decor or dimensions. The black-and-white Italian marble tiled floor gave an almost exotic feel to the vast entrance space. It was the most unusual of the very strange and oddly shaped rooms in the house because it was the best lit by natural light. A green stained glass ceiling, twinned with two huge, thirty foot high frosted windows on each side of the double front doors, lent an almost greenhouse feel to the place. It was like the designer had built the house the wrong way around, and some late redesign by the owner had put the front of the house facing southwards. It also gave the house a north facing garden, which all gardeners know is the least desired aspect.

Tracey always felt if she was still on the exterior of the house somehow here, and always expected it to be strewn with brown crisp curled leaves. It had a definite outside feel to her, like some Victorian Folly that should be in the rear garden. It would at least explain the cold breezes that swept around the vast entrance hallway on regular occurrences, even on still airless days. Her surprise at the hallway was always countered by the sight of the grand staircase, that swept up to the first floor of the house, like a can-can girl teasing with her delights of more wondrous sights to come. The original carpet had long since been worn threadbare from the hundreds of feet that had walked upon it, and years of insects chewing on it. In the sixties the rock star had replaced it with a Persian type design, that gave alternate steps a differing colour of red with gold weave, to gold with red weave. It also gave the staircase a sophisticated appearance that drew the eye upwards. The childhood fairy princess in her wanted to rush up those steps, holding bundles of her crinoline dress in each hand, into the arms of a tall, dark, handsome gentleman.

"So where do you want to start?" asked Peter from directly behind her. All the Polish caretaker saw was a *bloody* great hall that was a *bugger* to keep clean.

Tracey shook her blonde hair, coming back to herself. She had nearly forgotten the caretaker was still in the hall with her. "Let's start with the big rooms first, they are the ones that will sell the house to a new tenant."

Tracey made for the set of double doors to her far right, her heels clicking on the floor like pistol cracks. Peter pushed himself off the front door he was slouching on, wondering what the attractive, stern estate agent lady looked like naked. His trainers made little sound on the hallway floor. Tracey threw open the ballroom doors and entered, looking even tinier in the mass empty space. Peter sloped after her. His back seemed in a constant state of slouch, as he wondered how long this would all take. He was dying for his next cigarette.

Tracey was thorough, even though she wasn't happy with the caretaker following her around the whole time ogling her backside as she walked.

Upstairs, downstairs, the cellar, kitchens, and parlour they went looking for damp, mould, and who knew what else. Peter was literally gasping for a cigarette, and his easy-going patience was running thin. He'd started to mutter at every door they came to, and in each room, they examined until Tracey pulled him up on it. At last, they were on the home stretch, as they entered the music room via its east door.

It was a room decorated with friezes of Victorians playing oboes, cellos, violins and harps. All had kept their colour as the room had no windows, so no access to natural light. The ceiling and architraves were stained yellow with smoke from before the house converted to gas. The place had never really been decorated, as any musicians had used the acoustically superior ballroom to play their instruments. The place was dusty, which gave a clogging sound to the voice of anyone who sang in it. As a music room, it was not fit for purpose.

A grey, once white, sheet covered the only thing in the room, a black grand piano. Tracey didn't care for this dingy room at all, but turned on the brass light switch by the door anyway. She swaggered across the room, her nostrils immediately sniffling and reacting to the dust-filled atmosphere. She walked over to the piano, just to annoy the caretaker, who she knew smoked like a chimney. It was the only pleasure of the last half n' hour, and she would be glad to get out of the stark, deserted mausoleum of a house. She was sure it had been a spectacular sight back in its days of grandeur, but she wasn't sure how many hundreds of years ago that might have been. It would take a great many people in garish ball costumes, and a lot of light and music, to make this place seem alive.

She turned on her heel, facing the caretaker, who was leaning against the doorframe, and wasn't pretending to hide his boredom. She decided she would be as dour mouthed as he if she had to spend any amount of time on a regular basis in this house. She was halfway back to the doorway when she heard a click, followed by something hard falling a short distance.

She turned to find the source of the sound. Peter stood up straight, entering the room to follow her gaze to a curved alcove just around the open door. In the sky blue painted alcove sat a chubby, naked cherub, playing a horn or it might have been a pipe. When she had entered the room, giving his tiny bloated penis a cursory glance, both marble hands had been up holding the horn, which he played from carved, white lips. The right arm now hung down by its side, like it was an old, loose-limbed doll, and not a carved marble statuette.

Tracey and the caretaker closed in on the cherub in his alcove from different sides. Peter was on the side of the fallen arm, so hesitantly grabbed it at the wrist to return it to its former position. He was surprised when it clicked back into place. A louder click then came from somewhere behind the alcove. They were both amazed when the alcove, and the pedestal it sat on, moved out three inches from the surrounding wall to reveal a black crack of darkness behind it.

"*Co kurwa, do kurwy nędzy,*" Peter swore in his native tongue as a breeze blew through the gap behind the alcove.

"It's a secret door," Tracey said, her interest suddenly piqued by a new and intriguing part of the house. *Who knows it might even help sell the place to a client having secret passages and rooms.*

"I've never noticed this before, but it is a big old house—probably contains years of secrets," Peter said, moving closer to the dark gap in the secret door to peer inside. He could see nothing in the strip of darkness except a thick, sticky web patchwork. Surely the work of a thousand spiders over many generations.

Peter unclipped a small Maglite that was attached to a key ring that dangled down from a back-belt loop in the rear of his old work jeans. Turning it on he passed the beam up and down the length of the crack. He could only see the edge of a hidden wood-panelled passageway beyond.

Meanwhile, Tracey was mentally hopping from one foot to the other, desperate to know what lay beyond the secret door. She had a sudden rush of childhood excitement, remembering the books she used to love back then: *The Secret Garden* and *The Lion, The Witch and the Wardrobe*. She felt an almost sexual throbbing of anticipation between her legs, the thrill of something out of the norm happening to her lonely, monotonous life.

She could almost see her late father in her mind's eye, sitting on the edge of her bed, reading her bedtime stories. It was something they had shared and enjoyed before her mother cheated on her father, and he had left them. No more bedtime stories for his one and only princess, then nothing for months until his suicide. Other *uncles* and pseudo fathers had come and gone after that, but no one like her gentle, loving father. Tracey had moved out at sixteen, the day after her second stepfather tried to touch her up in the shower. She took her clothes, jewellery, and the cherished books her father had read to her. She still had them in almost pristine condition today.

"Come on then–there's a passage inside."

The Polish caretaker's words shook her from the childhood memories that had defined most of her adult life and her relationships. She moved to the wall, as Peter leaned into the door and shoved it wide open, getting a good many cobwebs on his shoulder for his efforts. The secret doorway was lined with dark red bricks before the woodlice chewed mahogany panelling took over. Peter was at the door leading the way. Tracey felt a little irritated at this, but it gave her time to fish her mobile from her handbag and turn on the torch app.

The dark wood panelled walls led two yards into an ancient looking shadowy stairwell. The passage opened up into a twelve foot by twelve wooden staircase, with a moth-eaten carpet which had been chewed away in most places. Long dangling cobwebs choked the corners of the stairs leading downwards into the unseen darkness below. Old, iron wall sconces were set in the middle of each descending wall, and some still had yellowed half melted candles fixed into them.

Tracey didn't mind the tall caretaker going down the dark steps first. She hoped he would walk into any invisible cobwebs as she tried to keep her distance from the walls, and the dirty wooden balustrade. They continued on in silence, exchanging only looks about the secret place in the heart of the old empty house. The wooden steps creaked in protest like they objected to shoes on them after so many years without use. They seemed solid and as well built as the house above and could be easily restored to their former glory to the Estate Agents' trained eye.

The only sign of anyone having been down here in the last two hundred years was an old leather football boot lying on its side, showing metal studs that were all the rage when Bobby Moore first captained England. The decor didn't change the lower they descended, but the cobwebs became less and less until the wooden walls looked new, and untouched by the ravages of time and hungry insects.

Tracey was also glad the hidden stairs didn't have any bad smells which usually came with such uncleaned and unseen places. In fact, when they had walked down the twelve sets of stairs that lined each wall, she was sure she could smell freshly sawn and polished wood.

"How far down does it go?" Tracey said as they turned another downward corner to find yet more sets of steps leading down into the darkness below.

Peter shrugged, leaned over the side of the balustrade and shone his tiny torch down into the well, but could only see more stairs. "It seems to go on forever."

"Well I hope not, I have another house to see later." Tracey's initial gung-ho, explorer- girl feeling had given away to boredom. Her calves had begun to hurt, and she was sure her left heel was forming a blood blister.

It had taken another twelve turns of the deep stairwell

before it bottomed out. The stairs ended, with almost pristine and intact carpet leading to another passage ahead. She had no idea which way they were facing. She followed the tall caretaker into the passageway, where he had to duck low to get through the archway. Tracey, who stood only five foot three in her heeled shoes, had no such problems.

The passage widened so she could catch up and stand next to Peter. Before them was a dividing wall and two passageways that set off in the same diagonal direction from where they stood.

"Left or right?" Peter asked her, just in case they got lost and he could have blaming rights.

"I'm on a schedule here, so you take the left one, and I'll take the right, and I'll be in Scotland before yer." Tracey had no idea why she had said the last bit of the old song, and just put it down to nerves. The place was creepy and dark, and in the bowels beneath the house, who knew what went on down here in years gone past.

"Eh?" Peter turned to her, looking very confused.

"Just go left, man." She frowned at him and rolled her eyes. She didn't wait for him, moving down the right-hand passage. "We'll meet back here in five minutes, okay?"

"Okay," he replied. Glad to be free of *the stuck-up tight arsed bitch* for a while.

Tracey held her mobile out before her, lighting the way. The only sound was of her heels clicking hard on the floor that was now flagstones. Her passage straightened after only three yards, and that led on for thirteen feet or so until the passage turned left. This went on for another thirteen feet and then turned left again. Another passage of the same length and dimensions led on ahead. She stopped, pulling a laser tape measure from her large bag, and measured the corridor length, exactly thirteen feet as she had judged. Tracey smiled and mentally patted herself on the back for her professional and well-trained eye.

Letting out a lungful of air she continued on her way, noticing she was perspiring slightly. Either the walk down the long stairs had caused this, or the secret underground passageways were getting warmer. She wondered how far down she was going, glad that the underground station did not run under this property. Another turn brought her to a shorter, wooden panelled corridor, and a dead end.

She quickened her pace, wondering if this was some sort of maze built deep underground. Finally reaching the end of the passage, she saw there was a little wooden chest, the size of her handbag, sitting on a polished black stone, pedestal. The chest looked old, oblong, with a curved lid fixed in place with iron strips and nails.

"Hope it's hiding a diamond tiara or something," she said to herself, reaching for the lid. Thoughts of taking what was inside, hiding it in her handbag, grew, and all the holidays in St Lucia she could purchase with her treasure. The little chest had no lock, but she lifted the lid with ease. Inside was a velvet base, with indented slots for four keys. In one of the slots sat a long, strange key. It looked gold but was probably just brass. She reached in and picked it up, weighing its heaviness in her palm. The end of the key that fitted in a lock looked normal enough, but the end she held was forged with a crescent moon shape in the handle, and an odd raised tiny square that ran along the top edge.

Tracey turned it over in her hand, wondering where the key fitted. She looked around the passage, but could see no keyholes, no other secret doors. She put the key in her purse and turned to head back the way she had come. She undid another button on her blouse, feeling even warmer. Maybe Peter's passage led to some answers about the key, or what the passageways were all about.

Hurrying, she retraced her steps back to where the two passageways split. Then she followed the way the caretaker had taken. His passage was shorter, maybe only ten feet in length, and it only took three turns to reach him.

He was standing in front of an arched doorway, with stones lining it instead of wood panelling. The door matched the little chest in colour and had the same iron bands across it, and similar fittings. A large, black, iron lock was set in the centre of the door, with a large black handle. Above the door and set in a stone lintel were carved four symbols: a black circle, a white one, a red crescent moon facing one way, and a blue crescent moon facing the other way.

"I tried to open it, but it's locked shut. It's thick, well made," Peter said as she walked up to him.

"Lucky you have me around then," she said, fishing out the key she had found. "Give this a try."

"Where did you find that?"

"At the end of *my* corridor, in a little chest, come on, *chop-chop.*" Tracey beamed at him proudly, before urging him on.

The key looked large, even in Peter's hands. He pushed it into the lock and turned it. The clicks at first were tiny, almost inaudible. They grew, spreading out from the locks like a ripple effect as if the key had been tossed into a pond. With every click, there followed a whir of expanding noise behind the door like it was mapping the dawning of the Industrial Revolution. Getting louder and louder until Tracey had to clap her hands over her ears to keep out the droning metallic clangs. Something akin to the working of Big Ben was happening behind the door. Even Peter stepped away from the door, his face wincing against the cacophony of noise, but he did not want to put his hands over his ears and show any weakness in front of the pushy estate agent.

Then the noise stopped.

And there was silence of a sort.

Though the workings of the vast mechanisms behind the door had stopped, the ringing in Tracey and Peter's ears did not. It felt like someone had hit two tuning forks and were holding them up to each side of their heads.

The estate agent and the caretaker of the old house looked at each other, with eyebrows, one plucked and the other bushy, raised.

Peter reached out and turned the large round handle and the door moved inwards two inches. The hairs on the back of his neck were up. He had a deep-rooted, old world feeling that this was a bad idea, but he had to see what was beyond the locked subterranean door. Licking his lips, he pushed the heavy door inwards and stepped back to stand next to Tracey.

They both gasped in unison.

The room was totally red.

Floor, walls, ceiling, and all furniture was bright red. The only thing out of place in the crimson colour scheme was a plain, old looking, arched-topped door in the wall opposite. A brown wooden door, with a black metal lock, that nearly matched the one they peered past, into the room.

"Okay...somebody liked red then," Tracey said, moving forward, past the rigid figure of a suddenly and rooted to the spot Peter. She moved over the threshold into the red room and stopped about a yard in. She looked around, expecting to spy something apart from the other door that wasn't in keeping with the red theme, but she was out of luck.

To her immediate right, in the roughly twelve by twelve-foot square room, was an upholstered, red leather, wing-back chair. Beyond that, in the corner, was a hexagonal table on a matching pedestal, painted, she assumed, bright red. Along from the table next to the leather chair was a red oblong table, with four red wooden chairs neatly set around it. The only object on the table was a red metal candlestick, with three prongs holding three bright red wax candles. Up along one wall and shielding one corner of the room was a dressing screen that looked Chinese. It had oriental patterns of brick red, blood red, and claret, but was mostly deep red. The pattern had no images to it, just lines in reds of varying hues running down the lacquered wood. It had long red metal hinges that showed no gaps of the corner behind it.

In the opposite corner was a single bed. It too was made of painted red wood and had sheets, covers, and pillows to match. The only other things in the red carpeted room were a desk and chair. The red desk had a red paper blotter on it, and two more of the candlesticks, nothing else

Tracey scratched her arm out nervously and moved across the red carpet towards the brown wooden door. Peter still hovered in the doorway, not liking the feel or decor of the red room at all. Tracey tried the other door, but it was locked. The metal handle felt icy cold in her grasp, and she pulled her hand back quickly. Rubbing her palm to warm it up she bent over to examine the keyhole, which wasn't a usual keyhole shape. It had more of a cross shape to it, but as she leant closer, a sudden noise disturbed her.

At first, she thought it was coming from behind the locked door. Her ears pinpointed that the sound was emanating from behind the Chinese screen in the corner. As she listened, she thought at first the sound was breathing, but as she took a tentative step closer, it sounded like someone was muttering so fast that all the words were converging into one whispered stream. Then she realised that it seemed to be one word, repeated over and over so that she couldn't really discern where the middle, start, and end syllables of the word were. To Tracey's ear, it sounded anything but English.

"Absconditus-absconditusasconditusabsconditus."

Peter stood in the doorway watching as Tracey crept closer to the red screen in the corner, like she had heard something behind it, that he had not. His boots hesitated at the threshold of the red room, only half an inch away from the thin red carpet. He did not know why his whole body told him not to go inside. Perhaps coming from a small village in Poland he was more superstitious than the city-living woman. Then it suddenly dawned on him, like a double slap on each cheek of his face, how could the red room be so well lit?

The corridors and stairs coming down had been pitch black, and they needed light to see. The red room was clear and well lit. His eyes flicked to the candles on the table, all three burning brightly like the red had picked up on his thoughts and projected an explanation. Yet even with those, and the lit ones on the desk, the room should not be so bright. There were no electric lights on the ceilings or walls.

And if the candles were lit, who had lit them?

His eyes opened wide as Tracey moved closer to the red screen, her painted nails reaching out to pull it aside.

No, there must be someone inside the room.

Peter ran into the room, hearing the strange mutterings as he raced forwards to get his body between the estate agent and the screen. He managed to shove her back roughly against the other door, but his failing right arm knocked the red screen over, sliding painfully down his right side and leg to the floor.

Something cowering in the shadows leapt up at him to bite hard with grinding teeth, down on his right wrist.

Somehow Tracey had pulled the large caretaker from the red room deep in the bowels of the house. His right hand had been gripped in the teeth of whatever had attacked him. As she grabbed Peter by the arm, the teeth released their hold. Tracey had shoved him out of the door and had the presence of mind to pull the door to the room shut and locked it before the creature got out.

The key to the red room clattered to the stone floor, but she left it there, more concerned with pulling out a travel pack of tissues to put over the stump where Peter's right hand used to be. He wailed and screamed in agony, but Tracey ignored this, and the blood splattering onto her expensive shoes. She helped the Polish caretaker around the corridors and let him lean on her as they took what seemed like aeons to climb back up the hidden staircase. She could not let her mind wander or think what the thing had been that had attacked Peter. Using her mobile phone for illumination. She could see that she had no signal beneath the house, so they pressed on. Peter wanted to stop more than once, but fright of what lay below, and fear of him bleeding out on the stairs, kept them going.

Images of the creature flashed into her mind, but she forced them out, in case they stopped her in her tracks and sent her mind off to places she did not want to visit. Her mind was suggesting the creature was a hairless man. She knew that she had to get back out into the sunlight to banish it all from her mind. Images of a blood covered body, teeth biting through skin, veins and bone, flashed through her mind. She countered them with thoughts of the trees, roads, cars and buses of London that were just up and above them.

Even the old music room, even though it was still within the empty house, would be preferable to the darkness that clung to every corner of the corridors and stairs. Peter groaned, his increased reliance on her pushing her down with his weight. His breaths were short and shallow, but she pressed on up the stairs, coaxing him on, knowing if he fell she would never be able to get him to his feet again.

Then out the dark nightmare, she saw the last staircase which led up to the light coming from the behind the secret entrance in the music room.

"Come on, you stupid man," she urged, but her words fell on deaf ears.

Peter fell three steps from the top of the stairs. As he went down, his good arm was around Tracey's shoulder, he was forced down with him. With a squeal of pain, and then despair, she put her free hand out to stop her fall. It did cushion her hitting the steps, but sent her mobile flying off across the stairs above her head, and over the side, to fall into the void below. She heard it smash on the stone floor below, leaving her and Peter in near darkness.

"Peter, get up, you've got to get up," she cried, tears running down her usually well-presented face. He did not respond.

She tried to pull at the back of his overalls to get him the last three steps, but he was an unconscious dead weight. Scraping both her knees, she had no choice but to leave him and go get help. Sobbing with fear, pain and frustration, she hurried up the steps, slipping once, as she made a mad dash for the light behind the secret door. Three, two, one, and she was squeezing through the gap, and into the dull light of the music room. The images on the walls and the horn blowing cherubs seemed to be mocking her as she ran for the open door to the corridor. She had lost one shoe, but she didn't stop. She kicked the other off as she raced past the grand staircase.

Her throat was tight with tears, and her breath laboured as she ran faster than at any time in her life since her last school's sports day. Then she was out through the open door, ignoring the cold steps on her feet, or the crunch of the leaves underfoot, as she raced around the path to the side gate. It was closed, but not locked, and she barged into it getting another deep splinter in her already blood covered right palm, her momentum spinning her around as she raced into the busy mid-morning London street.

Tracey stopped only to scream her lungs out.

CHAPTER THREE

Nick Hobbs rubbed at the stubble on his chin and scratched at his itching groin as he travelled up the escalator to the exit of the tube station. A tired, middle-aged woman looked down her nose at him as she travelled down in the opposite direction. Nick saw her expression and blew her a kiss. The woman blushed red, and turned her haughty nose away from him, towards the advertising screens on the walls.

Smiling, Nick fished out the remains of a packet of Polos from his pocket, popped the mint into his mouth, before fishing out his Travelcard from a pocket of his jeans. He couldn't recall ever visiting this particular tube station before, it was hardly one of the well-known ones. But there were plenty of things he didn't recall these days, which was probably for the best. He did recall the twins from last night in every vivid detail, right down to the last mole and freckle. Of their names he was much hazier–Alice and Alyssa–possibly.

He passed through the exit barriers into a very small ticket area. The tube station had only a ticket office on one side, and two little kiosk shops selling shoe repairs in one and papers, sweets and drinks in the other. The exit/entrance was nothing more than a wide maw of a hole. Nick walked through from the subterranean metal and tile world of the Underground, into a sunlit world that was too bright for his bloodshot eyes.

"Wow, too bright," he said to no one in particular. He fished a pair of aviator sunglasses from the outside pocket of the crumpled blue jacket he wore. As he pulled them out, he dislodged something else, which fell onto the pavement. Two obviously bunking off schoolgirls walking past gasped and then giggled to themselves as they saw the luminous pink lady's thong lying on the concrete slab next to a discarded crisp packet. With a tired, but wide grin, Nick swept his hand down to snatch up the underwear, smiling at the girls who were looking over their shoulders at him. He winked, popped the thong into a nearby bin fixed to a lamppost, and then put on his shades and continued on his way.

A brisk morning shower had coated this part of North London while Nick had been on the tube. The sun was now out and streaming across the large double-laned crossroads ahead. Nick stopped at the crossing and took in the world around him. A tired traffic-fumed junction stared back at him. Beside the tube was a tyre shop and opposite it rows of expensive looking Edwardian townhouses that had seen better decades. On the angle across from where he stood was a large, fenced off residence, hidden by old trees and high hedges.

The green walking man on the pedestrian signal flashed, and the shrill noise indicated it was time to cross the road. Once across he came to a line of weary looking shops and businesses set back in recessed doors, with dirty plaques giving him only the slightest chance of guessing their business. Kebab shop gave way to a betting shop, taxi cab firm, newsagents, a Polish deli, curry house, a fried chicken place a long way from Kentucky, and a corner coffee shop. None of them branded or big names, and Nick could understand why. This was a part of London not worth rebranding, a place where a community lived, but rarely got visitors like him. It was a thoroughfare, a traffic tributary to pass through on route to somewhere much more interesting and vibrant.

Steam rose from the bonnets of parked cars and vans outside the shops he passed, as the hot sun condensed the rain into low vapours. Nick wiped sweat from his top lip. The Polo in his mouth hadn't helped his dry mouth. He checked his watch, saw he was running late, but went into the newsagents anyway. He stepped aside to let a tall, gaunt man with grey hair leading to heavy mutton-chops, leave the shop before he entered.

"Thank you, my good man," the man said with a theatrical air, mixed with a taint of a Lancashire accent.

Smiling at this, Nick approached an open cooler next to the counter and fished out a carton of orange juice. He plonked it on the counter, pulled across a copy of the Sun and then pointed up behind the Asian woman in a blue sari. "Packet of menthol cigarettes and a box of matches, please."

The woman fetched the cigarettes and matches and placed them on top of the newspaper. "Do you want a bag with that?" she asked as she rang up the total.

"No, I'm fine thanks," Nick replied, handing over a tenner from his pale leather wallet. He took his change, cigarettes and matches, and put them in the pocket vacated by his sunglasses and the thong. He tucked the newspaper under his arm and was already unscrewing the top of the orange juice carton before the newsagent's door chimed shut behind him. He chugged down a third of it as he slowly made his way across the slick pavement to another crossing that would lead him to his destination. Another third of the juice went down as he waited for the green man to lead the way again.

A few people walked by, a mother with two toddlers in a double buggy, an old man with vacant eyes waiting for his life to end, and a couple of dudes in close quarter conversation over something playing on a mobile phone screen. They, and the shops were left behind as Nick crossed the road and turned left. He followed a high wall, built with yellow bricks. They revealed a twenty foot high, black painted, cast iron set of gates. Nick passed by a set of bollards set outside to stop tube commuters from parking there during the day, and in through the open gates.

Into the cemetery.

He finished off his juice and dropped the carton into a large green bin as he walked by. Fished out his cigarettes and opened the new packet as he left a concrete area with two brick buildings on either side. He popped another Polo into his mouth before he put the cigarettes between his lips and stopped to light up just inside the next part of the cemetery. He used matches over a lighter, and he loved the first smell of a lit match: it was up there with frying bacon and the scent of an aroused woman. He sniffed up the phosphorus funk before he took a drag on his menthol cigarette.

Double Minting he dubbed it ages ago. Taking in the menthol smoke over the Polo mint, and down into his lungs, wait, and exhale long through the nose. Sometimes, if he had the patience, he would, as a little game, suck the Polo hole wider to fit over the end of the cigarette between his lips. It was his cancerous detox to rid his taste buds of whatever he'd been drinking or eating the night before, and it had served him well over the years.

He breathed out again and continued along a gravel path between two long strips of lawn. This went on for thirty yards or so, before coming to a wide, even, rough dirt and stone track. It split off in three directions. Left and right on curving paths that soon disappeared behind rows of ancient, withered, yew trees, infested with ivy and blackberry bushes. Surrounded by the obviously trimmed virulent vines and foliage were tombstones, angel statues, small crypts, and even more strange edifices to the dead.

Taking another drag of his minty cigarette, Nick took the path ahead of him. It seemed wider and better maintained than the other two paths. Nick liked the crunch of the stones under his shoes. The path seemed strangely dry and dusty, given that it had obviously rained hard for a while before he got here. Maybe the overhanging trees, forming an almost ceremonial cortège over the path, or the angle the rain had come in had something to do with it. Benches were situated every fifty yards or so down the wide path, on concrete slabs over the encroaching wild grass and vines. He counted three along and stopped next to it, looking around the place. The path was devoid of all human life. Behind the bench, an angel statue on a tall plinth towered over the leaves, next to a large sycamore tree. The pious countenance of the angel stared down at him, its mouth open, and arms stretching for him in disapproval of his very presence there. Nick pulled his paper from under his arm and dropped it on the slightly damp bench, giving him somewhere dry to sit.

Nick sneered up at the angel and blew smoke up towards its ivy skirted body.

"Abdiel doesn't seem to like you, Nick." An old, rich voice said from behind him.

Nick managed not to jump in fright, or at least show fear as he turned around to see the owner of the voice. The tramp pulled his ragged, stained clothes through the bushes and creepers, as he emerged from the gravestones opposite. The man was black-skinned and had a bushy black beard that seemed to merge with the dark shirt and collar under his thick, grey coat. The heat and a light breeze from behind the man wafted his sweat and urine smell deep into Nick's nostrils. He had to take a suck on his cigarettes, and blow it quickly out of his nose, to get the unclean smell from his system.

"Abdiel?" Nick asked, turning back to the angel, wondering why most angels in cemeteries and graveyards were female.

"Sounds like something you take to get rid of indigestion."

"One of the angels who remained faithful to God during the war in Heaven, and took on Satan," the tramp said, finally extracting himself from the clinging bushes to come and stand next to Nick. Forcing himself to breathe through his mouth, Nick turned away from the angel with a sneer as he sat down on the newspaper covered bench.

"I thought Abdiel was a dude anyway," Nick said, delving back into his brain to remember all things biblical–something he tried to avoid at all costs these days.

"Man, woman, child, angels are celestial beings Nick, not bound by human gender tags," the dirty tramp said, sitting down on the far end of the bench. "Anyway, I think the stonemason who carved it just liked chiselling out a woman's shape."

The old tramp laughed until he coughed, which made Nick smile.

"I brought the sandwiches, as usual, where's the wine?" the tramp said, pulling a crumpled brown paper bag from the folds of his coat. Nick was pretty hungry, but not that desperate to try the old tramps' food.

"I forgot," Nick said, dropping the butt of his cigarette between his shoes before he ground it into the dirt with the twist of his heel.

"You always seem to forget lately, is it Alzheimer's?"

"Fuck off," Nick swore. "Anyway, why are you dressed like that, and what is that smell?"

"Language," the tramp retorted. "I'm in disguise."

"But why?" Nick forgot to breathe through his mouth, caught a whiff of his companion and almost gagged.

"Because I don't want to be seen dead with you Nick, that's why. I have my reputation to look after." The tramp opened the brown bag and pulled a wholemeal sandwich, with some meat and mustard inside.

"Hmmm, nothing changes then. You need my help again, but you are too ashamed to be seen out with me. A guy could get a complex you know."

"Put away your ego boy and have a sandwich," the tramp said, thrusting the bag towards Nick.

Nick focused on what was between the two slices of cut bread instead. "What's in them?"

"Pork," the tramp replied with a mouthful.

"That is so wrong in so many ways," Nick said, shaking his head, and staring at the twisted cigarette butt between his shoes. "So why have you dragged me across London to this bloody place, you know the decor gives me the creeps."

The tramp waited until he had chewed and swallowed his sandwich before speaking. "I know. That's why we always meet in cemeteries, and this one is rather splendid I think."

"So is it something to do with this place?" Nick asked, raising his hands and trying to ignore the feeling that the angels were staring at him with their round, stone eyes.

"Oh no - nothing to do with this serene little holy enclave - no. But it's close by, son, can't you feel it?"

"No," Nick said. "And don't call me son, you know I don't like it."

"That's why I say it, Nick, and get you to meet in cemeteries because one day you might just get it into that thick skull of yours who's in charge here."

Nick, with anger twisting the nerves in his face, turned to the old tramp but held his tongue. It wasn't worth going over old ground again.

"Cat got your tongue?" the tramp asked, sitting up rigidly, looking less of a crumpled old tramp, and more of the person behind the disguise.

Still Nick didn't bite.

"Then let's begin," the tramp said, pulling a padded envelope from the deep folds of his coat. He tapped it three times on Nick's knee before Nick snatched it out of his hands. "The house next door is the one I'm very much interested in. You'll find all the information you need to proceed with your investigation, including the lease deeds, signed in your name for six months, with an option for another six months if you so desire. You will live there, and find out its secrets, for me." The tramp then pulled another thick envelope from his coat pocket and held it an inch above Nick's right knee.

"What's this?" Nick asked, putting the first envelope on his lap to receive the new one.

"Thirty thousand pounds in cash, call it pocket money for your stay, *son.*"

Nick swallowed down the urge to punch the old tramp in the face. He waited five seconds to calm a little before speaking. "So what's so special about this house?"

Nick opened the first envelope to find a lease agreement, with his name forged on it so any comeback would fall on him. There were cuttings from two local, and one national newspaper, about a recent attack in the house, and not much else, apart from a set of keys on a key ring. One of the keys was large, and old looking, and had half a handle part and some raised lines on the length of it.

"What's this key open then?"

"A room that isn't always there," the tramp replied.

"What is that supposed to mean?"

"It means inside that house is a room that comes and goes like the tides of the sea. And in that mysterious oddity of a room, lies a door on the other side."

"And where does *that door* lead?" asked Nick, getting fed up of receiving the usual run-around from the old man.

"I don't know," the tramp said, slapping his kneecaps and standing from the bench.

"What do you mean, you don't know?"

"My words are plain English aren't they, Nick, I don't have an inkling, and I need to know."

"What if I don't want to play spooky house sitter?"

"Not quitting again before the hard work starts are you, Nick, that's so...so, you." The tramp looked at him with a bit of shame in his dark eyes.

"Fuck off," Nick shouted, throwing the envelope filled with cash at the tramp, who let it hit him and then fall onto the path.

"As you wish." The tramp nodded and moved off across the dirt path. Nick watched with fury in his eyes as the tramp left the track, behind a tall, thin mausoleum with a lion on top. He vanished from view into the trees beyond.

Nick stood up, and thought about chasing after him, but instead bent down to scoop up the envelope full of cash. The money, at least, would come in handy, funding his playboy lifestyle for a while, and at least he had a place to crash. He vowed not to investigate the house, though, or the mystery room inside.

A vow, like most of the ones Nick gave, that didn't last very long.

CHAPTER FOUR

The Scotsman was glad to close the front door of his luxury Monaco home behind him and get inside, where the air-conditioning was on full icy blast. His huge Doberman, Mr Smith, looked up from where it was lying on the cold, tiled floor of the entrance hall, saw it was his master, and put his head back on his crossed paws to sleep again.

"No, it's okay...don't get up," the Scotsman said to the dog, in an accent that barely retained any trace of Melrose, his town of birth. Accents could leave a trail back to his old dead self, birth certificates, church records, schools report, friends he had in his youth. Luckily for him, he had an almost comical knack for doing impressions and accents to a tee. Which, added to his ability to shoot a rifle with unerring accuracy, and his rather plain *Average Joe* looks, had kept him alive into a retirement most me in his former profession ever attained.

The Scotsman dropped his house keys, Ferrari keys, and his thick wallet into a crystal bowl, liking the scratching sounds the metal keys made on the side, like skates on ice. He had a bowl like this in the hallway of his mother's house back on Stuart Road, in Melrose, and it brought back what happy memories he had of that pre-adult life he so cherished. Before his oil rig worker father was killed in a helicopter accident on his way home after three months away from them, before his grief-stricken mum became the *town bike!* The only difference was his mum's bowl cost £2.99 at *Woolies*, while his one cost 60,000 Euros. The feeling of scratching something so expensive made his hard face soften. He'd pay a million pounds if he could have that old cheap crystal bowl instead.

He took off his sunglasses and stepped down into his huge living room, filled with expensive treasures bought with the blood money he'd earned over his career. The sunglasses went on a round, glass occasional table next to his huge L-shape sofa. His jacket went next, draped over a dining chair, on an upper connecting side of the warehouse-esque home. It was next to his white and stainless steel kitchen but looked out onto a wide balcony that ran the side of the hillside home and overlooked the Costa Azzurra.

Ignoring the stunning view, he woke up to every morning, he proceeded through a doorway into the main bedroom, only to find he was not alone.

"How the hell did you get in here?" he asked, putting his fists on his hips and his $3,000 designer belt.

The brother of the dog sitting in the hallway sat up on his Super-King sized bed, always more excited to see his master than his sibling. The Scotsman smiled, and walked up to the end of the bed, tutting at the state of his twisted covers. He let the dog jump up, paws on his shoulders, and give him one lick of his face.

"That's enough now, Mr Wesson," he said, rubbing behind the dog's ears. "Now out you go, you know you shouldn't be in here."

The Doberman gave a loud whine, then leapt down off the bed, and padded out of his master's bedroom to go drink from his silver water bowl. Scratching his temple, the Scotsman padded over to his en-suite bathroom to freshen up before dinner with Alina tonight. He got to the bathroom door and suddenly stopped.

The hackles on the back of his neck began to rise.

He knelt, feeling under the nightstand beside his bed, to retrieve the Sphinx 9mm taped underneath it. He pulled off one resilient piece of tape and flicked it on the cream carpet. His left hand gripped the pistol, even though the sticky residue of the tape made his hand feel tacky and uncomfortable. Then aiming at the object of his paranoid action, he rounded his huge bed and made for the centre mirrored wardrobe door that was two inches ajar. The other seven wardrobe doors were closed flush, as he had left them this morning, reflecting back his fifty-five-year-old, wiry frame, as he approached, pistol out before him. If any of the other wardrobes had been open wouldn't have been as much of a concern to his, but this one was special. Mr Wesson in his room, the special wardrobe open, when both doors were closed when he left this morning. It pointed to the fact that someone had been in his house and knew exactly where to go.

The Scotsman gripped the edge of the mirrored wardrobe door with his right hand and pulled it open, pointing the pistol into the recess of his jacket closet. A light went on automatically when the door was opened more than three inches, and it showed no one hiding inside, or anything looking like it had moved.

He knelt down and looked up under his hanging jackets, from casual to sport to dinner, checking if anything had been tampered with, or moved. None looked like they had. He looked around at the shoeboxes on the floor of the wardrobe, but all were where he had placed them. Each with the slight scratch on the top left-hand corner, and all pointing as he'd left them.

Then, with some relief, he began to carefully pick them up, checking for wires underneath, or any subtle change in weight, but he could find nothing. He took them all out, one by one. Placing, as he always did, five to the left hand of him and five to the right. Then he pressed his forefinger of his right hand into a knot in the wooden floor of the wardrobe. There was a click, followed by a hiss, and a four feet by four feet section of the floor lifted up like a lid to reveal a steel safe underneath, with a keypad and a metal handle next to it.

He quickly typed a seven-figure sequence of numbers into it that only he knew, an old telephone number he'd once had when he went by his birth name, so many years ago. A light next to the keypad went from red to amber. The Scotsman waited for a second and then typed in two more numbers - his age–which turned off the explosive device inside the safe. The light turned from amber to green, and he turned the handle and pulled the safe lid up.

Inside were four deep piles of cash in dollars, pounds,

euros, and rupees, each with a passport of that country on the top. There were two other items - a wooden cigar box, and an old, metal tobacco tin. He prised open the tin first to find inside three keys of safe houses he owned under various pseudonyms around the world, and a key to a safe-deposit box in a bank in Switzerland. He replaced the lid and the tin back in the safe, and then put down the pistol. He lifted the cigar box out with all the reverence of a holy relic and placed it on his knees to open it.

Inside were two wedding bands belonging to his late parents. He had to get a Saturday job with the milkman to save up all year to buy back his mother's from the local pawn shop. His mother had sold it to buy booze when her looks and attention from men began to fade. He was sixteen when he came home from school, after his English Language exam, to find her dead on the kitchen floor. Her bloated stomach filled with Johnny Walker Black label, sleeping pills, and half a bottle of bleach from under the kitchen sink.

Under the rings were pictures of his parents from happier times, before his father's death, with him in the centre of them both. The only other thing in the box was an old, black walkie-talkie from his hired assassin days. The only object he hadn't thrown in the River Thames and kept after he retired, to remind him of what he was—a cold-hearted killer for money. This was the walkie-talkie we used to talk to his M16 contact during the troubles in Northern Ireland. His code-name had been Danny-Boy, and the British government's most secret section *Box 17* had given it to him to receive orders for drops. Drops where he would send someone else to collect and leave at a different location for him to finally collect two days later. Inside would be orders on whom they wanted dead and pre-payment in US dollars.

The one the IRA had given him was lost in a hedge somewhere in Crossmaglen, where they tried to double-cross him as the Troubles came to an end. His codename with them had been Emerald, and he had taken payment to kill politicians, soldiers, and informants. They too paid in US funded dollars, and so he had made the start of his wealth, killing for both sides, and made sure he doubled his money. But he was a loose end that neither side could afford to have hanging over them now they were going legit and forming governments. So they tried to assassinate the assassin, like in all good *Le Carre* books. But he was hard to kill, and though wounded, escaped to Monaco, and once medically stitched up, and well again, decided enough was enough. His investments had made millions, and the thrill of taking life after life of fathers, sons, brothers, even sisters and children, was making him sick to his stomach.

He had retired ten years ago.

But he kept the walkie-talkie as a reminder of who had been, next to the pictures of the boy he had been. Even now he was a different animal to those formative parts of his life, a calmer person, with a life, pleasures, and a young girlfriend to lavish diamonds on. He had a home, his dogs, and a place to call home after all these years.

He put the walkie-talkie back in the cigar box and closed the lid. He leant forward to place the box back in his floor safe when he heard a familiar hiss from inside.

He stopped, arms outstretched, hovering over the floor of the safe.

The unmistakable hiss of the walkie-talkie inside the cigar box happened again.

Shuffling back in shock, he placed the cigar box on the carpet next to his pistol and extended his right forefinger to flip it open. Inside, the tiny red light on top of the walkie-talkie glowed like it was on, but The Scotsman was sure it had been off, and the batteries hadn't been changed since he last used the thing, over a decade ago.

Through the constant hiss, he could make out the low tones of someone singing, but he couldn't catch the tune. His mouth was dry, so he licked his lips, and with trembling hands reached down to try and turn the sound up.

As his fingers reached for the radio, the volume raised significantly, and the whistles and hiss of static faded into the airwaves until he could hear one strong voice singing in strong Scottish Melrose tones. "...just got back from the Isle of Skye, Donald where's ya trousers..."

The Scotsman cried out in fear, closed the lid of the cigar box, and threw it into the safe. He slammed the safe shut and locked it, before fleeing the bedroom, leaving his boxes and pistol behind on the carpet. He ran, shaking from head to foot, into the living room, slamming his bedroom door shut behind him. He slid open a balcony window and rushed into the heat of the day, his breathing coming in fast hectic breaths. His hands felt like two blocks of ice, as he clamped them on the rail, trying to get his senses and mind back in order.

He was crying, for the first time since he was sixteen, at his mother's funeral. He stared at the hot sun that warmed his cold, clammy face, then to the sea below. Trying to calm down, and fathom how he had heard his long dead father's voice singing the song he did when he was home from the *rigs* and carrying him up the wooden hill to Bedfordshire, coming from his walkie-talkie.

CHAPTER FIVE

Nick sucked a piece of pork stuck in a gap at the back lower part of his front teeth. He finally got it loose with the tip of his tongue as he exited the cemetery. He was very good with his tongue and mouth–all the girls said so. His teeth were naturally white, and all his own, without a hint of bleaching.

He had his jacket held by one thumb over his right shoulder. The earlier rain clouds had been burned away by the hot summer sun. It was getting humid and hot in this part of North London. Nick smiled–hot summers–he loved nothing better. He preferred the sizzling baking heat, pure and brain aching, not like you got in Asia with seventy-five percent humidity. Today the sun burned down on the top of his head, and it felt good.

He should have turned left of course, which would have taken him to the house in question right slap-bang next door to the cemetery, but he didn't. His green eyes spotted a corner pub across the street and tucked down a side road. It had uninviting green tiles, with a brown stripe around. Nick didn't care about the outside decor, some of the best pubs, clubs and dives had shitty facades. He crossed the road, even though he was itching to have a look at the house the tramp wanted him to investigate. But he rarely got such treats in his life anymore, things new and interesting to pique his interest. So he entered the gloomy confines of the pub and saw only the lunchtime patrons and regulars propping up the bar.

He ordered a pint of IPA before he'd even realised it. His body and throat were hoping for a little respite from the booze, and maybe an orange juice. Nick paid and sat down in a corner booth, as far away from any other living soul as he could manage. He dropped his jacket, with its bulging pockets stuffed with two envelopes, on the long bench seat next to him. Taking out the thinner brown envelope, he flicked the tails of his jacket over to cover up the wad of cash in the other.

He took a sip of the cool beer, delaying the moment of opening the first envelope. It was part of the fun of life, to wind himself up a little. Like sex; get right up to the precipice of climaxing and then stopping or waiting until the last moment of pain before taking a much-needed toilet break. The sheer joy that trembled through his body when the act was finally done was always worth the pain of delaying to the last moment, like ants were running up and down his spine.

Nick took a deep breath and let it out slowly, knowing he could not delay any longer. He opened the envelope and placed the contents on the table before him, near his resting left hand, and away from any sticky beer rings. He flicked the house keys off the papers but paused to pick up the large, strange looking key. The lease was no interest to him, so he picked up the first of the cuttings from *The Daily Star*. It was all sensational, large on headline, small on facts, apart from identifying Tracey Sunderland, a pretty blonde, estate agent aged 39, on what she was supposed to have seen, and what had bitten off the hand of a Polish caretaker. Tracey, now an ex-employee of a local estate agent, said they had found a secret room in the bowels of the house, painted red.

A room that police couldn't find, even after an extensive search.

The Polish caretaker had been flown to recuperate in a mental asylum near his family home in Krakow. He was a gibbering wreck, and couldn't utter a single word in English, or Polish, that made any sense.

The two local clippings told Tracey's story in more vivid detail. How she had found the key in a box and the red room, and inside they had discovered some red painted madman who attacked Peter Podolski.

The very key Nick now held in his hand.

The police had found the secret passage, the box, and corridors as she described to them, but no signs of any doors, or weird red rooms. They had even taken her into custody to charge her with the attack, but had little evidence to pursue the case. Her employers had dropped her like a stone, and now she was scared to go out, apart from trips to the local jobcentre.

The second piece showed a picture of the house itself; an old, dour looking, rundown place, known locally as being haunted. The article had sketchy details, and no direct quotes from Tracey Sunderland, just badly written third-hand reporting and two spelling mistakes. Nick put the papers down and took a long sip of ale, his eyes fixed on the picture of the house he was about to become resident in.

"The Ritz, it ain't," he muttered into his glass, before drinking some more.

He looked around his new *local* and gave a wry smile to his surroundings, with its drab décor, and even drabber looking patrons. His fingers rubbed at the brass key but got no supernatural vibrations from it at all. It didn't feel special, or odd at all, only the look of it–like it was not finished off properly. He ran his thumb up and down the raised edge of the key, wondering if it had some significance, or was just part of its quirky design.

He put it down and had a cursory glance over the lease, nodding with approval at his forged signature on three different pages. He didn't bother looking at the cash in the other envelope. He knew that the tramp wouldn't give Nick any excuses not to investigate the house.

But it already had piqued his interest, and it took a lot to get Nick interested in much else other than booze and fucking these days. Hell, he would have done it for free.

Nick downed his pint, and then shoved everything back in the envelope and shrugged on his jacket. He picked up the envelope with the newspaper clipping, lease, and keys and got up. He was intending a trip to the men's toilet but then spotted the food board being put out on the side of the bar.

His stomach rumbled angrily like he had a ravenous Kraken in his stomach. He looked from the exit to the specials board to the corridor leading to the toilets. His face lined with indecision.

Another pint, a steak and kidney pudding, and a trip to the men's later, he was finally giving in to the pounding urge in his brain to explore his new abode. His urgent need to get inside was only tempered by the padlocked side gate he had to open, and the chain he had to pull through just to get into the grounds. He noticed a bare inch of black and yellow police tape at eye level as he finally pushed open the gate.

Looking back at the type of area he was going to be living in, he turned and bolted himself inside. He hoped he never did anything stupid like misplacing the padlock key.

As he entered the grounds of the house, it felt like he had entered a different season altogether.

Summer ended two steps under the high canopy of trees that drained the daylight and surrounded the whole house, like *Entish* guardians. Brown leaves were strewn about the weed and wild rose covered front drive.

Haven't got around to replacing the Polish caretaker then, Nick mused as the soles of his shoes crunched the dry leaves into the stones of the driveway. An ivy choked fountain lay in the centre of the front garden, directly in front of the house's entrance. The house was built of old stone, giving it almost the appearance of a castle. Tall chimneys rose high above its rooftops and were shaped in a way that made them seem like six habit wearing monks looking down at him as he walked up the drive.

Nick shivered. Monks gave him the creeps at the best of times. He always identified them with silent, hidden vows, brooding under their cowls like pious pricks waiting for death. Soon he was out from under the shadow of the trees, and in front of the imposing house. Its windows were large, with small panes and lead rims, showing nothing back but black reflections.

He trotted up the stone steps to the front doors and fished out the set of house keys. Two locks, two keys, and he was in, but that didn't take away the gloom. There was light alright, sunlight streaming through a glass ceiling. Covered with moss and grime that gave the sunlight filtering through it a green tinge. It fell into the centre of the large entrance hall, across its white and black marble tiled floor. The natural light showing up the dust in the air as it shown across the vast, wide staircase that swept up to the floors and rooms above. This bright dazzling centre made everything around the edges seem shadowy and pushed to the limits of Nick's peripheral vision. The doors, arches, and vase filled recesses seemed to have double shadows, like a child's drawing, where the shading is overdone.

Nick walked to the edge of the centre of the light. He suddenly stopped and laughed. Something came to mind, and he stuck his right hand out into the warm light air, half-expecting some *Indiana Jones* style trap to spring up and spear his guts with wooden stakes. He walked to the side of the circle of light, edging his way around it. His eyes were adjusting to the contrasting glare and shadows, and he could see to his right a set of double oak doors, at least ten feet high. A long corridor led off down past the staircase, into the darkness beyond, and traversed the whole length of the house.

The place was silent. Any noise from the main London artery road right next door, filtered out by the thick stone walls and encircling boundary trees. Another set of double doors faced the pair he stood next to, across the grand entrance hall to his left. These rooms, plus two at the back, must make up the odd castle-like shape to the house. A rectangular central core, with four squares in each corner.

Nick began to tick through a mental list in his mind, of what he might need for his stay, starting with Absinthe, and ending with Zip-gun. His next thought was whether there were any decent, un-mould-ridden beds for him to sleep on. The tramp would never have considered this, or Nick's comfort at any point. Nick would rather buy a camper bed than to sleep on some cold, damp mattress that fifty people had peed, cum, and died in. Looking down the long depths of the hallway, he recalled that the secret passage was in the old music room somewhere on the ground floor. All he had to do was find it. He ummed and aahed for a few seconds, deliberating between bed checks, or running full pelt into the heart of this mystery.

He had teased himself too much already today and set off down the dark corridor in search of the music room, where his investigation would commence. The corridor was long and straight and finished in an endless dark. Nick could have turned on the lights to see how long the corridor was, but where would the fun be in that? He opened two doors on his right: the first being a cloakroom or some sort and the second a large WC split in half for each sex presumably. The plumbing offended his nostrils so he exited that room sharpishly.

So he tried the door opposite.

"Bingo," he said, as he opened the door to find the right room after only his third go. It could have easily taken him longer in a house this size. He entered the room, switching on the lights, glad of the fact no one had been around to hear him say *bingo*. Only a large piano gave away the musical history of the place until he noticed the walls covered with images of full-figured women of the time playing various instruments, with Pan and few other woodland denizens. The secret door in the south wall did not live up to its description. It was two inches open and covered from top to bottom with zigzagging police tape. Behind its wrappings, there was a sky blue painted alcove, and in it sat a fat nude cherub, playing a horn, its left arm broken off and lying on the marble plinth by its toes.

Nick pulled off the tape, taking more care than the police to protect the decor of the music room. Even with careful, slow tugging, some of the two hundred and sixty-year-old wall friezes came off with the tape.

"Philistines," Nick muttered as he rolled the sticky tape into a ball and tossed it behind him into a corner. Then he spat on both palms, rubbed them together, before reaching his hands around the secret door. It pulled open easier than he expected. He thought it must have had a lot of recent use after the attack a month ago. He saw a low passageway lined with foundation bricks, which soon became wooden panelling. There was enough light from the music room to make out a bannister not far into the darkness. Taking out his mobile phone from his jacket, he turned on the brightest setting of his torch app and set off into the hidden heart of the old house.

A musty smelling wooden staircase led down and around into the darkness below. Nick leaned over the side of the small balcony at the top, making sure he put as little weight on the old wood as possible, in case it decided today was the day it broke. He could not see the bottom. He shone the light from his mobile, but this showed only two centuries of cobwebs and little else.

Seeing little else to delay his descent, he trudged down the solid wooden steps, noticing the footmarks in the dust caused by the many police boots going up and down it during the investigation. It also left the sides and corners of the steps covered in two inches of grey matter, consisting of dust, mice droppings, dead flies, spiders and their many webs. This and the lack of any lighting apart from candle sconces on the walls indicated to Nick that this secret passage had remained secret for many decades at least.

There was nothing for it but to trudge down, turning left and left and left, at least twenty-four times before he finally reached the bottom. A red carpet was laid on the bottom of the staircase, and something odd hit Nick's keen eye immediately.

It was clean down here.

Not just clean, but pristine. From the carpet to the staircase, to the wood panelled walls, everything was polished and shiny clean, like it was put there yesterday. He touched the round end of the balustrade as he stepped off the last wooden step. His fingers came away without dust on them, and the faint aroma of beeswax. He rubbed his fingers together and looked around, but apart from the carpet, and the passage leading off to his right it was empty. He was pretty sure that the police would not have cleaned the place, apart maybe from clearing up the caretaker's blood.

It was the first real mystery in this house of conundrums.

But that didn't bother him, in fact, it turned on his investigative mind.

He looked up without his using his mobile and could only see the suspended darkness above his head. He bit the corner of his bottom lip trying to work out how deep underground he was. Surely as deep as the tube he'd come on. Luckily the underground line ran somewhere across the road to the east of the house, or this place might have been ruined when the tunnels had been built. Still, he took his time, shining his light into every corner.

Once convinced there was nothing of interest to find he moved off down the passageway. He had to duck low to get under the arch and into another strange area of the house. The carpet stopped at the entrance and he felt cold, hard flagstones underfoot. The wooden panelling gave way to rough, grey bricks, that looked like they had been hewn from solid stone, rather than manufactured like modern bricks. The passage quickly widened and divided at this point, like some sort of underground stone maze. Nick pondered which diagonal passageway to follow.

He took the one to the left, hoping it would lead to the core of what lay at the deep epicentre. One half turn and three proper L-shape turns later, and he found himself at a dead end.

Except the door that Tracey Sunderland and Peter Podolski claimed to have been there, wasn't. The stone floor was scrubbed clean in a roundish spot near the wall. Nick knelt down, instantly feeling a deep-rooted cold, rise up from the flagstones, through his jeans, and into his kneecap. Lowering his mobile and his face nearer the edges of the flagstones, he could still pick up traces of dried, brown blood.

Frowning slightly, he stood up and sucked at his teeth. Nick reached out with his free right hand to touch the cold wall in front of him. He felt a shiver run up his arm and a vibration, like the foundations of the house jumped at his touch, and then nothing. Nick stepped back and moved his left arm up and around where the estate agent and caretaker claimed they found a door, but there was nothing there at all. Not even the suggestion of a secret door.

He knocked around every other stone next to the cleaned part of the floor with the bottom of his fist. He could find no trace of the door at all. The police found no trace of it either.

The tramp had said it was here, with a room and another door inside it. He could be a nuisance, but his instincts on things like this were never wrong. The end of the corridor brought no further clues or signs of a secret door, so Nick retraced his steps back to where the passageways parted. He took the right-hand side, slightly longer passageway. This seemed to follow the same direction as the first one, but it ended with something of interest.

At the end of the second passageway, sitting on a polished,

black stone, waist-high pedestal, was a small wooden box. He reached it, the police having left it there as it had no real significance to their GBH assault investigation. It looked a simple oblong box, dated from Tudor times he surmised. He lifted the lid to find four velvet covered slots, which looked like they would hold four keys.

Suddenly scrambling inside his jacket pocket, he pulled out the first envelope and tipped it over, so the large heavy key slipped out first. He managed to tip it back quickly to stop the papers falling out. Putting the envelope back in his inner jacket pocket, he quickly tried placing the large, strange, brass key into the slots. The first indent did not fit, but the second was a perfect match. He tried it in the other two slots, but it was a bit out in dimension in each, but only by a millimetre here or there.

Putting the key into the second slot, Nick picked up the box and decided to take it with him. Maybe in natural light, it would yield some clue to the keys it once housed, or its maker. He was getting cold in the passageway, and his fingers felt numb as he clasped the wooden box to his side. He fancied one more look at where the door should be, but the increasing bone gnawing cold changed his mind for him. He made his way round and out of the passageway and traipsed back up the dark staircase. The sciatic nerve in his left thigh was burning by the time he got back up to the top balcony.

Once he was along the passage and ducking down to get out of the secret entrance it was back to normal again. Nick walked towards the open door and then stopped. He turned. He took two steps back to the cherub and his secret passageway behind. He moved his head towards the door and then finally indecision left him. He decided to go over and push the secret door shut. The breaking of the cherub trigger arm meant it didn't close flush anymore, but at least it wasn't wide open.

Something about the creeping cold down there made him want to close the secret alcove door and keep it down there. He warmed up as he made his way back up to the vast entrance hall. The sunlight from the glass ceiling bathed the sweeping start of the grand staircase in summer's warmth. So he turned off the light on his phone and sat down on the wide steps to examine the box.

The rays soon warmed him up, as he turned the box over in his hands. It didn't seem that remarkable; old, yes, but worth no more than four hundred pounds maybe. It wasn't expertly made, or made of any especially rare wood, just a thing to house the keys inside.

"They are the key to this matter," Nick said to himself, and then groaned out loud at what he had said. He opened the box again, and there under the lid were two letters burned into the underside of the wood: NC.

Nick looked at the initials, glad to have found something, but not sure if they would be of any use in solving what was going on. A door and a room that seemed to come and go. He examined the key, with its odd ridge along the top, but no spark of insight came to mind. Standing up, and holding the box under his arm, he preceded up the wide and impressively opulent, grand staircase, in search of a bedroom to use during his stay.

He found most of the large rooms with the four-poster beds had been trashed over the years or suffered from damp, mildew, or a touch of both. He found a smaller, more tidy room on the west side of the house, about halfway along. It had a bed with no mattress, but there were a desk and an open fireplace he could use if the summer turned for the worse. It, like the rest of the house, interfered with his mobile phone signal. He wrapped the box in an old net curtain, he hid it up the fireplace on a ledge above the flue.

Once he knew it was secure, Nick took a tour of the rest of the house, including the basement kitchens, cellars, and the rear gardens. He left the library for another day, thinking this might be a place to dig up some clues about the origins of the house, and the family who once lived here. At about six-thirty, he locked up and made his way over to his new local pub, and ordered another pint of IPA, and a rare steak and chips for dinner. While he waited for his food he went on the internet and ordered a whole raft of things he might need during his stay. These included four bags of plain flour, two cameras with time lapse features and tripods, a tiny camcorder, EMF meter, Absinthe, food, including a big jar of Marmite, pickaxes, hammers and all manner of other things, ending with the most luxurious camper bed money could buy.

Nick always travelled light, but he was never short of a bob or two, so just ordered things in as required. He was just looking at the varying delivery dates when his dinner arrived, and all thoughts about the house left him.

"You're keen," a woman's voice said as his steaming dinner was placed on the table in front of him, followed by a cheap white serviette and his cutlery.

"Eh?" Nick replied, looking up from the screen of his phone to find a woman in her late fifties, with bushy copper-red hair, standing over him. She must be the landlady, he'd seen her loitering around the bar area with a glass of wine earlier in the day.

"You've been in twice in one day, you staying around here then?" she asked, her lip curled up on the side every time she finished speaking.

Nick smirked. "Maybe I can't resist a redhead who owns a pub?"

"Get away with you." The landlady (Nick could spot them a mile off) eyed him suspiciously. She touched the back of her hair and pushed out her ample chest all the same. She turned to the balding landlord who had served Nick's drinks both times today. "'Ere, Jim, got a charmer here, says he only comes here to look at me and not the beer."

Not exactly anywhere near what I said, Nick thought, *added a bit of poetic license there girl.*

"Tell him the opticians is only two doors down on Abbey Street," was Jim's terse reply to his wife, before he took a new customer's order.

Nick could see the glare through the muscles in the landlady's cheek, but when she turned to face him, it was polite smiles again. "So you going to be a new regular here then?"

"Can't see why not, I'm renting the big old house over the street next to the cemetery." Nick let out his reply, like a fishing line in the river, and waited to see what it would catch.

"Really?" she said, the lines in her furrowed brow looking like a relief map of a farmer's ploughed field. "The estate agents did tell you about the place, cos I know how those buggers might not give you the full facts."

"They told me about the attack the other month, yes," Nick smiled casually and sipped at his beer. "Why, does it have more of a chequered past than that then?"

The landlady blew out her cheeks. "You could say that. We've only been here twenty years, but some of the regulars, the older ones, could tell you a tale of two that would make you not want to step back inside even the gardens of that house."

"Anything you could tell me would be interesting, I don't even know the name of the place."

"Most people don't even notice it, they just walk on by. Most people around here just call it the *Haunted House*, but what does Lionel call it, Jim?" She asked her husband, who obviously still had one ear on the conversation, as he finished serving.

"Forky's House," Jim replied, handing over a beer to his customer.

"Forky's House," the landlady repeated, turning to look down at Nick again.

"Unusual name?"

"'Tis isn't it. Dunno what it means really, must be the name of the bloke that built it I suppose. But it's got a rum history of death and murder. Some American airmen were murdered there during the Second World War apparently, and some rock star topped himself there during the sixties."

"Billy Ryan," Jim called over helpfully from the bar, while giving out change to the man he was serving.

"That's it, Billy Ryan, bit of wild man of rock back in the day," the landlady recalled. Then she looked down at Nick, her mooning face coming back to the present. "Anyway, better not scare you off, or you'll never come back again, and your pie will be getting cold."

She bustled off back to the bar and disappeared through a door into the back of the pub. That was the last Nick saw of her that night.

Nick ate quickly and finished his beer. He raised a parting

hand at Jim as he left, but the pub was busier now, the early evening rush started, and Jim did not see him leave. The sun was still shining, and the streets were nearly deserted. The commuters had long since left for home, and the people going out for the night were still at home, getting ready.

The roads were still busy as he crossed at the crossing, with its constant soundtrack of beeps that always ended before you reached the other side. Nick wondered if they had done a time-and-motion study on it, but using only Olympic sprinters. The sun was warm on his face as he walked past the large fence to the gates. He unlocked them, and moved inside, thinking he'd have to leave them open tomorrow, as some of his deliveries would start arriving. He hoped the doorbell still worked and knew he'd have to keep an ear out for the door all day. That meant no trips down to the dead-end, secret passages until night-time tomorrow.

"Maybe I'll hit the library tomorrow then," he muttered to himself as he closed and padlocked shut the gate behind him.

Nick turned around.

He was back in *gloom-land* again.

The high, surrounding fence and tall, imposing trees let little of the evening sun even touch the house. It should be bathed in reflected sunlight, but only the chimney and odd angles of the roofs seemed to get any sustained light. The walls, windows, and the grounds were only punctuated with spears of summer sunshine like they had to be thrown with almighty effort by some sun god.

Exhaling, he pulled out his phone as he walked down the shady path to the front steps. He tapped in Billy Ryan's name on the internet to see what he could find. He came up with a few sites, and images of the wild guitar man of sixties rock. Mostly about his band, their hits, and his wildlife, and the women he bedded. Nick's right shoe was on the first step up to the front door when he stopped dead, noticing another piece of information about the dead rocker.

Death Pictures of Famous Singers From the Sixties Who Died Too Young.

Nick scrolled through images of Eddie Cochran with his

head smashed in after his fateful car crash in April 1960; a
picture of Stuart Sutcliffe on a mortuary slab from April 1962,
Patsy Cline's mangled corpse from a plane crash in May 1963,
Dinah Washington lying dead in bed with sleeping pills on the
bedside cabinet from December 1963. The list and the sick death
pictures went on, with names upon names of singers that Nick
recognised from Jim Reeves, Johnny Burnette, Cole Porter, Sam
Cooke, Nat King Cole, Woody Guthrie, Otis Redding, Frankie
Lyman and good old Billy Ryan. The list seemed endless, and
Nick wondered how many singers made it out of the sixties
alive. Plane crashes, heroin overdoses, booze, pills, clubbed to
death, shot, drowned and car crashes. All were shown on this
morgue of an American site.

There was Billy Ryan, head first in a water fountain, his long
hair spread out on either side on the water's surface. His hands
clasped around the thing like he was having the last slow dance
of the night and a daffodil sticking out the crack of his arse.

Nick made it onto the second step and then stopped.

He looked up, and before him was the very same fountain
from the grainy black-and-white photo on the site. It was covered
in green algae, bindweeds, and ivy now, but it was the same
fountain that Ryan had died in, his veins burning with snorted
industrial strength cleaner. Nick looked from the morbid, death
picture, to the serene and dirty fountain.

"Not the best way to go for sure," Nick said to himself. Then
something in the picture caught his eye and using his right
finger and thumb he enlarged a certain part of the photograph.
Nick moved down the steps and closer to the fountain. He stood
roughly where the photographer had taken the picture of Billy
Ryan's last repose. The image of Ryan's left hand was blurry so
enlarged, but he could still make out that the rock star held a
key in his death grip.

A key, which was the same as the one in the box in the
fireplace, or maybe even one of its missing siblings. Nick picked
up a nearby piece of fallen branch to poke around in the dried
up remains of the green sludge and crusted dirt inside the
waterless fountain. He pushed back ivy and found a dead bird,
but nothing else was there, no key.

A stab of light shone down from a gap in the canopy of trees and lit up the base and side of the fountain. He looked up at the lance of sunlight and nodded his thanks to the heavens. Prodding with the branch and his hands found no sign of any key from a picture over fifty years old.

"Worth a punt, eh?" he said as he stood up, dropped the branch, and rubbed his dirty hands onto the hips of his jeans. "Probably in some police evidence bag somewhere on a dusty shelf."

Clicking off the site, he jogged up the front steps to unlock the front doors. Once inside the large black-and-white tiled hallway, he was again surprised to find that it let in more of the sun than the front garden did. It almost made the place feel a little liveable. Nick went over to a brass fitting on the wall, full of light switches, and turned them all on, one by one. It was like turning on the Christmas lights in Blackpool, as the shadow-filled darkness was banished from the corridors, halls, landings and passageways of the house.

Nick was sure he heard at least two light bulbs blow, both upstairs and down, as the house's fifty-year-old wiring strained at the sudden over-usage of electricity. "Towels," he said to the east music room entrance. Something else he needed and forgot to order for his stay. He wasn't sure how long it would take to glean the dark hidden secrets of this house, but Nick had come to realise it would not be a five-minute job. He half expected to hear ghostly music wafting from behind the music room door. Half expected a ghost would entice him in, but there was no sound in the house apart from the soles of his shoes on the floor as he walked away.

He went upstairs to his bedroom. Before entering, he found the nearest bathroom, only a couple of doors down on the same side of the corridor. The large bath was the abode of spiders and didn't look too inviting, but the sink and toilet were both functional. He pulled out a narrow blue box from his inner jacket pocket and set it on the porcelain sink. He opened the plastic box to reveal a toothbrush in two pieces, that he slotted together, and a miniature tube of toothpaste which he applied to the brush and started to clean his teeth.

After three minutes he spat into the sink and turned on the cold tap. It rumbled for a second, then brown water erupted and then stopped.

"Bollocks," Nick swore, knowing he'd have to pop over to the local shop and try and get some bottles of water, and maybe toilet paper too before he could bed down for the night.

CHAPTER SIX

The dream was more boring than repeats of *Mastermind*.
It was always the same.
Never deviating from its repetitive narrative.

Nick was alone, in a desert of parched, cracked clay, with a dune bowl of sand surrounding him as far as the eye could see. And he couldn't see much but sand, an orange bleached sky, and a burning sun at high noon. The flat, baked surface ran for a mile or so in every direction. The shifting dunes could never be reached - Nick had tried many times, and it was like the ground was a miniature treadmill, and his walking, or running, would never get him closer.

So Nick did what he normally did. Showed a little patience and waited for the dream to end. He used to pull an imaginary pack of cards from his mind in the old days. He sat crossed legged on the parched earth and played games on his mobile phone. He pulled his arms out of his blue jacket and draped it over his head to get a little shade, to see the screen better, and get the searing sun off his head. Normally he loved the sun, heat, but this Death Valley of a place was too hot for him.

The dream seemed to last an eternity every night. No wonder he tried to stay up to all hours indulging his carnal desires, sleep gave him little rest. He'd just finished a game of solitaire and was wondering what game to play next when he heard a noise. He'd never heard noises here before. Even his footfalls were near cushioned silence. Nick looked up from under the shade of his jacket, and for the first time, he could see something ahead in the distance. Four figures, dark shadows walking towards his position in the centre of the desert. Nick stood and shrugged on his jacket. He cupped his eyes with both hands and tried to focus on the figures. They were distant, dark blobs in human form, too far away to see clearly. They seemed to end at the knees, as the ground quivered in the heat haze, erasing their legs and feet. Nick wasn't sure whether to feel trepidation or elation at having visitors to his nightmare world. He moved forward, walking slowly at first, and then into a little jog. He felt his lungs burning as they drew in more of the baking air. The four figures seemed to be walking at an angle towards him, so the gaps between their bodies decreased.

Their legs inched into view, and their colour, each seemed covered head to foot, including faces, in different hues: black, white, blue and red. Nick ran. As he did the bodies of these four human sexless shapes merged into one, as they drew closer. All hues were gone now, so only one shape remained.

There before him not more than four hundred yards away was a boy.

"Oh my little prince," Nick said, sitting up in the two armchairs he'd pushed together to make some sort of bed for the night. There were tears in his eyes. He was clawing at his chest, his nails leaving lines of red marks as his outpouring of grief overtook him. "Oh, my poor boy."

It took nearly fifteen minutes for him to calm down.

He left his bedroom and headed for a different bathroom, only finding out it was already morning when he entered the un-shuttered room. The sun was up early this time of the year, so he had no clue to what hour it was. He washed his face, armpits, and stinging chest in the cold water. This lessened the effect of the nightmare, and now at least it faded from his mind. He looked in the dirty-edged mirror above the basin and saw the criss-cross marks on his chest where he'd scratched himself. He hadn't done anything like that in years. He wondered why his nightmare had suddenly evolved. Maybe the answer was the house.

If it did indeed hold a room that could magically disappear and reappear, what could it do to the subconscious mind? Nick wetted and flattened down his hair as best he could, and then went back to his bedroom. He opened the shutters over the high windows, to welcome in a new morning. Nick wore only his boxers, as the night had been humid, even for such a large, shadowy house like this. He dressed in yesterday's clothes, hoping that new clothes were the first of his deliveries to arrive today.

He was just tying up his shoelaces and thinking of breakfast, when the doorbell was rung three times, followed by rapid knocking on his front door. Any thought of not hearing it was dispelled, the noise echoed through the empty house, crashed to the rear and backwards until they met in one cacophony of sound.

Was it food, drink, booze, the camper bed or cameras, he thought as he raced down the grand staircase. The light here was dim at this hour unlike the afternoon, where it bathed the stairs in warming sunlight.

It was a small box to sign for: only 5″ x4″ x4″ and contained his EMF meter.

He put it on the staircase and sat down next to it. He finished off the bottle of water and the packet of Hobnobs he'd got from the late opening newsagents across the road. He didn't want to stray to far from the front door today, so headed for the double doors on the west side of the house. Unlike the empty ballroom he'd ventured in yesterday, this room was full of furniture. All covered over with dustsheets.

"White sheets. Can't have a proper haunted house and ghosts without the obligatory white sheets." Nick said, pulling off the nearest one to reveal an ornate armchair. He put on a happy tune from his mobile as he worked. *Soundgarden* blared out as he pulled off another sheet, and another, to reveal a trio of occasional tables, and another armchair. Enjoying himself now, Nick weaved through the furniture at a faster and faster pace, whipping off sheets from tables, sideboards, sofas and the like.

He finished at the same time as the song on his phone died to nothing. He sneezed four times in succession, down onto the pile of dusty white sheets at his feet. He rubbed at his nose, wiping any wetness on his knuckles onto the seat of his jeans. Now he had somewhere to sit. He was about to go over and open up two of the many windows in the huge room when the doorbell chimed again.

Nick hurried as a large bulk of his next day delivery order arrived. He had food, clothes, drink, but no booze or camper bed yet. Leaving the opened, and unpacked boxes in the hallway, he returned to the vast sitting room to open the windows. This was a job-and-a-half it turned out, as it involved using a large pole with a double hook on the end. He'd only managed to open one after ten minutes when the doorbell went again. He rubbed at his neck, which ached a little from craning his head upwards for so long and put down the pole.

The booze and heavy tools like the hammer, sledgehammer, pickaxe arrived next, but no sign of the camper bed. It took most of the morning to get the windows open, while most of the things he ordered were delivered. Then he swore to himself, as he knew he would have to shut the bloody things again that evening.

He spent a hungry afternoon, not daring to go out unless he missed a delivery van or two. He did unpack the boxes using a knife he found in a near empty drawer in the kitchen. He filled an empty room next to the sitting room with the cardboard debris, nearly to the high ceiling in places. At least it was out of the way, but the hallway and stair carpet were littered with cut plastic tags, box stuffing, and dropped bits of packaging. He found an old broom, with overused bent bristles in the cloakroom and decided to sweep up as he waited for the rest of his deliveries. It had been years since he'd done anything menial like sweeping, and he quite enjoyed the novelty of it.

By six o'clock the hall and stairs were swept clean and bathed in warm afternoon sunshine. Nick sneezed. Looking at all the swirling dust motes in the sunlit parts of the hall, he retreated into the airier sitting room.

He, therefore, missed the dust motes swirling and collecting into the vague form of a man, on the stairs. Before a breeze through the open sitting room door dissipated the formation into floating nothingness again.

CHAPTER SEVEN

The Scotsman turned over and woke up, finding he was not in his own bed.

He sat up, naked, as a thin silk sheet dropped off his torso. He was in his mid-fifties, but he kept himself fit and trim. He didn't have a Hollywood six-pack, but he had a firm gut for someone over fifty. His hair was maybe going grey, but he thought he was still okay looking.

"You okay there, Steve?" The question, and the blonde hair and naked form of his twenty-nine-year-old girlfriend asked, at least confirming whose bedroom he was in. Steve was his Monaco name, after the actor he loved, Steve McQueen.

"Yes, because I'm with you," he said and reached over to kiss her as passionately as a man with no heart could manage. "What time is it?"

"Early, just after nine, sweetie," she replied, nuzzling up to lay her face on his hairy chest.

Early, he mentally shook his head. When he was in the French Foreign Legion, back in the mid-seventies, they were up at 5 a.m. every morning to do a full pack run. *The girl doesn't know she's born.*

"We should get up in a bit, I'm starving."

"What is starving?" she asked in her Eastern-European accent, both of them were exiles from their home countries.

"Hungry, you know."

"I'm glad you changed your mind and comes over last night, Steve," she said turning her head to suck at his small right nipple as her hand wandered under the sheets to between his legs. "I am also hungry, yes."

He'd done the right thing on fleeing his place, as his girlfriend made him forget about the walkie-talkie for the rest of the day.

CHAPTER EIGHT

The camper bed did not arrive that day. He checked his phone, it had a three-day delivery time span. Grunting to himself that he never noticed this before he headed out to the pub to have his dinner. Bangers n' Mash was the order of the day, eased down with onion gravy and two pints of IPA. Treacle tart and custard followed, and Nick found he was sweating by the time he finished both hot meals. It was still very warm out, as he left the pub at about nine, after a little chat with the landlord and lady.

He decided to pick up a couple packets of cigarettes, and two large bottles of water, before retiring back to Forky's House. He couldn't get over the name, it sounded like some trashy American frat-film from the early eighties, rather than the name for a posh mansion in the middle of North London.

Nick exited the shop with two packs of cigarettes in his jacket pockets, two packets of Polos, and two Mars bars added to the two-litre bottles of water he carried in a thin plastic bag, too fragile for the weight it bore. He could feel the thin handles stretching and cutting into his right palms only a few steps down the pavement. He had just passed a thin, dark alleyway between a tanning salon and a bookies when he heard a punch being delivered, and the woof of air from someone's lungs. Nick stopped at the entrance to the alleyway, it was lined with several foul smelling bins on one side.

A tall figure he half-recognised rose up to his full height of about six foot two, towering over his smaller, and darker clothed assailants.

"How do ya like that then, ya fucking poof?" snarled one youth from under his hoodie.

"Not the sorta fisting you like eh, *Gandalf the Gay*," laughed another youth with a matching grey hoodie.

"Really, children isn't it a school night?" The tall man was dressed in what looked like a dark red dressing gown, over a pair of beige trousers, and sockless slip-ons. "Won't your mothers be wanting you home for tea?"

His voice was booming and authoritative, but Nick could hear the nervous fear at the back of his throat. None of them had noticed Nick, they were too intent on playing out this homophobic melodrama in broad daylight.

"Fucking tea, that what you fucking gays drinking ain't it." Only one of the hoodies had not spoken yet, he stood, watching the tall, older man, with evil intent.

"Don't your mother's make you fine boys tea then, before they pop off to walk the streets all night to give fellatio to any passing man for a fiver." Some of the strength and bravery had returned to the older man's voice, mocking the youths.

"What did you say?" One of them punched the tall man in the stomach again, doubling him over.

"I said your mother are whores, and the best part of your no-mark, absent fathers, dribbled up the crack of your mother's derrieres," the winded man retorted.

"Right that's it, I'm gonna cut you another hole that you can get fucked up." The quiet one pulled a knife from his pocket, and flicked it open, advancing on the helpless man.

"I wouldn't do that if I was you," Nick spoke for the first time. "Blood is a devilish thing to get out of clothes even at low-temperature washes."

"Who the fuck are you?"

"I'm the bloke who is working out which one of you I'm going to kill first," Nick replied, pointing from each youth to the other in turn, and back again.

"Kill us, you're fucking off your trolley, mate."

"Oh I never joke about murder," Nick said, setting down his bottles of water on the pavement, and rolling up the sleeves of his jacket as he entered the alley.

"You were only joking about murder I assume, sir," the tall man asked, as the last of the beaten youths hobbled out of the alley, with his own knife sticking out of his left thigh.

"What day is it today?" Nick asked, picking up a fallen hooded top to wipe the blood off his knuckles.

"Tuesday."

"Then I was joking. I only murder on Monday, Sundays and Wednesday mornings."

"We better leave before they come back with more chums, or call the police," The tall man said, patting Nick gratefully on his left shoulder.

"Do they know where you live?"

"Sadly—yes."

"Then over to my house then, I have tea, and something harder I think," Nick said and led the man out of the blood-covered alley, and across the road to Forky's House. The defeated youths were nowhere to be seen.

"Now there's an offer," the older man muttered, false bravado coming back to his loud, thespian tones. They crossed at the crossing, the traffic was lighter now, so they walked across without invoking the flashing green man. The older man followed in Nick's wake for a while, and then as he got his breath back his long legs soon caught up, and he came alongside. They rounded the corner of the high wall of the house, and Nick stopped.

The man cruelly dubbed *Gandalf the Gay* by the youths thought it was to check the coast was clear. So he dutifully scanned the roads, houses, shops and tube station for any sign of his attackers, but could see none. It was only the rattle of the chain and padlock that caused the older man to crane his neck around like some bald eagle, then his body twirled around with silent grace as his eyes caught what his rescuer was doing.

"I haven't been rescued from a fate worse than death by a cat-burglar have I?" he asked, raising his bushy grey and black mottled eyebrows.

"No," Nick said, finally opening the padlock, "this is where I live."

"You reside, here?"

"For a while at least." Nick nodded, and showed an open

palm to the tall gentleman, showing him the way in.

"All by yourself?"

"Yes."

Nick could see the hesitation in the older man's body language. A flicker of real fear on his sallow, but warmly engaging cheeks. Then a loud shout came from the direction of the tube station. Both men looked round but could see no one.

"I'm going to fucking kill the queer-cunt," a loud, older teen voice echoed across the street.

"Then I accept your kind invitation," *Gandalf* said, as he hurried past Nick into the dark confines of the tree-lined grounds.

Nick quickly shut and locked the gate and led the shaken man down the drive towards the house. He could see his new acquaintance was shaking and unnerved but was that due to his run in with the queer-bashers, or the thought of entering Forky's House?

"So would I have seen you in anything then, Lionel?" asked Nick, as they sat in opposite chairs in the sitting room. Nick poured red wine into two tumblers he'd purloined from the pub when no one was looking: something else he'd forgotten to order. The man he'd saved, now properly introduced as Lionel Hawthorne, hadn't looked like he'd wanted to venture too deep into this house. So the first room on the left, the de-sheeted sitting room was the ideal place.

Once inside, the man had calmed a little and told Nick he was actor and thespian of no small renown. Indeed, talking about his favourite subject, himself, had brought the colour and passion back to Lionel's cheeks.

"Well, dear, where do I begin? Stage, television, films and theatres, I've done them all. *The Bill, Doctors, Casualty, Corrie, Doctor Who,* I've worked with Gielgud, Dame Peggy Mount, and Lawrence Harvey. Even did a film with John Wayne once, bloody awful thing it was, but there you go. I've trod more boards than a sailor on shore-leave, my new friend. Ah, the stories I could recount." Lionel leant forward with his half-drained wine so Nick could reciprocate with a clink of stolen glass.

"New or old *Who*?" Nick asked, sitting back on his carved and gilded framed seat.

"Oh, the classic *Who* my dear boy. I appeared twice you know with Pertwee, now that was a man, and later on with McCoy, you know the Seventh one." What Lionel did not impart was he played an Ice Warrior, in one and a passenger on a spaceship with one line, before he died in the later episode. The time his actual face appeared on screen added up to all of thirty-seven seconds.

"But, where are the manners my mother taught me, and my father beat into me? Thank you for helping me out of that spot of bother back there. I only went out for a pint of milk for my *Crunchy Nut Cornflakes*, and to get a tin of cat food for Othello. Hence my evening attire," Lionel explained, letting his open hands run down the length of his red dressing gown.

"Othello, your black cat then?"

"Ah-ha no, white body with a black face, like many Othello's in their time." Lionel laughed, and Nick found his large, over-the-top laughter infectious.

"So, have you lived around here long?" Nick asked after the laughter had died, and their wine tumblers drained some more.

"Oh, well, best part of fifty-two years. I was born in Leeds, but my mother brought me down here to escape my father's fists. He was very handy with those on women and children he termed as *Nancy-Boys*."

"Sounds rough," said Nick, taking another sip of wine, and wondering if any of the food supplies he ordered contained a packet of Cheese n' Onion crisps.

"Ancient history, my dear boy, my father drank himself into an early grave last century...all alone, and with no mourners at his grave." Lionel waved his hand in the air in a dismissive manner and drained his glass.

"Another?"

"Be rude not too." Lionel stretched forwards as Nick topped up both of their glasses. "In fact, my poor departed mother used to clean this place, back in the day when they could get people to stay here."

"Really, did she clean for Billy Ryan then?"

"Oh, yes, and I used to help her out during the school holidays. Saw some sights, we did cleaning up after him. Had my first kisses here you know, with a drunk girl from a chocolate ad, Vogue model, and then a nice young drummer called Sebastian, he was my first if you don't mind me lowering the tone."

"Not at all," Nick smiled at the older man's reminisces.

"This place could do with sprucing up, old thing. I'll get my little Romanian cleaner girl to come and see you, she is always after more hours and extra work."

"Thanks." Nick nodded. "So were you shocked when Billy Ryan died?"

"*No,* it wasn't a big shock that he died the way he did. I was at Art College at the time, but it was my mother who found him in the fountain. Nearly did her in, seeing him like that, but it was only a matter of time with Billy, he'd snort anything up that ruddy great hooter of his."

"So you know all about the place really, Lionel." Nick began leaning forwards to put down his tumbler of wine. "Did you know about the secret door in the music room and the stairs going down?"

"No," Lionel said, a little too quickly, and stood to retie his dressing gown around his long thin frame. "Look, I'd better be getting back to Othello, and hope those young hooligans haven't broken into my flat."

"Okay. I'll walk you over there and see you safely inside if you like?"

"I'm not a child that has to be escorted back to my bed, Nick. I'm a sixty-five-year-old man, who's lived around here most of his adult life." There was a hint of trembling anger in Lionel's voice.

"I didn't mean to offend." Nick raised his hands in peace. "I just didn't want you getting beaten up again, that's all."

"I know," Lionel said in a softer voice, putting his hand out on Nick's shoulder. "You'll have to excuse me, it's been one of those nights, *my dear.* It's not often a handsome young man comes to my rescue anymore."

"Hey, let me at least walk you to the gate and make sure the coast is clear." Nick offered, reaching up to squeeze the older man's shoulder.

"That would be acceptable." Lionel Hawthorne nodded.

They left the sitting room, and Nick noticed that his new friend did not look down the dark corridors, or at the stairs, but kept his focus constantly on the front doors. The sun had set, and the front of the house felt stuffy, close, and dark as pitch. Outside the unlocked gate, the streets seemed quiet enough, showing no signs of angry youths out for gay blood.

"Will you be okay from here?" Nick asked as they moved to the edge of the curb, to be buffeted by the sharp breeze of a passing double-decker bus.

"Yes," Lionel said in a loud voice, which he lowered when the noisy bus had passed by. "Thank you once again for the wine and the help in the alley. You'll have to pop over one afternoon for high tea, Othello and I seldom get visitors these days."

"Sounds good to me. What flat number are you?"

"Seventeen B, above the kebab shop. Just ring the buzzer anytime you like if you want a chinwag. Just make it after eleven a.m., if possible. Othello does like to sleep in."

"I certainly will," Nick replied with a genuine smile. "Just one more thing, Lionel, before you go?"

"Yes, my, dear boy. Ask anything of me, my brave hero."

"Did your mother, or you, ever see some oddly made keys around the house at all when you cleaned there? Large, brassy thing, with only one loop at the bottom end, and a funny ridge on the top?"

"I saw many sights in that house, Nick, but I don't recall a key like that. Right better be off, *toodle-loo*." Lionel was off across the road and over on the other side before Nick could call out goodbye. Lionel gave one quick wave, before entering a side door next to the kebab shop and disappearing quickly from view. Nick scratched his chin, and, humming an old Billy Ryan tune, returned to his new abode.

CHAPTER NINE

It was warm and stuffy upstairs, so Nick stayed on the sofa in the sitting room. His eyes blinked open to light filtering in through the tall windows, his eyes focusing on two tumblers, and an empty bottle of red wine on the table in front of him. That night's desert dream already fading from his thoughts. His back had fared a little better than on the two pushed together chairs upstairs. He sat up and ran both his hands through his hair. Then he considered braving the water supply for a much-needed bath.

He had only risen to his feet and sneezed out dust from his nose when he heard the doorbell chiming. Confused, he looked down at his mobile phone to see it was a quarter to nine in the morning. He picked it up, and slipped it into his trouser pocket, yawning as he walked out of the sitting room.

It must be a delivery, hopefully, my camper bed, he thought, as he yawned again wider, making his jaw click. But as he reached the door he stopped dead, his hand on the large doorknob. *But I'm sure I locked the gate and padlocked it shut last night?*

Seeing he would get no answers by staring at the front doors, he unlocked and opened them, hoping it was a man in uniform carrying a box with his camper bed in it.

It turned out it was not.

It was a short, pretty girl, with long, dark hair flowing down over the jacket she had on. She was high-cheeked, with dazzling topaz-blue eyes that seemed to stare right through Nick. She wore jeans and UGG boots, but the clothes did not detract from her overall beauty. She smiled as he opened the door wide, to step out onto the cold stone steps. It was thin, business smile, that ended on her cheeks with dimples.

"Are you Mister Nick?" she asked, with an Eastern European tinge to her English accent.

"I guess so." He laughed at the switching of his Christian name to a surname. "And who may you be?"

"I am Crina Popescu, I clean for Mister Lionel across the road. He says that you might need a cleaner for this house too?"

"It certainly needs a good dust and hoover," Nick said, eyeing her up and down, as a prospective employer, and for other more base reasons. "But how did you get through the locked gate?"

"I climb over wall." She showed her dimpled smile again.

"Very impressive." Nick nodded. "You must really want this job?"

"I need money, yes," Crina said, tipping her head to the left, before licking her top lip nervously. "This is big house, lots of rooms to clean, lots of money."

Nick couldn't help his smirk opening up into a pleasant laugh. "I admire your honesty, Crina Popescu, so would you like the job?"

"You haven't even heard if I am any good, or what monies I will charge you?"

"You work for Lionel, and he's a top bloke, that's reference enough, and I only intend to use half-a-dozen rooms here. Shall we say weekdays, three hours a day, including you cook me a midday meal? Say twenty pounds an hour. That sound fair to you Crina?"

"I don't even charge half of twenty quids usually." The shock of the hourly rate forcing an honest reply from Crina's full lips.

"Ah, well, I think you are worth it, Crina Popescu, and I'm fucking minted," Nick said, coming down one step closer to her. The Romanian girl backed away to match the advance of her new employer. "So what do you say can you start eleven a.m. tomorrow?"

Crina thought for three seconds. Obviously weighing some domestic conundrum in her mind, before answering.

"You have a deal," she finally replied, moving forward to extend her pale right hand.

"Deal," Nick smiled out of the side of his mouth as he

reached forward to shake her hand. He noticed that as her wrist
came out of her sleeve, there was an old white and pink scar
that ran across the main vein there. "My word is my bond, and
my handshake a contract."

Crina frowned, not sure what her new young, thirty years
old she reckoned, employer was talking about. She nodded and
took her hand from his warm, comforting one. "Thank you,"
she said, just for something polite to say.

"Do you want to pop in now, or wait until tomorrow to see
the mammoth task in hand, or do you have any questions about
our arrangement?"

"I have somewhere I have to be, another cleaning job," Crina
said, taking one more step back, her heel digging a small rut
into the stones of the driveway. "And only one question, what
is half-a-dozen?"

"Oh, six, it's also my favourite number," Nick replied, before
thumbing back inside the house with his right hand. "I'll go
fetch the keys to open the gate, and let you leave in a more
ladylike manner."

Crina nodded and waited on the gloomy drive for Nick to
return. Before he did she crossed herself twice, and once again
for good measure.

Crina's arrival and swift departure was a stroke of good fortune
for Nick. A yellow and green delivery van was parked as he
opened the gate, and he'd hardly heard her say goodbye before
he was accosted by a tall, uniformed delivery man, with dreads.
By the time Nick had signed for a large, heavy, oblong cardboard
box, Crina had walked off to wherever she was going next.

He was slightly miffed that he never saw her jean covered
behind walk away, as he lugged his box back to the house. But
his pondering, lascivious imaginings of her body were soon
dispelled, as inside the box his deluxe camper bed had arrived
at last. Scattering white polystyrene chips all over the hall he
raced upstairs to his chosen bedroom and set about putting it
together.

When he'd accomplished this feat of assemblage, Nick felt
like a true hunter-gatherer, and then he was hit by a nagging

hunger in his belly. Leaving the torture of a bath for another day, he washed his face, gave a cursory wash to his body, put on a new shirt and underwear he'd bought, and headed out to find some morning sustenance.

The kebab shop, pub, and other restaurants were not open. He wasn't in the mood for what the Polish Deli had to offer or the Newsagents, so he walked over the next road to the corner coffee shop. Nick ordered a double espresso, a large cappuccino, two bacon and egg baps and an apricot filled tart. He sat down on one of the metal tables outside in the warm morning sunshine and began his breakfast. The espresso went down first to wake him up, followed by the two greasy baps. Then, with mind buzzing and belly sated, he ate the tart and drank his other coffee at a more sedate rate. He watched the world in this part of North London hurry by, off to work, shop and other places. While he just drank in the sights, sounds and different languages of the place. With the last dregs of cappuccino left in the large cup, he slapped his knees and stood, sending crumbs falling from his lap onto the warm paving slabs.

He had work to do.

He took another disappointing trip down through the music room's secret door, to the parallel corridors in the depths of the earth, but there were still no signs of a doorway there.

He headed back up to explore the library. He wanted to try and glean any clues from the books inside on who built the place, and what purpose the hidden steps down to the passages had. He left the music room via the west door. As soon as he closed the door behind him, he heard the unmistakable sound of the piano being played. Not a tune as such, but just random keys being hit, by some rank amateur.

Nick spun round and pulled open the music room door so quickly he couldn't get his foot out of the way, and the door wedged only a quarter-way open. There was no one to be seen sitting, or standing, by the piano, but swift movement caught his eye from the east door of the music room. He thought he saw a short person, or a male child, quickly close the door as they exited into the parallel corridor.

He heard a child's giggle as he got his foot out the way and raced across the music room to the eastern doorway. He pulled it cleanly open and ducked into the corridor, looking left and then right. It was only when he flicked his head to the right did he see a pair of legs and shoes round the large bannister of the grand staircase. Nick ran down the unlit corridor, coming into the bright hallway, where his shoes on the flooring echoed around the quiet house.

The hallway was empty, and the doors to the ballroom and sitting room were both closed shut. With his hand on the round, carved end of the bannister, he looked up the stairs, but could see no signs of an intruder, or hear any footfalls anywhere. Rubbing at the stubble on the top of his lip he moved into the centre of the hallway, facing the wide steps of the carpeted staircase and held his breath to listen.

All he could hear was the pounding of his heart in his ears. The house was more silent than his still body could ever be. He held his breath as long as he could, but the quiet, vast house offered up no sounds at all. He could not get the sound of his racing heart out of his eardrums. Only when he exhaled did a sound come, almost if it was waiting for that precise moment. A child's laughter again, coming from the west corridor, where he had begun the chase. Nick ran as fast as he could down the wood-panelled corridor.

He noticed it at once, the library door that had been shut only moments ago was open into the passageway.

He ran on, skidding to a halt past the open large wooden doorway. With his heart pounding, he took a deep, calming breath, and entered the library. It wasn't as large as he remembered but was from skirting board to architrave it was filled with purpose-built bookcases. They were filled to the brim with books that had probably not been touched in over a hundred years or more. There were a couple of reading tables, but nothing more in the way of furniture, not even a chair. It was musty and filled with volumes of knowledge and works of old fiction, but there was nowhere for anyone, not even a child to hide.

Nick moved inside and walked around both reading tables,

but there were no children hidden behind, or under them. He looked at the windows, but they looked like they had been untouched in over half a century. Cradles of cobwebs hung in the high echelons of the windows, but nothing else.

"Who are you, little one, and what do you want of me?" Nick said to the rows upon rows of books, making him feel slightly embarrassed. There came no answer, no giggles of prepubescent children, nothing but silence in the library.

Nick waited in the thunderous silence and wondered if this room had a secret door also.

The door of the library slammed shut with such force it rattled the old glass in the windows. Nick had no time to let the shock take over his body as he raced over and grabbed the knob. As he did something fell behind him and landed onto the wooden floor with a stifled thump. Nick, his hand still held fast onto the doorknob, turned his body and neck to see what had fallen.

On the floor, in between the two large windows, was a bound ochre coloured hardback book. Sucking his teeth in indecision, Nick quickly decided to push open the library door first. He poked his head out around the door, his hand still gripped on the handle, but the dimly lit corridor was empty in both directions. Closing the door again, he strode over to the fallen book. He did not touch it at first but looked up at the bookcase in between the two large windows. There, on the highest shelf, was a gap that matched the size of the spine of the fallen book. Ignoring the black slit between the rows of volumes with unreadable titles, titles obscured by the height of the shelves and the dust that covered them Nick looked at the book on the floor.

He crouched down. It had landed on its plain back cover, which retained more of the original orange colour than the faded spine. He finally picked it up and looked at the title: *The Four Feathers* by *A.E.W.Mason*. He flicked the first page open to find it was a first edition from 1902. There came another thump from behind him, that made him raise his shoulders up into his neck. Nick turned to see another hardback from a middle shelf had fallen from a bookcase to the left of the closed door. Holding the first book in his left hand, he hurried over to pick it up and found it was a copy of *Dickens Bleak House*. Another book fell, three bookcases along to the right of the door, this time from only two shelves up.

"For fuck's sake," Nick cursed and hurried over to gather up this third book, that some unseen hand had chosen to tip out onto the floor. Nick looked around but could see no sign of anyone else in the library with him, no one visible. The third book was one he had never heard of before: *Travels with a Donkey in the Cevennes* by *Robert Louis Stevenson*: obviously not one of his classics.

"Anymore for anymore?" Nick asked the empty library as he stood up, clutching the three old books to his chest.

No one answered.

No more books fell.

Nick waited. He stood still for five minutes, before walking over to the nearest reading desk, and setting the three fallen books side by side on it. Nick stared at the books, and wondered why the child-like spirit that seemed to have taken an interest in him this morning had wanted him to see these books? Or were they just random showings of its ghostly telekinetic powers?

He had heard of two of the titles and two of the authors, but apart from this being a bit of a bleak house, he could not understand what clues they could hold. He leafed through their thin dusty pages and then hung each upside down, but no secret pieces of paper slipped out. He scratched his head and decided he'd had enough of the ghostly literature-throwing child for one morning. Gathering up the three books in his arms, he went out into the rear garden to think.

The garden wasn't neglected by any means, it was tidy enough but bare and dull of colour. There seemed to be a lot of grey slab stones for paths, leading to a fountain. The stone used was covered in green moss, and yellow lichen, matching the limp, green-grey foliage, and dull white flowers that made up the tired looking borders. The huge, guardian trees that bordered the place on all sides, only let in chinks of light through its dark green armour, and whatever grew there loved the shade, and was hardy to the extreme.

Nick wandered down to a small six-sided pavilion that

seemed to be the only suntrap in the rear garden. It looked like it had been there years. It had been repaired in several areas, some better than others. It also had been repainted on numerous occasions, with gloss white paint for the side, and bright sunshine yellow for the roof. It looked totally out of place in the gloomy garden, like a Goth in full-gear on a sunny tropical beach.

On closer inspection, Nick could see the many layers of paint might be the only thing still holding the pavilion upright. The bright, warm, summer sunlight surrounded the pavilion, the paved avenue around it, and two small oval lawns set in front of it. The pavilion had three walls at the back, wooden panels on a rough stone base. The other three sides of the hexagon had wooden posts to hold up the roof but were open to the sunshine. Nick rapped on the nearest post with his knuckles to test its sturdiness before stepping inside.

The back three walls had stone slabs, laid on extended parts of the grey stones walls, about two feet off the wooden floor. Nick sat down on the stone bench facing the house, as this was fully bathed in the sunshine, unlike its fellows. He closed his eyes, leant his head back on the wooden panel behind, and drank in the early morning sunshine.

He laid the three books from the library down on the bench next to him, forgetting about the dark ghostly house for the time being. He let the rays of the sun flow through him, the heat on his exposed skin just about perfect-hot.

"Think I'm gonna spend a lot of time out here," he murmured to himself, letting his mind wander.

His mind drifted from one thing to another. To sex, sun-kissed beaches and back again. He yawned, nodded, and fell asleep in the comforting sunshine.

He dreamed of the desert.

Of four riders on four horses.

Both rider and horse, each one colour; white, black, blue and vivid red. As they rode forward, out of the shimmering reflective sea of sand, they merged into one entity.

One person.

One child.

His dead son.

Nick awoke from his dream, or nightmare, with a start. His hands and arms jumping into his body like he had been struck by lightning. This involuntary twitch sent the three books from the library falling to the floor of the pavilion. Nick glanced at his watch, he reckoned he'd only been asleep for about thirty minutes or so. He rubbed at his warm face and leant down to pick up the fallen books. They had landed on top of each other, like a fan, showing only some of the book titles.

Nick stayed his reaching hand, an inch from the spine of the first book. *Bleak House* was at the bottom of the pile, so only the words House was showing. The Stevenson book lay in the middle of the pile so only the key part of *donkey* was showing and *The Four Feathers* lay on top.

"Four…key…house," Nick read aloud. "Forky's House. Four Keys House."

Nick gathered up the books in his arms and raced down the garden. His hot cheeks glad of the shade nearer the house. He ran back upstairs to his bedroom and dropped the three warm books on his camper bed. Then he grabbed his mobile phone, keys, and wallet, and ran downstairs. He was out of the house, tapping away at his mobile phone for directions to a certain estate agents, the local council planning offices, and the local library.

The local library was within walking distance, the council offices, and estate agents further afield. So, looking at the directions on his screen, he turned right on the main road, went past the cemetery, and down the street to his first port of call.

At last, some of the ghostly mystery of the house was pressing him into action.

CHAPTER TEN

The Scotsman, known in Monaco as Stephen Carlisle, woke suddenly as something heavy landed on his chest. He opened his eyes, just in time to see a long, wet tongue lick the side of his face, from his jawline to his eyelid.

"Ged-off," he said, some of his native tongue forcing its way out, as he sat up, and pushed Mr Wesson off the spare bed. The dog whimpered a little at its admonishment, and trotted off, out the gap of the half-open bedroom door. The Scotsman wiped the wet drool from his face with the bedsheets and then swung his bare legs out of bed. He stood and padded out of the spare bedroom to find Smith and Wesson sitting and waiting by their empty food bowls. He emptied out a large tin of the finest dog food into each bowl before heading for a shower.

He walked past the closed master bedroom door and scratched at the crown of his unwashed, short hair. For a man who had no place for fear in his life, he had avoided sleeping in his own bed, two nights in succession. The walkie-talkie talking to him with his father's voice seemed like some silly fairy-tale to him, and it bugged him why the episode had bothered him so much. Was it subconscious guilt surfacing after all these years?

The old him had never felt any guilt. He did his job and was paid well. Was he an evil man because he carried out such assassinations, or were the shadowy powers-that-be, more to blame for ordering them? Maybe he was going soft in his old age, or slowly losing his grip. He had everything a man could ever want; cars, women, his dogs to love him, a luxury house, and lifestyle any man would chew their right arm off to have. Maybe it was a new kind of guilt, a rich man's guilt. He had more money than politicians had sense, maybe he was falling into the cult of celebrity, trap. If you have everything, all there was left was to feel guilty about it.

He washed the shampoo out of his hair, turned off the shower, and shook himself to get off the excess water. He pulled on a thick white robe and used a towel to quickly dry his hair. He watched the last of the shampoo and water disappearing down the hole in the shower base.

"Fuck guilt," he muttered to himself and made for his main bedroom. He flung the door open and strode over to his wardrobes. He pulled open the one that contained his hidden safe and the walkie-talkie. Set the walkie-talkie down on his bed and looked at it.

No sound came from it.

He picked it up and opened the back to confirm what he knew: it had no batteries inside to power it. No way could it have spoken to him the other day. He tried to turn it on, but no light showed. It was dead, like his old life.

He threw it back into his memory box and knelt down to put it away in the safe again. As he did, a muffled voice spoke from inside the cigar box.

"You cannot escape the past or who you are, Donald."

The Scotsman dropped the box on the carpeted floor and scrambled back to a safe distance away. He leant on the side of his bed and saw that the walkie-talkie had fallen out of the lid of the box, with a picture of his long dead father.

"Who are you, what do you want?" he hissed at the walkie-talkie. The little bulb that should not be on, it flickered red, off, and its neighbour next door flicked on green.

"Don't you recognise your own kin now, son?" the static-laced voice answered.

"Dad?"

"Aye, lad, tis me, Donald."

"What do ya want, pappy?" the Scotsman asked, using the term he had called his father before he died.

"Peace, lad."

"Aren't you at peace in Heaven then, with mammy?"

"No, lad, we rot in purgatory for the sins of the son we begat."

"No…," the Scotsman whined, "don't say that."

"Well, it's true. There is no place in Heaven's grace for a couple who raised such an evil soulless child as you, Donald."

"Don't say that, I loved you both." Tears were running down his cheeks as he shouted at the walkie-talkie.

"As a child, before God took me, and your mother fell from grace, yes. But as a man you became an abomination before His eyes, and He cast me down here to share your awful burden with ya mammy."

"What can I do to help? I'll repent my sins, confess all my crimes…" He trailed off, it was hard to speak.

"There may be a way," his father said. in a kindlier voice.

"Anything, please tell me. Pappy."

"I will come to you again soon and bring another with me. My forgiveness is not enough…" The voice of his long-dead father was fading and the static rising in volume.

"When, pappy?"

"Soon, son…soon…" The voice and the static faded away into nothing. The light on top of the walkie-talkie turned from green to red, and then even the red light faded away to nothing. The Scotsman was sitting on the floor of his bedroom, still sobbing into his sheets, when his dogs padded in. They slowly moved close up to him. He quickly pulled them in close and hugged them tightly. A little surprised at such overt affection, Smith and Wesson licked his face and pressed their bodies closer to his.

CHAPTER ELEVEN

The library idea was a godsend to Nick.

In fact, the upstairs of the building was a local museum, and he was soon introduced to a charming local studies woman in her late sixties, called Margo. She was very interested to hear that he was investigating the local haunted house. She referred to it as Forky's House and recounted the story she knew of the French doctor who flipped-his-lid (in her words) and murdered several wounded American servicemen during the war. Her older sister once told her all about it, the stressed surgeon going mad, and embarking on a nightly killing spree.

"So what is the proper name of the house? Forky's House is just a nickname isn't it?" Nick asked as the older woman, in a long plaid shirt and matching jacket, sat together, poring over old maps she had found.

"You know, I don't rightly know. It's always been called the haunted house, or Forky's House, to my knowledge."

"But your older sister who was born before the war, what did she or your parents call it before this Doctor Forque went doolally?"

"I don't recall, but these various maps of the area should tell us something. It was a large house, even when this was a village in dear old Middlesex before London swallowed it up." Margo raised her spectacles, and hunted through the maps of the area, before sounding an excited, "aha."

"Found something?" Nick asked, inching the small chair he was sat in around the table, and closer to the local studies lady.

She popped on her half-moon specs from a beaded chain around her neck and pointed to a familiar looking square on the map. "This map dates back from nineteen-oh-seven, and here is the house in question, simply referred to as the Gates' House. Now that adds up, as the Gates family were wealthy landowners around here. I've seen their surname on many an old title deed."

"So do you know how old the house is?" Nick asked, wondering if there were any more old maps under the pile that might shed some light on the history of the place.

"Well by the looks of it, I'd say it's Georgian, but let's plough on and see what else we can find, young man."

Nick smiled at being called a young man, but Margo didn't notice, she was too busy digging through the maps she had brought out of storage. She seemed to be enjoying looking back at the house's history as much as Nick wanted to know the information.

"Ah, here we go," Margo said, straightening her posture, and turning another map around so Nick could get a better look at it.

Nick looked at the map and was surprised at how few buildings were shown on it. The pub was there, the house, of course, the cemetery, churches, and even farms.

"When is this one from?"

"Eighteen thirty-three, we have more, they all say Gates House on them, but this one names it as something completely different: Four Keys House. That's an odd coincidence isn't it, as some people call it Forky's House still to this day. Obviously, over the years language changes, the spelling of English words alter, it's most fascinating don't you think?"

Nick nodded in reply. "Do you have any maps even earlier than this?"

"Well, let's have a gander shall we?" Margo said as she dug into her pile of photocopied maps on the table in front of her. "I wonder what name the place will have next, eh?"

Nick just smiled back in response. His mind was trying to figure out how the name of the house kept changing over the years, but always seemed to be known as Four Keys House or a close approximation.

"Two more," Margo suddenly cried, enthusiastically pulling

two smaller maps from the bottom of her pile. Nick looked around, at a teacher and gaggle of young school children, who looked over from a history outing they were on. Nick noticed that the teacher was young, had shoulder length, wavy auburn hair, and very kissable, pouty lips. His musings about the teacher were interrupted by Margo slamming the two maps down in front of him, over the other two maps he had already seen.

"What years have we got here, Margo?" he asked, looking at the two, harder to read, and slightly less to scale, drawings of the local parish from long ago.

"Well, two very similar maps, only five years apart." Margo leant over the table and tapped the right-hand map. "This one is from Seventeen Sixty-Two, and still names the house as Four Keys House."

"And this one?" Nick said, tapping the left map.

"Is from Seventeen Fifty-Seven, but the newly built house goes under another name: Clovis House."

"Clovis House," Nick pondered the name change. "But why change the name of the house so quickly?"

"Well, I do run a little Genealogy business on the side, but it will cost you a remuneration of my time to look into the history of the place, and who built and owned it."

Nick reached into his pocket and took out a roll of cash he knew to be five hundred pounds. He opened Margo's liver-spotted left hand, gently turned it over, and placed the cash in her palm. "Will this do for starters?"

"Erm, yes," Margo stammered. "Starters, fish, main and desserts as well I should guess."

"Hope this puts me top of your priority list, Margo," Nick said, taking an old till receipt from his jacket pocket and using a pen lying on the desk, to scribble his name and number on. "Here's my mobile number to call me with anything you dig up."

"I don't have a mobile myself," Margo said, looking at the number in one hand and the cash in the other. "What if I need to call on you, what is your address?"

Nick stood up from the small chair and looked down as she gazed up at him.

"Four Keys House," he simply replied, and left her to it.

His next port of call that day was a bus ride over to the estate agents that handled the renting out of the house. He had to wait fourteen minutes for the bus, but it gave him plenty of time to think about the house and its ever-changing names. While he was in possession of one key, it sounded like there were three more keys to find, somewhere?

The maps told him so, the local legends suggested it, and the ghostly boy conveyed this via the fallen books. Nick looked up from his musings to see the estate agents whizz by. He rang the bell, and was in luck, as there was a stop only thirty yards away, at the end of another local parade of shops. He jumped off the bus as it hissed to a stop, and he walked past a post office and a bank, to where the offices of Sims, Maynard, and Lee were situated. This part of London was only a stone's throw from the house but seemed set in a more affluent part of the borough. Nick pushed open the glass door to the large fronted estate agents. Nick could only spot one property advertised on the glass that was under a million pounds. There were four desks, three of them occupied by men, tailored in the same matching corporate suits. The fourth desk, near the door, was empty of a person and the usual desk clutter, like it wasn't being used at the moment. One of the men got up from his desk to greet him.

"Yes, can I help you?" his smile was genuine enough.

"I hope so. My name is Nicholas Hobbs, and I'm renting out one of your houses."

"Forky's." The man nodded. "I hope everything is to your satisfaction, if you need any help to make your stay more comfortable, please don't hesitate to tell me or my colleagues here. I'm Mr Sims, by the way."

Nick noted the man had butted in, and spoken very briskly, to deflect any oncoming trouble that he might have with whatever Nick was going to say.

"Yes, everything is fine," Nick said, using his most reassuring tone of voice. "But there is something you could do for me, a couple of things in fact."

"Fire away, we are here to serve."

"I've become attached to a certain painting in the drawing room, and I'd like to buy it. I wonder if you could give me the contact details of the house owners, so I can maybe try and convince them to let me purchase it. Also, I found a purse belonging to a Tracey Sunderland, and her business card says she works here, could I have her address to return it." Nick knew that the man wanted to butt in again on at least two occasions, that's why he had spoken quickly, and without stopping.

"Well, Mr Gates, who owns the property, is a very private man, but we can easily pass on your request to the solicitors we deal with about the picture. Sadly, Tracey quit her job here a couple of weeks ago."

"Well then, you will have no qualms about giving me her address so I can send her purse back to her. On the matter of the picture, if you can get Mr Gates solicitor to contact me in due course, that would be great."

"Erm, yes…okay." Mr Sims stammered a little and then showed Nick over to his desk. He sat down, looked up Tracey's address, and wrote it on the back of one of the company's business cards. Nick sat down, took a business card and scribbled his name and mobile number on it. Nick and Sims then exchanged cards. Nick was smiling. Mr Sims looked a little more hesitant to be giving over his former employee's address. The thought of losing the first resident at Forky's House for decades quelled his concerns.

"I look forward to hearing from Mr Gates' solicitors in due course," Nick said, as he rose to his feet. He shook the man's hand and left the shop with a waved, "goodbye."

He walked along the road to a bench by the bus stop and sat down. With such little information, feigned interest in paintings and pretend purses, he'd dug up some useful stuff. Namely that the Gates family still owned the house that they had surely renamed.

He pulled out his mobile and tapped in his current address onto the Land Registry website. There he clicked on the check who owns a property, part of the page and typed in the postcode of the house. Two clicks later, and a payment of £3 bought up the details of a solicitors in Ipswich, Suffolk.

That was a bit far to go today. So he typed in the directions from the estate agents' postcode to Tracey Sunderland's home. He found it was only two streets away. Smiling at his craftiness, he stood and headed off in the direction the map on his phone sent him.

"Isn't modern technology wonderful," he said to himself as he turned left at the next junction.

Nick found himself outside Tracey Sunderland's home after less than a three-minutes' walk. It was clouding over, but the temperature was still in the high seventies. She lived in a modest two up, two down, but even modest was selling for well over four hundred and ninety thousand in this part of town.

Conning the estate agents out of information had been like taking candy from a baby. Nick wasn't as cock-sure of his approach this time. He walked up the small drive next to a parked car, with no plan in mind. He would come up with something on the spot if she was in. He rang the doorbell, under a small covered step, and then retreated back to wait for an answer to the chimes.

Nick had almost given up after another ring on the bell, a knock and a minute went by. He was about to walk back up the drive when the door opened a few inches to reveal a tired woman, who seemed to Nick to be weighed down with a heavier gravity than the rest of the inhabitants of planet Earth.

"What do you want, I'm rather busy?" the woman asked, her voice as distressed and tired as the well-worn, white dressing gown she had on. Nick could see her ankles and tiny feet were bare. Her hair looked like it had not seen water, shampoo, brush or tongs for a while. She had flaking black eyeliner on, but no other makeup, and the tired red lines on her right cheek of someone who had just woken from a long slumber.

"My name is Nick Hobbs, and I'm investigating Forky's House." Nick decided, for once, honesty was the best policy.

"I've talked to too many reporters already about that place. Now I have no job, credibility, or according to most people around here, no marbles left, so goodbye." Tracey stepped back in order to close the door.

Nick had less than a second to come up with something quick. "I'm staying there now, and I've seen the ghost of a little boy."

The door wavered a half inch from being closed. No part of Tracey Sunderland could be seen in the gap between door and jam.

"I want to know about the red room you saw." Nick kept it simple, knowing too many, or too few, words would result in the door being clicked shut.

Still the door quivered, within a quarter of an inch of being closed.

"I think the ghost may be my dead son," Nick said; a last throw of the dice.

The door opened. Tracey's face seemed even deeper etched with worry, but her blue eyes were open now and had hope in them. "Wait here, I'll get dressed, and we'll go out for coffee. I'll be ten minutes, tops."

The door closed.

It did not reopen for twenty minutes.

When it did, a very different Tracey Sunderland stepped out.

She had obviously had a quick shower, dried and tied her long blonde hair back in a pigtail, and put on some make-up. She had on tight jeans, trainers and a thin cream top with long sleeves. She had bags and rings around her eyes from lack of sleep or too much alcohol, but Nick couldn't help but notice her curves.

"This way," she said, heading off down the drive, and then turned left.

Nick hurried after her.

"My name is Nick by the way, really." He held his hand across his body for her to shake, but she declined. He thought it best to introduce himself again to get the conversation flowing.

"Tracey, but I guess you know that, or you wouldn't be bothering me."

"I didn't mean to drag you away from whatever you were doing, but I just need to ask you a few questions, if I may, about what you saw."

"I needed to get out. I've been stuck in there for a week, and the place is starting to smell like I feel."

Nick laughed a little, and even she cracked a grin, which lessened the lines on her face, making her look attractive.

"So, where are we going this fine sunny day?" Nick asked as they turned the corner into another street of houses and apartment blocks.

"To a local greasy-spoon, I know. I'm sick of low-fat Weight Watchers frozen meals. I want a fucking fry-up and builders' tea, on you, and then we'll talk."

"Sounds good to me."

Nick had the fat-boy special, like his lunchtime guest, at Ali's Cafe. He'd wiped his lips and chin three times, but it still felt like he'd washed his face with olive oil that morning. Tracey, who obviously hadn't been eating or sleeping well lately, wolfed her food and washed it down with two mugs of tea.

"That should put back some the pounds I've lost over the past few weeks," she said, before draining the dregs of her second cup. Her pink lipstick had long gone, but she looked less lethargic, and almost with-it now. "So what do you want to know?"

"Firstly, why you agreed to talk to me." Nick leaned forward, his elbows on the laminated table.

"Damned if I know." Tracey shrugged. "Maybe I just needed to un-pause my life, and start living, rather than existing, again. I'm talking a load of old shit, aren't I?"

"No." Nick shook his head before he winked. "Well, only a little bit."

"I can live with that," Tracey said and smiled back at him. "So you want to know about the red room then?"

"If you feel comfortable talking about it."

"Don't think I'll ever be comfortable talking about it, but I have to get it out there and move on. I'm hoping my nightmares will stop, or the sleeping pills the doctor prescribed me actually kick-in at night." Tracey turned her tea mug round and round as she spoke.

"So you never found, or knew about the secret stairs before that day?"

"Nope." She looked into his eyes. "Are you a reporter then or what?"

"A weird, beardy, smelly old guy, pays me to investigate haunted houses. The unsociable hours and working conditions are crap, but it beats the usual nine-to-five, eh?"

"And you said you lost your son?" Tracey's blue eyes flicked up from her mug to catch Nick's, before darting back to her empty plate.

"Yeah, a long time ago, but it still hurts here," Nick said thumping his heart with his right fist. "I think about him every day, and what he would have turned out like if he lived."

"Can I ask what happened to him?"

It was Nick's turn to meet her eyes and then look down at the pieces of uncooked bacon rind on his white plate. "He was murdered."

"Shit, I'm sorry." Tracey reached across the table and took Nick's right hand and gave it a squeeze.

"Hey, it was years ago, but that's why I need to find out if there is such a thing as life-after-death. Is his soul at rest, or does he linger somewhere? So please tell me what you saw in that room. Any fact or detail you can recall, please it's so important to me." Nick turned his hand and squeezed hers in return for her comforting tactile gesture.

"Okay, well I found a key, in a passageway around the corner from where me and Peter found the doorway. It was an odd thing with only one loop at the end, like a part was missing, or had been cut off. The door had…circles, and half circles, on a stone lintel above the doorway…four of them. We opened the door, and I went inside. The whole room was red in colour. Not lit red, every object had been painted or chosen to go in there because it was the same red colour. Weird, huh?"

"So what was exactly in the room?"

"A desk with a three-pronged candle holder on it. A bed with red sheets, a chair, and a table. In the far wall was another door, that was locked, and there was a red Chinese-like screen for getting undressed behind. That's where the madman was waiting." Tracey sat back in her plastic backed chair, letting her fingers slip out of Nick's hand. She swallowed hard and breathed in and out for a while.

"And he was painted red too?" Nick ventured in a soft voice.

"Either that or he was naked and covered head to toe in blood or something. He was chanting something before he attacked Peter and bit him." Tracey paused again to lick her dry lips. She tipped her tea mug towards her, but it was empty.

"I know it's hard, but can you recall anything he said?" Nick learnt forwards, both elbows on the table again.

"Not now, only in my nightmares. It sounded Latin to me, but I never did that at school. The thin, red guy had no hair and bit off Peter's hand. Only then did we manage to run out of the room and shut and lock the mad bastard in."

"So there was nothing else in the room that you can remember?"

Tracey shook her head.

"And literally everything was red?"

Tracey nodded and then looked up from her plate. "Except the door opposite to the one we went into. That was brown... well natural wood colour."

"Thank you," Nick said, reaching across to squeeze Tracey's hand again.

"What for?"

"That must have been hard to say."

"It gets easier." Tracey shrugged again. "It feels more like a bad dream. Especially when the police came back and said there was no door there at all. Lucky for me Peter survived and stayed sane long enough to collaborate my story, or I might have been done for it."

"Is the caretaker in a bad way then?"

"I just had an email from his mother in Poland this morning. He hung himself in his hospital room yesterday afternoon." All the colour had drained from her face.

"Shit."

"Shit indeed. Now walk me home will you?"

Nick paid, and they walked slowly back to Tracey's house.

"So what will you do now?" Nick inquired as they walked up the drive to her front door.

"Put this place on the market. I own four properties near

Farnham that I can earn a living off. One is unoccupied at the moment. I can sell this off and make a tidy profit. I'm tired of London, and life." Tracey laughed, but there was no humour in it.

"Sounds the right course of action to me," Nick replied, as Tracey fumbled through her bag to pull out her front door key.

"You wanna come in?" she asked, as she unlocked the door and pushed it inwards.

Their eyes met. Both of them grinned and then looked down onto the pebbled path in the same instant.

"I'd better not," Nick said, pursing his lips and thrusting his hands into his pockets.

"I understand," Tracey nodded, "I'm not looking or feeling at my best."

"It's not that," Nick explained. "I just don't want to screw up your life any more than it is now."

"Honest, and good looking." Tracey nodded and pondered. "Nah, you're right. You obviously aren't my type at all."

They laughed again to break the sexual tension.

Nick raised his right hand in a wave and then turned on his heel and departed. He didn't look back but did count to himself. He got up to five before he heard Tracey Sunderland's front door close shut.

CHAPTER TWELVE

Nick went home after his day of investigating. He was feeling tired of body and mind. Even so, he took a walk downstairs to the secret passages, but only a door-less wall greeted him. He promised himself later in the day he would set up the special cameras he bought and revisit the place Tracey and the late Peter claimed to have found a door to a red room. He went back up to the sitting room. A quiet sit on the sofa turned into an hour's nap, and he woke feeling more tired and groggy than before.

He felt hot and sweaty so decided to brave one of the house's antiquated showers. He found one in the master bedroom that seemed cleaner than the rest. The water came out cool, but clean, and the curtain smelled of bleach. It was summertime and hot, so the cold shower did him good for two reasons. He masturbated in the shower and thought about turning up on Tracey's doorstep tonight, with red roses, to accept her invitation inside. He thought about her as he wanked, but as soon as he was spent, the idea of visiting was becoming less and less of a sound judgement call. He had other things to do - a mystery haunted house to fathom, with its missing, secret red room.

So he started off with the four tiny cameras that came with night vision settings. They were relayed to a laptop, with quartered black screens so he could see what was showing on each, all at the same time. He placed the first one in the library, a no-brainer really because of the activity there. Then down to the corridor where Tracey's mysterious disappearing door should be, but wasn't. The last two took a bit of thinking about.

After much consideration and changing of his mind, he

placed one at the rear of the house, pointing down the ground floor west corridor that led to the library. The last, after even more ponderous deliberations, he placed on the first floor at the front of the house, pointing down the upper east corridor. This wasn't an ideal spot, but at least he had three floors covered. He could easily have done with two more cameras, but the surveillance set he had bought had only come with four.

He did have a digital camera on a tripod set up on the top of the grand staircase pointing down. This was fitted with a motion sensor and would only snap off pictures with an eye-watering flash if anything larger than a rat hurried past. Which meant it had taken five pictures of Nick so far, with an ever increasingly annoyed look on his face and lots of red-eye glare. He soon learned to exit the sitting room (his base of operations), head down the west corridor, through the music room, and upstairs if he needed, via the much less grandiose servant's stairs.

He brought his camper bed, some of his clothes, and food supplies down, so he had little need to move about later that night, except for toilet visits. The camera down in the depths refused to work at first. So he had to ring the helpdesk number provided. They suggested using one of the signal boosters in the set as some old houses with thick walls made it hard for the laptop to pick up the signal. It took a booster in the music room just through the open secret entrance, and one right down at the bottom of the steps to get a picture. It showed a dark green lifeless world, a wall with no door. Nick hadn't really expected much else.

Nick was hot and bothered by the time he had finished and was shocked to see it was ten to seven on his mobile. With a change of shirt, he set off out to the pub for a spot of dinner before his vigil tonight. It was warm out, and it felt good to have the sun on his face as he entered the pub. The landlord and lady both said hello as he entered and poured him an IPA before he'd even asked for one. He had Hunter's chicken for dinner, but ordered lemonade after the first pint, or he knew he'd get drowsy later on.

He was thinking of leaving when Lionel's tall, imposing

frame entered the pub, with a man a third of his age, with wide, adoring eyes for the thespian, behind round-framed glasses. The lad bought himself a Coke, and the actor a large dry sherry before Lionel spotted Nick and made a bee-line for him. The younger man, who was failing badly to cultivate a goatee, trailed after him.

"Budge up, Nick, there's a good fellow," Lionel boomed in his resonant voice, so everyone in the pub, including the punters in the lavatories, could hear.

Nick exhaled, smiled politely, and did as he was told. Lionel took centre stage and the young man perched on the other end, looking delighted to just be in a pub without being asked for ID. Nick saw that the lad looked even younger than late teens, close up.

"How are you, Lionel, anymore... trouble?" Nick inquired, fetching over the dregs of his pint to his side of the table.

"Oh, not a dickie-bird, on that front thank you, Nick." Lionel nodded appreciatively, and then continued in a louder more confident voice, "This is my new, young friend David Hewlett. He runs a Doctor Who appreciation site on the interweb and has travelled all the way here from Maidstone to interview me about my roles in that award winning show."

Nick reckoned if Lionel's voice had warbled any louder, he would have rattled out some of the pub's windows. "That's excellent," Nick replied and drained the last gulps of his pale ale.

"Social niceties, David," Lionel prompted, but the penny did not drop straight away. "Shake hands with the nice man."

"Oh," David said, and reached over a sweaty palm, for Nick to crush and shake.

"Well, I'd better let you get on then, Lionel. I've got a big night investigating the house, so..." Nick got up from the semi-circular booth, nodding to David and Lionel.

"Thank you," Lionel nodded. "Do let me know how you get on. Pop round for high-tea tomorrow if you have the time, old chap."

"Okay." Nick waved first at the table, and then at the landlords as he left the pub and trotted off back to Forky's

House. It was just after eight, and the sun was still low in the sky, making his shadow long, like a rack torture victim.

The house was wallowing in deep shadows. Only the hallway and the sweet spot in the rear garden really benefitted from the fading sunlight. Dust motes hung and danced in the sunlight that angled across the hall to bathe the ballroom door with its radiance. The lights showed years of lacquer applied to the thick heavy wood, the doors, and matching wall panels. Nick stared at the lines, flicks and flecks in the wood, wondering how many trillions of different unique patterns there were in the world, just laid out in sawn wood.

Feeling small in the universe for the first time in a long time, he retreated into the sitting room to fire up the laptop and check the cameras before night fell. Unseen by him or his cameras, a pattern of black shadows detached themselves from the sun-kissed doors and converged with the dust motes caught in the air before them. Together they formed a vague human-like shape, tall, like a man covered with a hood and cloak. The ghastly figure edged to the boundary of the sunlight, towards the closed sitting room doors, with a growing menace and purpose. Once out of the sunlight its form faltered, and flash from the tripod mounted motion camera sent it scatterings in all directions, so nothing of its form remained.

The cameras on the screen where all working perfectly, even the cellar one. It was already gloomy inside the sitting room, so Nick turned on the light, as dusk covered this part of North London. One by one the sensors on the remaining three spy-cameras turned from natural light vision to a murky green. Apart from the odd bit of static, there was nothing happening. Nick opened a can of Coke and flicked through his phone to see if he had any emails or missed any interesting news. He was playing angry birds within five minutes, as he waited for the sun to set.

A quarter of a can of Coke pitching into his groin woke Nick from his slumber. He stood, swore, and rubbed at the small coke stain on his jeans. Putting down the offending can, he flicked the sticky, wet remains off his hands, and then rubbed them down the side of his legs. The shutters were still all wide open, but dusk had been replaced by full darkness. He grabbed up his phone that sat on the sofa to check the hour, - it was a quarter to midnight.

"Bollocks," he said, as he dropped his mobile back on the sofa. Nick continued to rub his sticky hands on the back of his jeans as he went over to close all the shutters. A good look at the green night-vision images on the laptop screen showed nothing. He exited the sitting room and took the long route upstairs to wash his hand and change his trousers.

He returned a few minutes later, via the back of the static digital camera on the stairs. A quick check revealed only one photo had been taken, and that had been much earlier when it was still light out. The picture captured the stairs and hallway below. One side was lighter than the other as it was bathed in sunlight through the glass roof. Yet there was a blur in the centre of the image, where sunlight and shadows met.

Nick enlarged that part of the photo.

He blinked twice and then enlarged it a little more.

Caught on camera was the partial realisation of a hooded figure or at least the top quarter. It showed part of a dark cloaked body, with a clearly visible pale hand, below a covered hooded face. Nick swallowed hard and stepped back from the camera. Of all the ghosts and the spirits of the dead, he never expected to see that foul figure again.

He hurried downstairs, ignoring the flashes coming from the camera behind him.

He stopped dead at the very spot the camera had captured the hooded spirit. Behind him, the camera ceased its flashes and picture whirls for a moment.

The house seemed even quieter than normal if that could be possible. No cars could be heard rushing past on the junction outside. No sound entered the dark house or seemed to be permitted to leave it.

All was darkness, empty and devoid.

Nothing living or good resided in Forky's House.

Sensing nothing, not even a cold-spot, Nick stormed back to the sitting room, with only two flashes from above to mark him leaving.

Nick sat on the sofa, and then he was up again within seconds. He paced around the room twice, clockwise, and then again anti-clockwise. His fingers going through his hair, as so many dark thoughts, circled in his mind. At last, he sat on the sofa again, and pulled his fingers down from his hair, over his eyes, and into his mouth, pulling it open. Then his eyes caught the screen of his laptop, and he froze. All thoughts of the hooded figure, half-caught on camera, were gone.

In the top quadrant of the screen was the view from far below in the secret passages below the house. In the picture, coloured green by the night vision camera was a door that had not been there fifteen minutes ago. Nick grabbed his mobile, a small power torch from the coffee table, and flew out of the room. He had to take the long route back to the bedroom to fetch the key he had hidden and then return by the same route to the music room. He turned on his torch and entered through the secret door. He held onto the rail to stop himself hurtling down the steps in his haste to reach the bottom. Panting hard, and the torch flicking up and down in his hand as he ran, he finally reached the end of the inner passageway.

His last steps were just to slow himself to a halt before the large, impossible door that stood before him in the wall. A wall that earlier that day, and every other day he'd spent at the house, had been just a plain stone wall, with no signs of entry at all to a red room beyond. He hesitantly stepped closer and reached up to touch the stones that lined the arch of the doorway. They were cool, solid and real.

The lintel was so high he could only touch the bottom of it on tip-toes. He stepped back to look at the indented symbols, the black circle, then a white one, a red crescent moon facing one way, and a blue crescent moon facing the other way. He reached forward to grab the large black knocker. It was warm to the touch. He lifted it up until it was horizontal, and then let it fall. It hit the door with a thud but left no mark on the aged wood. His hand went to turn the handle next to the lock. It moved, but the door did not, it was locked.

"Here we go then," he said in a low voice. Nick took the large key from his pocket and pushed it easily into the keyhole.

He turned it left, but it did not budge, and then tried it right, but it still did not move. "Come on!"

Nick jiggled the key and then hurt his hand trying to make the thing move in the lock. It was having none of it. He stopped applying pressure, fearing that the key might snap off. He pulled it out and looked at the indents in his palm where he had been trying to turn it.

He stared at the door, before focusing on the lock again. He made a thoughtful clicking sound in his mouth, as he wondered what to try next. Bending down, he pointed the beam of his torch into the keyhole. It illuminated the outer part of the lock but showed nothing but darkness within. Whatever angle he shone the torch from, it would show nothing of the inner mechanisms of the lock.

With his calves protesting, he slipped the key inside again. Nick pushed the key in as far as it would go and turned it to the left. Once again it did not move, and he pulled it out again with a swift, "Grrrrrrrrh."

Nick stood up to give his legs a rest. He back up to the wood-panelled wall behind and leant against it. Then he had an idea. He pulled his mobile from his pocket and began to take shot after shot of the door, and its position in the passageway. He searched his pockets. What he really wanted was a knife, but he could only rustle up a fifty pence piece. He was reluctant to leave the door that had suddenly appeared here from nowhere. With the coin, he etched grooves in the wooden panels either side of the door. He wanted to at least make sure he knew its position if the thing vanished again.

Putting the coin away he reached up with his mobile and took the best picture he could manage. The flashes left little orange and blue streaks in his eyes. He suddenly kicked the door in frustration. It was solid, dense wood, and all he managed to do was hurt his right big toe.

"Fucking open, you fucking stupid thing." He kicked the door again but made sure he used the heel of his shoe this time. It did not even judder in the lock, so solid was it made. He had planned to stay and watch the thing all night, but the rage inside him got the better of his rational mind. He ran upstairs, simmering like a boiling kettle. But the stairs took their toll, and his anger was lukewarm by the time he emerged back into the music room.

He'd bought a pickaxe, axe, and sledgehammer, and had been of a mind to fetch them all. He wanted to do extreme damage to the door and walls below, but it seemed less of a plan now. The thought of carrying all those heavy tools down there killed the idea and his anger.

He was thirsty and hot. So he made for the sitting room to have a drink and strategise on what would be his next course of action. He opened a can of *Irn Bru* he'd picked up from the newsagent and gulped down half of the can. He stared at the laptop, showing four green images of the house. Nothing showed up on the other three, but the door was still there in the other one.

Nick tapped the coffee table with his fingers and then leaned to his left to pull his mobile from his trouser pocket. He brought up the images of the door he'd taken and flicked through them slowly. He stopped at the one with the lintel and used his thumb and forefinger to enlarge it on his mobile.

"Black, white, red and blue," he said to himself, looking at the carved symbols above the doorway arch. He searched for them on the internet but came up with little of any use.

"So we've got a black, full circle, a white one too. Then a half-moon shape red…" Nick's words died before he got to the last colour. He had just said what they looked like without thinking. "They are phases of the bloody moon. Black, no moon, white full moon, a red half-moon, and a half blue moon. But what does that mean?"

Nick scratched a psychosomatic itch on the crown on his head and leant over to pull the key from his other pocket. He moved it closer to his right eye and closed his left. On the brass under the loop of the handle, in the unworn grooves, were faint flecks of red paint. He tapped the key twice again his forehead and stood up.

"This place was originally called Four Keys House. I have one key, a red key. There are four symbols representing four phases of the moon, each had a different colour. A key for each colour. A key that will only open the door it seems when the corresponding moon is in the sky."

Nick laughed out loud in the silent house. He put the key and his mobile into separate pockets and raced into the hallway. He ignored the flash of the camera high on the landing above and ran over to the front doors. He unlocked one and ran outside into the darkness. It was still mild, and the pebbles crunched under his shoes as he skidded to a halt by the fountain.

Billy Ryan's fountain, he thought, and he craned his neck skywards. It was a dark night, with little clouds in the firmament, and no moon at all shone down on him or the house. He spun around looking up at the stars above him muttering. "No moon, no moon."

A shrill screech broke the near silence, a fox. The traffic outside had died down at last.

Nick looked down towards the fountain. "Oh, Billy Ryan, silly old rocker Billy Ryan, where did your key go?"

He did some dancing spins back to the steps up to the open front door. His mood was an utter contrast from earlier, down below. The door had four phases when it would appear each month. All Nick had to do was either wait for the right time or find the missing three keys. He did a hot shoe shuffle up the steps and shut the door with a bang. Another flash of the camera went off as he hurried back to the sitting room and pulled his phone from his pocket. He searched for the next phases of the moon, and when they would occur. Today was the ninth of June, and the website he found showed a large black circle, depicting no moon tonight. Sadly, the new moon had passed before he'd arrived, and his red key would not be any use until the last day of this month again. Yet his theory should be corroborated on the sixteenth of June when the blue half-moon should make the door reappear.

Nick took the key out and placed it on the coffee table next to the laptop. He looked at the screened and grinned as the doorway showed on camera two. "Now all I have to do is find three more keys."

He looked around the sitting room. He felt a lot better than earlier when he'd kicked the shit out of the door and hurt his toe. He had seven days before the doorway would appear again. Seven days to search the house room-by-room and top-to-bottom. If the other three keys were not in the house or grounds, he had no idea where to start looking for them. They could be anywhere, buried in a rubbish tip, sitting in someone's kitchen drawer, destroyed by fire or lost forever in another country even.

A sudden thought came to him, and he picked up the notes the Tramp had given him. He checked the date of the attack in the red room; it had been on the fourth of May. Using the website he found, Nick scrolled back one month. The half-moon was due on the third of May. But that would roll onto the next day after midnight, and some days you could see the moon clearly in the sky anyway.

"These things are so complicated," he said to himself as he took another swig from his can of drink. He was wondering if he had any chocolate in the sitting room when he heard a crashing noise from the hallway. More noises of something bumping and crashing followed, as he ran to the sitting room door and wrenched it open. The hallway was empty of anyone or anything as far as he could make out. Nick hurried over to switch on the lights, nearby at the front door. The cause of the noise was easy to spot. The smashed remains of the camera from the landing lay halfway down the grand staircase. It looked like it had been bashed from side to side. It was crumpled, broken open, and parts of its inner workings lay strewn across the steps.

Nick ran up the stairs. It felt awkward to his gait as the steps were deep and made him nearly hop from one up to the next. He knelt and picked up the camera. It was freezing cold to the touch, even though the night was warm. Something plastic and intrinsic to the workings tumbled out from the gaping hole in its solid plastic side. The rear digital screen was cracked in several places, and the digital memory stick had melted in its slot. The camera soon cooled.

There were forces at work in the house that did not like his presence.

But Nick wasn't one to scare easily. He had lost the only thing that he ever loved years ago. Any ghosts paled into insignificance compared with that.

CHAPTER THIRTEEN

Nick awoke on his camper bed in the sitting room just after nine that morning. His desert dreams were already fading from his thoughts. The underground doorway had vanished from the green screen of his laptop. He quickly put a fresh pair of boxers, pulled on his jeans and trainers, before heading down the secret stairs.

He took only the key, his mobile, torch, and the lit cigarette in his mouth.

Sure enough, the door that had been so real and tactile last night had vanished. He found his coin-scratch marks in the panels about four feet apart, with no sign of the stone lintel or doorway arch. It was just a smooth, wood-panelled passageway that went nowhere. Nick rapped his knuckles on the wood, which sounded dull and solid. He pressed his left ear against the wall, but could hear nothing.

He took a few *after* photos and then trudged slowly back upstairs. Nick washed and made a cup of coffee, before sitting down to fast-forward through the night's recordings. He had to sit through each, in turn, so started with the one in the secret sub-cellar. On a fresh notepad he jotted down the time the door appeared, and the time it blinked out of existence again. He even slowed it down frame by frame, one instant it was there and the next gone. It had been there for a good six hours this time, which he noted. *If the door blinked away with him in it, would he had to then wait a month to get out again?*

Then he thought about the *Red Man* Tracey had described to him. Had he been trapped like this in the room years ago? Why hadn't he escaped? Maybe because the secret passage had not been open for fifty odd years.

"But how could he survive in there for so long without food and water?" Nick asked himself, leaning back on the sofa with his half-drunk coffee resting on his chest. "We are talking about a magical room that appears only a few times a month, maybe time does not move as fast inside the room. Maybe time only starts again when the room is back in this reality, or the door is opened to this world?" Nick sat up and put down his coffee mug next to the laptop.

He whizzed through the next two recording with all the lacklustre zeal of a man who continues reading a book after his favourite character dies on page one hundred and two. The library showed nothing all night. The camera pointing down the ground floor west corridor picked up little, apart from him moving in front of it now and again. The last camera, set up on the first floor east corridor, had shown nothing of any interest; so he nearly missed something. A dark blurred image shooting along the corridor and then out of sight toward the static camera about the same time it was destroyed. Nick rewound the image and slowed it frame-by-frame just before it appeared. Not all of the thing could be seen, only parts, like he was watching it through a slatted fence. Yet it had the looks and gait of a creeping man, dressed in dark clothes. The closer it got to the camera, more could be defined of its countenance. Nick had expected a hooded figure again, but it was not so. This man was tall and thin like a beanpole. Dark smudges under his nose and on his chin must be a goatee beard, and on his head was a large Victorian hat. His clothes, or what Nick could make out, were period too.

Nick saved the frozen image. He was slightly perplexed by the number of ghosts that haunted the house. There were rumours of murdered American airmen and the murderous Dr Forque. He wrote down details of all three restless spirits he had encountered so far in the house. Were they related in any way to the red room, or were they some metaphysical distraction of an old house, with a tainted history?

Could it possibly be a former owner or resident of the house? How could Nick find this out? He had enough trouble with the red room that popped in and out of existence with the phasing of the moon. He half expected to see a spectral Billy Ryan walk through the wall, strumming his guitar.

"Fuck this place," Nick said, closing his laptop as he rose. He grabbed his wallet and jacket and headed out of the house to seek answers or at least a hearty breakfast. There wasn't too much choice, only the newsagents and coffee house were open. He was just walking past the side door that led to Lionel's upstairs flat when the door opened. Lionel, wearing an orange kimono with red lotus flowers on it, came out onto his front step, his long thin arm around the young man who had interviewed him yesterday.

The young fellow saw Nick, blushed bright red from his cheeks to his hairline and hurried off, clutching his backpack down the street towards the tube station.

"Now don't be a stranger," Lionel called after him. When the embarrassed youth turned to briefly acknowledge this call, the ageing actor blew him a kiss. This caused the lad to hurry even faster, back home to his mother.

"Good night?" Nick asked his friend as the young man disappeared into the busy tube station entrance.

"You know, my dear boy, I think I may have fallen in love for the three-hundredth time." Lionel touched each corner of his mouth with a long forefinger and then smiled at Nick.

"Looks like you opened that boy's world up to a universe larger than Doctor Who," Nick said with a grin.

"The closet is so much smaller on the inside I find," Lionel rumbled out a laugh. "What are you doing up at such an ungodly hour, Nicholas?"

"I'm hungry."

"Then come on in, sir. I was cooking up a fried breakfast, but my companion was in a rush to return home, lest his mother worried where he spent the night." Lionel extended his hand of friendship and ushered Nick inside. "I always cook for two in the mornings anyway, old habits die hard."

"Will there be bacon and tea?" Nick asked, following up the steep set of stairs, trying to avoid looking up the kimono of his thin legged host.

"And fried bread, sir, until the day I die."

"So...how is your stay over the road then?" Lionel asked, lighting up a post-breakfast cigarette, before offering a raised one from the same packet.

Nick borrowed the actors lighter from the doily covered breakfast table to light-up. They both puffed away from a while, before Lionel's bushy eyebrows inverted into a furrowed V, pressing to get an answer.

"Very eventful so far," Nick guardedly replied.

"In what way?" Lionel quizzed, as he crossed his pale, and near hairless legs.

"In the usual way," Nick smirked and took another drag of his cigarette.

"Oh, be like that then." Lionel rested his elbow on the arm of his chair and looked towards the ceiling. His cigarette held between the first two fingers of his right hand, the smoke curling up to the nicotine-stained Artex.

"I thought the place gave you the willies?"

"Oh, very droll," Lionel replied, with an expansive wave of his cigarette hand. "I may not want to step inside the place after the hours of darkness, but I do worry about you over there, Nicholas. Some terrible things have happened there over the years, and it leaves a taint you know."

"I know. I've seen some of the taints you refer too," Nick said, leaning back in his chair, and taking another suck on his cigarette.

"Ghosts of the past," Lionel said, uncrossing his legs and leaning forwards slightly.

"Yes, of my past and the houses. Not that I fully understand what they want from me yet, but it's still early days." Nick studied the actor's face. His features gave little away, but his eyes looked like they were hungry for more information. "Why are you so interested, because you used to visit the place when Billy Ryan lived there?"

"No, not in that sense anyway." Lionel shifted uncomfortably in his own chair and stared deep into Nick's unblinking eyes. "I just thought if there were ghosts there, then there is an afterlife maybe. Where my mother sits drinking tea all day, with her old brown stockings rolled down to her ankles, and one day I'll see her again."

"Doesn't everyone hope there is another place, where they will see their loved ones again, but is that all the information you are after?"

"Isn't that enough?"

"You want to know if I've seen the door deep under the house, and the room beyond it." It was Nick's turn to lean forwards, as he laid his cigarette to rest on the edge of an ashtray on the breakfast table. "Because you've seen it too, haven't you?"

"All right, yes, but only once, half a century ago. Fifty years makes things like that easy to dismiss as some drug induced dream forming as a memory. Billy Ryan showed me it once, and I've tried my darndest to forget what I saw ever since."

"And what did he show you?"

"A door that appears and disappears for no rhyme or reason. Behind which is a room the like I never want to see again, a room conjured by satanic black magic, an evil room in the heart of that decrepit house." Lionel had not spoken properly in such serious tones for years.

"Did he open the door?"

"Yes, but I wish he hadn't." Lionel seemed to be shaking, dropping ash onto the carpet. Nick had not seen such fearful looking eyes, outside that of a dying person.

"What was in the room, Lionel?" Nick was on the edge of the seat, his hands open and pleading with the man to say more.

"A completely blue room."

"A blue room you say, what else?" Nick asked confused.

"Oh, there was a bed and a table, desk and things. There was a door in the wall opposite, which seemed so close and yet far away at the same time. There was also a blue dressing screen with someone, or something, hiding behind it." Lionel's fearful eyes turned away from Nick and caught sight of the ash growing on the stub of his cigarette. He stubbed his out on a clear glass ashtray on an occasional table next to his chair.

"Did you go in, or see who was behind the screen?"

"I did not see him, or it, but I heard a man's voice speaking something over and over again, in a foreign language. Billy tried to push me in, but I ducked, and ran, and did not go back to that place until way after he died."

"So you didn't see who was behind the blue screen then?"

"Only," Lionel gulped audibly, "only the thinnest set of blue painted fingers grab the edge of the screen as I ran away. I went back there months after Billy died, using my mother's door keys, but I could not find the door again on two separate visits. In the end, I put it down to the booze and drugs he plied me with, and slowly forgot it." Lionel looked down, and his long fingers and clasped together tightly. "Have you seen it?"

"Only the door, but I have only one key, and I think there may be three others. You don't know where I could find them do you?"

Lionel shook his head. "I've seen some terrible things in my life, and acts of wanton hate towards people like myself, but never felt evil as a physical presence like I did standing at that open doorway."

"I'm sorry I made you recall it, my friend," Nick said, standing up. "I guess I'll take my leave of you now and leave you in peace."

"Better out than in, they say," Lionel remained seated. "I always found better in than out myself."

"That sounds more like you," Nick smiled and reached out his hand in friendship.

Lionel took it and gave it a gentle, tender squeeze. Nick walked towards the door of the living area of the flat, heading for the landing and stairs out.

"Next time breakfast is on you, my dear," Lionel called after him, getting some of his old colour back in his throaty voice.

"Deal," Nick replied and left him to his thoughts. Nick had enough things to think about. Four keys, four colours, and maybe four different rooms, or maybe the same room that changes with the phases of the moon. Who could tell? Nick wouldn't be able to until he got in there himself or found the rest of the missing keys. Outside, he lit one of his own cigarettes and walked on down the road, heading for the museum section of the local library.

After Nick had left the flat, Lionel got up, kicked on his slippers, and padded out into the landing. Then he opened one of three closed doors, the door that led to his mother's bedroom. The curtains were pulled, and dust clogged light crept in through the net curtains. The place hadn't changed since she had died, and Lionel never had the heart to throw any of her things away. He kept it as a mausoleum to her memory. It was much closer and less expensive than the plot and angel guardian in the cemetery where her earthly remains were buried.

He'd just flown back from Qatar, making a film with Omar Sharif and Kevin Costner, where he'd been well paid as the lead villain. He used most of it to give her the funeral and grave that she so richly deserved in death. Her life had never been a bowl of cherries, but Lionel loved her and taken care of her as best he could.

He shuffled over to a cuckoo clock on the wall next to a large brass cross. His long fingers hesitated an inch from its face and then moved to the side to open up a long side panel. Inside the long thin door were the hidden inner workings of the clock. Taped to the back of the space behind the pendulum and gears was one long odd shaped key.

Lionel stared at it for two seconds and then closed the side door again. He left his mother's drab bedroom, having no desire to handle the thing ever again. He was just making sure the key was still there, after all these years.

CHAPTER FOURTEEN

"Stop fart-arsing around you two." The Scotsman scolded his two dogs, who were tussling over a large bone by the pool. Both Smith and Wesson looked up and turned towards him, with hurt looks. Then Wesson dipped his head, scooped up the fallen bone and bounded off back inside the apartment. Smith's head drooped, and he padded two steps forward to the edge of the infinity pool. He dropped his head to within half an inch above the water and sniffed it. Not keen on the chemical smells coming from the tasty looking water, he padded slowly back inside, and out of the hot midday sun.

"Bloody animals," Steve muttered and reached back his left arm out of the pool to grab his gin and tonic from under the shade of a large white canopy. He nearly drained it all, as the ice cubes had already melted. He put it back in the shade and then plunged under the water to swim over to the other side in four long strokes. He pulled himself out and turned to sit in the full sunshine. The water and the drying sun did nothing to take away the nagging tick in the back of his skull.

The walkie-talkie called to him wherever he went. He took his girlfriend by helicopter to Rome the day before, hoping sex and distance would help, but it didn't. The bloody thing seemed to be his new *Jiminy Cricket* consciousness, that he long felt he never possessed. Souls, spirits, death, Heaven and Hell, were all fables for the weak-minded fools that paid his blood-money.

A new thought hit him, something even more worrying than the walkie-talkie that communed with the dead. What if the nagging thing in his head wasn't real? What if it was the start of something else, brain cancer, dementia, or a tumour causing him to hear voices. Steve stood up and made his way over to the sun lounger to grab his robe. He hurried inside, picked up his landline telephone, and dialled his doctor's office for an immediate check-up.

CHAPTER FIFTEEN

Nick's mobile rang as he was bounding up the steps to the first floor of the local library. The number calling him was unknown, but he answered it anyway.

"Hello, can I help you?" he asked, slowing down his ascent up the second set of stairs to the museum.

"Is that Mr Nick Hobbs?"

"Yes."

"This is Margo Cohen from the local museum. I've dug up a tiny bit more information for you already. Would you like to come to visit me at the library and I can tell you all about it?"

"Okay," Nick said, with a huge grin on his face, and ended the call as he bounded up the last three steps. He opened the wood-framed double glass door at the top and entered the small local museum.

Margo Cohen was standing by the information desk. A long curly white plastic wire leading up to a phone pressed into her bushy hair. She had a bemused look on her face and was looking down at the desk and saying. "Hello, hello. Mr Hobbs are you still there?"

"Yes and…no," Nick said, walking up to the desk.

"Oh," she said startled, "you're here." She pulled the phone from her ear, then looked from it to Nick and back, and finally replaced it on the receiver.

"Yep," he nodded, "just on my way up the stairs as you called. So what dirt have you dished up, Margo?"

"I'm not some cheap and tawdry gossip rag you know Mr Hobbs."

"Please call me, Nick," he said, showing her his pearly whites.

She smiled thinly. "Right, I guess you want to know what I have found out so far."

"Yes please."

Margo searched under some official looking letters on the desk in front of her and pulled a battered, buff hardback notepad from underneath. She licked her right thumb and flicked through to the correct page, where she had jotted some notes.

"Right, the house was built by a Nicholas Clovis, a local member of parliament and something big in the City. He was about forty when he married a much younger woman of this parish, one Anne Gates. They got hitched three years before the house was built, so maybe he thought he'd need a bigger place, for a wife and family."

"Did they have any children?"

"Not according to the parish records, no," Her nose twitched and then frowned. Then she popped her glasses on from where they had dangled around her neck, and she smiled and continued. "Probably didn't help that Nicholas Clovis died in seventeen sixty-two."

"Isn't that the same year the house name was changed to Four Keys House?"

"Yes, it is, well remembered," Margo smiled at him over her spectacles, like he was one of her pupils when she had taught history.

"Does it say what he died of?"

"Of a broken neck from a fall, that's all. So his widow lived there alone until she died at the ripe old age of one hundred and two. As Mr Clovis had no living relatives, and no children, the house passed onto Anne Clovis's great-nephew a Dr Henry Gates. He turned it into a little cottage hospital for a while until he died in eighteen-fifty. His eldest son didn't want the place and closed down the hospital. Dr Gate's third, and youngest son, took the place on as London was expanding by then." Margo let her glasses drop off the end of her nose and lowered her notepad.

"What was the third son called?"

"David Gates, but that's all I've managed to dig up so far."

"Good start, Margo. I wonder what else you will discover about the place."

"Time will tell Mister…I'm sorry, Nick. And remember, I still want that tour of the house." She fixed him with her beady eyes and pointed a bony digit at his chest.

"How about tomorrow?" Nick offered, leaning on the top of the information desk.

"I work until one."

"Half one then, I'll leave the gate open for you."

"You, sir, have a date."

"I look forward to it, Margo." Nick's phone chimed, and he pulled it from his trouser pocket to check it. It was a reminder that his new cleaner would be turning up very soon. "Look, I've got to dash, see you tomorrow."

"Half-one," Margo said to remind herself.

"Yep," Nick called over his shoulder as he made for the stairs.

Crina Popescu was waiting by the gate, checking the time on her mobile as Nick skidded to a jogging halt beside her. He could feel the sweat building up under his shirt, after hurrying back from the library.

"Sorry to have kept you. Have you been waiting long?" Nick fumbled his keys out of his pocket and un-padlocked the gate.

"Tens-minutes, but not to worry I will add it to your bill."

"Didn't want to climb over today then?" Nick asked, as he pulled back the chain and opened the gate up to show off the enclosed confines of the front garden.

"In about five minutes more, maybe." She nodded, the steady tone of her accented voice giving little away.

"Glad I turned up when I did then to save you the trouble."

Crina's long brown ponytail bobbed up and down across the old, faded jean jacket she wore over her cleaning things. She bent down, picked up a bucket in one hand and a plastic container in the other, containing sprays, bottles of bleach and other cleaning products. She followed Nick up to the house without uttering a word. Even Nick, who normally had the gift of the gab with all women, was silenced by her stern, but pretty, little face.

He let her in and showed her around from top to bottom, only leaving out the music room, as he was pretty sure he'd left the secret door open. He gave her a list of rooms that he used, that he would like cleaned every day. Then if she had time, after cooking him lunch, maybe tackle one other different room a day, so slowly the whole house would be cleaned up over time.

"So what foods do you like to eat?"

"Anything really. Surprise me with some Romanian delicacies."

"We have no delicacies in Romania, that's why I come here to England. So what food do you like to eat please?"

Nick grabbed the top of his T-shirt, fanning it in and out, and pondered with his mouth open. He suddenly couldn't think of one thing he liked to eat. Her blank subservient face and dull tones bored into his skull and seemed to suck the joy of eating from his mind.

"Chicken," he finally replied, latching onto a food that most people liked and cooked.

"Chicken?" she said, reaffirming what he said.

Nick nodded several times.

"What type of chicken? Legs, breast, wings, fried, sliced curried or roasted?"

"Roast," he replied, meekly latching on to the last word she had said. This woman, his new cleaner, seemed to emanate a grey coldness, like an aura of resentment towards him as her employer. Her voice, as she spoke, gave such inflexions, that she was doing him a big favour by working for him. Even her saying the word *breast* stirred nothing in his lewd mind but uncooked poultry.

"You want roast chicken every day for lunch?"

"Not every day...well not every week either, really," Nick said, trying to escape the chill that conversing with her brought. "Why don't you buy a nice cookbook from the shops, and charge it to my bill, and then we could run through the whole thing... trying stuff out?"

"Okay." Crina bent down and fetched a sponge and some surface cleaner from her bucket. "I clean now."

That was defiantly Nick's cue to leave, and he did. He

retreated to the library, thinking there might be some old cookbooks around the walls somewhere.

Crina watched her new employer hurry away. She smiled to herself and began to hum a Romanian children's rhyme her grandmother used to sing when she cleaned the house.

Nick decided, on a whim, to take down every single book in the library. Maybe he had read too many ghost and spy stories than was good for him, and that one book might have a key inside it. He started at the bottom and worked his way up. He checked the book titles on the off chance it might have something to do with the history of the house. Then he looked to see if there was a key inside, or a slip of paper with some vital, cryptic clue. He started out tidy, and reverent to each dusty tome, but that only lasted one whole bookcase. Boredom, frustration call it what you will soon got to him. So after only an hour into his search, he would start at the top of the bookcase and throw all the books down, shelf after shelf until he had a large book mountain on the floor. Then he would sit cross-legged in front of the pile and check through every one. The checked books were then flung back over his shoulder into an ever-increasing pile that *Smaug the Dragon* might like to curl up upon.

This is where Crina found him an hour and a half later, ensconced between a dwindling pile of hardbacks and a large mound behind that would make an epic bonfire. She placed a sandwich on a white plate on top of the flat part of the book pile in front of him. A layer of crisps ran around the edge of the white bread sandwich.

"What's this?" Nick asked, eyeing the plain looking sandwich with suspicion. A full roast hearty hot meal it was not.

"Chicken sandwich," she curtly replied. "You will have to give money to me for me to go shopping on my way home if you want more tomorrow."

"Right," Nick nodded. He reached for the plate and then saw the dirty state of his hands. Picking up the plate, he scrambled to his feet and went over and placed it on the reading desk. He handed her a fifty pound note from his wallet.

"You not like?" Crina asked, wondering if she should have

made a cheese sandwich instead.

"No, it will be fine for today," Nick said, rubbing his dusty hands down the sides of his jeans, and then showed them to his cleaner. "Dirty, see?"

"Yes," was her stilted reply. "I go clean now, again."

Nick wasn't sure if she was telling him or inquiring, so she could take her leave. She just turned on her heel and left him to it. Nick rubbed an itch under his nose, the dust on his fingers causing him to sneeze three times, like rapid-fire pistol shots. Shaking his head, he went off to wash his hands, before starting on his simple lunch.

He was still only halfway through his epic, and so far fruitless, library search when Crina popped her head around the library door again. "I am off now, see you tomorrow."

"Bye." Nick looked around from his search and found his wave was directed at an already empty doorway. He heard her light footsteps across the hallway, and then the door open and close. Once again, he was alone in the house, with just ghosts and volumes of dusty books.

CHAPTER SIXTEEN

The days between the last moon event and the next brought little or no new information to Nick's quest to find the three missing keys. Margo popped over the next day for a quick tour, which lasted nearly two hours. Nick steered her clear of the music room, to keep the secret staircase hidden.

The search of every book in the library had been a complete waste of time. All he had to show was blocked sinuses and the headache of putting all the books back. He did a shelf a day, knowing that this wasn't going to be a short stay at Forky's House. The wall far below was devoid of any doors, which at least proved his assumptions about the moon and its appearances.

Margo had dug up a few more titbits of information on the Gates family. Only ten years after inheriting the house, David Gates was tried and hung for the murder of his four-year-old daughter and her nanny. The information was sketchy at best, but there were newspaper reports of midnight satanic masses in the house by David Gates and unknown acquaintances. His wife moved out, and the house reverted back to his nephew, Peter Gates, the eldest son of his late older brother. There the story ran cold, and nothing much was reported about the house. Peter Gates leased it out to various well-to-do types over the years, but only on short leases.

The house went quiet for a long time.

He slept well, with only a few unquiet, nightly noises, and running of tiny feet around the halls. He dreamt of his son and the desert most nights, interspersed with the odd erotic fantasy about his Romanian cleaner. He had become fascinated by her and her ways. She seemed impervious to his usual charms, which most ladies adored. She seemed to gain a little more subtle beauty every day. He began to note if she wore make-up or changed the way her hair was pinned back, or her clothes that were just variations on a theme. Jeans and t-shirts, cheap and interchangeable under the cleaning smock she wore.

The clipped conversations they had were the highlight of his day. The only other people he saw on a semi-regular basis were Lionel, Margo, the newsagent and the people in the pub, where he ate most of his nightly meals. It was swelteringly hot, and he'd somehow managed to force down four Ploughman's Lunches in a row this week. That being the only salad option the pub served up.

Crina gave little away about her hometown in Romania, and nothing much of anything of a personal nature. He knew she lived in a flat somewhere, one tube station or three bus stops down, but not in which direction. Lionel was no use in supplying any further information either.

"Don't you dare try and fuck my cleaner," was all he would say in reply to Nick's inquiries about her.

So once more she had gone for the day. Her cleaning done to a fastidious standard, and a chicken salad with goats' cheese prepared for his lunch. He found himself pining after her already. The door frame was still quivering from when she closed it so hard on her way out. He put his hands to his face and turned on the spot. He had hours to wait until it got dark, let alone having to wait for the half-moon to show itself.

"God, I need a shag," he said to the stairs as he ran up them to put on his best shirt. The door wasn't going anywhere, but he was. He went *Up-West* and went from pub to casino, to bar to club, until one foxy lady in a killer red dress met his approving eye.

"Red is my favourite colour," he grunted into her neck as they fucked hard between two large wheelie bins in a tight alley behind the club.

"Glad of that," she panted, "cos I'm on my period."

It didn't seem to bother either of them, so they carried on to a natural conclusion.

Nick got back to the house on the last tube home, alone. He'd lost all interest in the red dress brunette after he had done his business. She was attractive but had given herself up far too easily for his liking. This made him think of Crina. His night out had scratched an itch, but on another level made him feel worse about himself. Grabbing a bottle of Scottish Springwater, the key, and his torch, he headed through the secret passage in the music room.

The stairs down were cooler than before, even though it was a rather humid night outside. The sweat under his armpits soon turned icy cold and made him wish he'd brought his jacket along. When he turned the last corner, the mysterious door was there again.

He touched the heavy wooden door. It was dry, but his hands came away feeling like he'd grasped a metal pole on a frosty February morning.

"Curiouser and curiouser," he said to the door, and then tried the black metal ring. He turned it, but like the previous door, it was locked. Frowning he took out the key from his pocket. He gave it a kiss for good luck and tried the lock. It went in, but would not budge an inch left or right. He withdrew the key, kicked the door for good measure and said, "Bollocks."

He took his mobile from his other pocket and took only one picture this time. He knew he had to wait until the end of the month until his key would work. He hastened back upstairs, chugging down his water as he went. He knew he had to step up the search for the missing keys before the end of the month, but he still had no real place to start looking. The only real clues about the other keys led to dead men: Billy Ryan and Peter Gates.

Feeling slightly puffed by the time he exited the secret door into the music room, he pulled out his mobile phone and scrolled down his contacts list. He wasn't getting anywhere fast, so he needed extra assistance. He was sure Margo would come up with the full Gates family tree in time, but he was getting antsy now. He spotted the contact he wanted, took a deep breath and dialled the number, even though it was so late at night. His call was answered on the third ring. He knew the person on the other end didn't go in for sleeping at night much, as that was when he did most of his nefarious business.

"This is indeed a welcome pleasure. I am your humble servant," a voice said, as slimy as a toad's back.

"Micheldever I have a job for you," Nick said down the phone, with a face like he was licking limes with the tip of his tongue. "Listen carefully, you oily runt, and I'll give you the details."

"As you wish Mr Hobbs." The grimy man on the end of the phone wrote down the information Nick was after.

Nick had to take a shower to cleanse himself after talking to the horrid little creature on the phone. He hated using the man, but the private investigator had ways and means lower than the sewers beneath London. Micheldever was a bent, old looking man, with jaundiced tone to his skin. Nick had used him in the past as a last resort, getting the information he required, but he always hoped the next time he rang that the odious little man had died of whatever ailment he was afflicted with.

Nick didn't get to bed until half-two. He at least had a bed upstairs to sleep on. He'd ordered a new mattress, and Crina had bought the right sized king-sized sheets for it. The camper bed was left in the sitting room, just in case he needed to pull an all-nighter again. He hadn't felt so frustrated in years, not even sex had eased his mind this time. He wanted Crina to join him willingly in his bed, with two of the missing keys hanging off her hard nipples, and the other wedged up her wet hole. He went to sleep dreaming of retrieving the keys with his tongue and lips from each part of her body.

His dreams soon turned arid and sand-filled as usual.

Nick woke the next day and groaned to himself. Why had he gotten Micheldever involved in all this? Why could he not have had more patience and found it all out by himself? He needed to find out where Billy Ryan's key had gone, and if any of the Gate's family who still owned the house knew about the missing keys. He cursed how lazy he'd become and hated being reliant on anyone.

He looked at the time on his mobile. It was only just after nine, so he pulled his sheet back over his head and tried to get more sleep in.

A creaking of his bedroom door woke him from his second slumber. He thought he heard whispering behind the door, and the sound of a child's feet running away down the hallway. Nick flung back the covers and swung his naked body out of bed. He padded over to his bedroom door, with a ball-aching erection, caused by an urgent need to pee. He rubbed at his rigid abdomen and pulled open the door.

Crina the cleaner was standing outside, dusting an old picture of a squire on an anatomically incorrect, oversized equine. She stopped, opened mouthed for a second, and then put her hand over her mouth to hide the first smile he ever saw her give.

"What time is it?" he asked, to try and make this delicate situation seem as normal as possible.

"Twelve o'clock. I let myself in. I thought you were out," Crina spoke from behind her mouth.

"Carry on." Nick barely nodded to her and took himself and his hard-on back inside his bedroom. He leant his bare back against the cool painted wood of the bedroom door to close it. "Great start to the day. Well done Nick."

He heard his Romanian cleaner tittering to herself, which didn't help his embarrassment, as she hurried off to another part of the vast house. Nick headed over to the window, opened the new curtain and the bedroom window. Then he proceeded to take a high arcing pee out over the rose garden below his window. With a lighter bladder and ebbing cock, he returned to bed. Nick pulled the covers over himself and wondered if he should be bothered getting up and dressed at all today.

He stayed in bed. Crina knocked at half-twelve with his lunch, and he told her to just leave it outside. He waited a full five minutes before tugging on a new dressing gown he'd bought, to go out to fetch it. It was a sliced roast chicken salad.

As he bent down to pick it up, he looked to see Crina walking around the corner at the back end of the house. She was gone in an instant without seeing him, but that did not worry him. The little, sullen, dark-haired young boy following her did.

Nick ate all the chicken off his plate, but left the salad, after finding a tiny, dead spider under the second leaf he turned over.

"And what was the cause of death m'lud," Nick chuntered on to himself, "death by drowning in honey and mustard dressing." He put the salad plate on his bedside cabinet and reached under the covers to scratch an itch. He decided to wait for his cleaner to leave before getting up. His mobile rang ten minutes later, and he grabbed it, thinking it would be Micheldever, but it wasn't. It was Lionel asking him if he fancied a late liquid lunch, so he could help read a film script he'd been sent. Nick told he would meet him there in forty minutes.

The corridor was empty as he padded off for his shower. He felt almost human and awake again as he towel-dried his hair. The front door banged shut as he was dressing, signalling that Crina had left at last. He hastened his dressing speed and kicked on his shoes to go out.

Lionel was in an even brasher and exuberant mood than ever. He obviously hadn't had a feature film script for a while and was laying it on thick about the twenty-line part he'd been offered.

"Funny though, I thought my agent must have died five years ago, old thing," Lionel laughed, giving Nick's left thigh a good squeeze. He was three rum and blacks into their afternoon drinking session.

"I thought you had died five years ago," Nick joked back.

"Oh, very droll," Lionel burst into heaving, Marlboro filtered laughter, that made the five other patrons of the pub turn their gaze his way. It took a few minutes before the older man calmed down and knocked back his drink. He was still chortling away as Nick got up to get in the next round of drinks.

They staggered back to Lionel's flat for coffee and biscuits at four. Lionel had found his singing voice, and Nick was glad to get him back in his flat. While the old thespian went through his range of Mikado Songs, Nick put the kettle on. They talked and chatted for another hour. The film would start in a week's time in Bulgaria. Lionel was an urgent replacement for another actor who had suddenly died two days ago. He'd be away for a month filming, so Lionel gave Nick a spare key to his flat so he could pop in now and again to water his plants. Crina would feed and take care of the cat for him, as he didn't trust Nick with living creatures.

Nick could not deny the actor's request and would miss him while he was away filming. With another key in his pocket, but not the type he wanted, he returned home, feeling light in his shoes. The takeaways and night-time restaurants were beginning to open, so Nick came back with a bottle of Irn Bru and a kebab in a thin blue plastic bag. He ate it at the vast table in the huge, dining room. He knew the haughty ghosts of the past would hate such food being consumed at a table that had seen such fine food over the years. It also kept the smell of the kebab far away from any of the rooms that he frequented.

He felt both good and bad after his booze session and takeaway meal. His chin smelt of kebab and his mouth of god-knows-what. In the bathroom upstairs he brushed his teeth with just water and washed his face. He'd bought a TV and Blu-ray player last week and decided to watch *Scarface* and the *Bad Lieutenant* in the sitting room. He was closing the shutters when a small dark shadow ran past the window towards the rear garden.

Nick ran to the next window but only caught a glimpse of a boy with black hair, running behind the winding borders of the rose garden. Nick was away-on-his-toes in an instant. Crashing out of the sitting room, before pumping his arms, and pelting down to the rear of the house. Double glass doors sat in the middle of the rear wall that led out onto a wide balcony, where garden parties had once been held. Nick ran over to the concrete railings and skidded to a halt. Scanning the sections of the rear garden, Nick could see or hear no signs of the running boy.

Then he heard footfalls beyond a line of crooked, intertwining pear trees that formed an avenue down the far side of the garden. Nick was off again down the wide, ornate steps into the garden proper. He followed the footsteps through the pear tree avenue. He could see nothing ahead but heard the soft giggling of a child, and the hard sound of shoes on the cobbled path beyond.

Soon he was in the sweet spot of the garden, the ovals of grass before the gazebo. Here the hearty sun shone down on everything, giving an almost magical, fairy feel to the place. It was so out of check with the rest of the shadowy, overhung garden, it felt like it was from another world, or another time. It was far more open here, with little box-lined paths curling off this way and that, back into the leafier edges of the garden.

Nick checked behind the back of the gazebo, but there was no one there. He stepped inside and looked around. Something that hadn't been there before caught his eye. On the centre bench lay a brass rimmed, hand-held magnifying glass. Nick picked it up and found the brass handle was warm to the touch, even though it was in a shaded part of the gazebo. He raised it to his right eye and looked through the convex magnifying glass. If he expected to see some distant parallel world instead of the garden, he was sadly disappointed.

He put it back down and searched the other side of the garden, but found nothing. Nick decided to leave the magnifying glass where it was. He was getting pissed off with the house trying to point him towards even more mysteries. He had enough of a mystery with the vanishing door, that and the gaggle of ghosts in the house was enough for him. He went back to the sitting room and put on *Scarface*. The bottle of Irn Bru sat on the sofa next to his mobile. He received no more calls or ghostly visitors that day.

Feeling embarrassed, which wasn't his modus operandi at all, Nick stayed out of Crina's way the next two days. He was beginning to get the feeling that his dark wish for Micheldever to shuffle off this mortal coil had actually worked.

Yet the call came two days after he had phoned him, while Nick was eating roast chicken in a garlic and tomato gravy, that Crina had called Ostropel. Nick wiped his lips with a napkin, took a deep breath and answered the call.

"You took your time," Nick began, dominating the call from the off.

"Yes, I can only apologise to you, sir. It was a most difficult task that you set Micheldever, and my news may not be very welcome." The private investigator's voice dripped with oily wet lips and sucking noises between the gaps in his teeth.

"So in two days, you have found out nothing?" Nick let the words hang in the ether before continuing. "You have never failed me before Micheldever."

"I can assure you, Mr Hobbs, I have sunk to even lower depths in this quest you have bestowed upon me. Deeper than the blackest pits of Tartarus itself has Micheldever dug, but no one knows of these keys that you seek."

Nick frowned and pursed his lips. If Micheldever couldn't found anything, then maybe the keys were lost forever. The private investigator had never failed in any task that Nick had set him in the past. "Have you found out anything at all then?"

"Yes. The coffin that held the body of the singer Billy Ryan was empty of both key and a corpse. I broke into two homes of his surviving family members, distant cousins, but they do not have the key."

"Back up a second. Billy Ryan's dead body wasn't in the coffin?"

"No sir, most perplexing it was. I even found his autopsy file and pictures. He certainly died, sir."

"What about the Gates family who own the house?"

"They are old money, sickeningly rich family, sir. Heavily guarded away in a huge mansion in Suffolk. Very powerful, and very influential in certain dark Masonic and political circles. I have tried my usual ways to gain entry but have so far failed. If the Gates family have any secrets, they guard them well, sir, from prying eyes and listening devices."

"So who is the head honcho of this powerful legacy?"

"Sir Boris Gates, a member of the House of Lords. A former Ambassador to the Vatican in his time, as well as running his family's vast business empire. Their mansion would take weeks to search, and then they could hold the keys or keys if they have any, in some Swiss Bank vault somewhere. How would you like me to proceed, sir."

"This Sir Boris Gates, get me all the information you have on his wife, daughters or granddaughters if he has any."

"As you wish, sir, it will be done."

Nick ended the call and returned to his lunch. He wondered why, just for once, things could not be easy and handed to him on a plate, like his lunch.

He took his plate and cutlery out to Crina in the ground floor kitchen. He had been his shy, retiring self for too long now.

"Do you dance?" he asked, putting his lunch things on the work surface next to her as she washed up.

"Excuse me?" she replied, her bare arms covered in white suds.

"Do you like to dance, Crina?" Nick leant his back against the work surface next to her and engaged his most winning of smiles. "God, they do have dancing in Romania, don't they?"

"Yes, we have dancing in Romania." She returned her gaze to the pot she was scrubbing. "Only last year, rock n' roll was the new thing back home."

Nick frowned and then got the fact that she was joking with him. It took a few extra seconds with her accented English for it to sink in.

"Very good." Nick laughed. "Very funny."

"Not that funny," she replied, with a hint of a cutting smile of the edges of her perfect full lips. "Why you ask about dancing?"

"Just wondered, that's all," Nick said, before pushing himself off the work surface and left her to her own devices in the kitchen.

"Funny fellow," Crina muttered to herself, before grabbing his plate and cutlery to submerge them under the soapy water in the Belfast sink.

Nick headed over to the newsagents to buy some more cigarettes, before popping into Lionel's place to water his vegetation. He sat in a wingback chair to smoke and blew smoke rings as he once again pondered the mystery of the missing keys. Billy Ryan's missing bones bothered him, and the Gates family bothered him more. He needed to get in with the sort of circles the Gates normally kept, but he didn't want to expose himself to them personally.

Another moon was happening soon. Not the one that he

really wanted, but without any of the other keys, he had little choice but to wait. He had taken a tour of the flat before he went, finding an old, brown, drab room, that obviously had belonged to Lionel's mother. Nick checked her jewellery box and drawers of folded old person's clothes but found no key she might have squirrelled away. The cuckoo clock on the wall chimed for two o'clock, so he decided to wander off back home.

An artistic whim came over him in the afternoon, alone in the gazebo in the bright spot of the garden. He dug out his mobile from his trouser pocket to order easels, paints, brushes and other things he needed. Nick hadn't painted for years, yet the scent of lavender and the sweet sun-cast place in the drab garden inspired him.

He could see months ahead in this strange house so an old hobby would help pass the time. Especially for the hours when Crina wasn't there, and Lionel was away. He wasn't used to being in one place for such a long time or having his short attention span stretched by house-sitting this haunted mansion. He sat in an enclosed garden, next to a busy hub road, in the capital city of Britain, but was still alone.

"Least I have all the ghosts for company," he said to himself, twiddling the magnify glass around in his left hand. But they weren't even that, they were quite shy most of the time, leaving Nick with plenty of thinking time on his hands. Then his thoughts would dwell on his murdered boy, and that wasn't good for him.

"The devil makes work for idle hands," he said, slapping his thighs, and putting down the magnifying glass. He got up and wandered inside the gloom of Forky's House.

After putting a line of books back on a shelf in the library, he wandered, hands in his pockets, up and down the corridors and passageways. He searched behind every picture he came across, hoping to find a key taped to the back. He was to be sorely disappointed.

For dinner, he made himself a cheese sandwich, and ate it in the suntrap gazebo, with his shirt off. This part of the garden felt so fresh and warm like he was on an Aegean shoreline. He sipped a fruity, chilled, white wine, closed his eyes, and let the heat of the sun wash over him, reminding him of better times. He stayed in the warm garden until the sun went down, and the wine was drunk. He took a long pee against one of the thick trunked sycamore trees and then tottered back inside.

While the heat and air outside had been fresh and carried on a warm southerly breeze, the inside of the house was dark, dank, and cloyingly stuffy. He checked his phone and then had to do a double-take, as it was nearly ten o'clock at night. He wandered to the entrance hallway next, to the double doors of the ballroom. He was about to turn at the staircase, to make for the sitting room, when he heard music emanating from the ballroom.

He stopped, and turned towards the closed doors, swaying a little. The music was low and constant, but an old tune that he recognised. He blinked and then moved closer to the doors. The music did not get much louder, but it sounded like a recording to him, and not a big band playing live. Nick scratched his hairline. His fingers wiggled nervously over the ornate door knobs. He put his forehead against the wood, where both doors met. The swing sound of Glen Miller flowed through the wood, vibrating against the furrowed skin of his brow. Nick took a deep breath and opened both the doors wide.

He'd expected the music to cease instantly, but it didn't. He expected to see a large empty dark ballroom, but it wasn't. He stepped through into another world, another era of the house, during the last war. The ballroom was full of low orange glow from the lamps around the walls. The polished floor was filled with hospital beds, trolleys of medical equipment, bedside cabinets, and white screens. There were at least twelve beds lined up against the walls, ten of which were occupied. A nurse in her forties was winding a gramophone on a table at the far end of the ballroom. There the Glen Miller sound was coming out loud and clear: *Pardon me, boy, is that the Chattanooga Choo-Choo? - Track 29–Boy - you can give me a shine.*

A jacket of a US airman sat draped over the end of one metal bed. A young man lay on his side, his injuries unclear, looking at a photo of his girl from back home. The next airman's injuries were easier to see, his left arm ended in a bandaged stump outside his pastel, tri-coloured cotton sheets. Nick walked on into the ward, aware that none of the US airmen were taking any notice of his presence. The next guy's head was swathed in bandages, with only a red raw, and slightly burnt off ear showing on the left side of his head. The next guy was asleep, with some sort of cage rising up over his legs under the covers. Two airmen sat in pyjamas next to each other playing cards. One was missing his right foot, and the other his left leg from the knee downwards.

The nurse smiled at some come-on they gave her. She just waved and walked quickly towards Nick. Having slightly overdone the wine, he could not get his legs to retreat around the side of an empty bed. The nurse walked right through him like he wasn't even there. Nick felt nothing and turned to watch her stride out of the ward and close the door behind her. He turned back to the wounded airmen, but still, none of them took any notice of his presence.

Sucking his bottom lip, Nick made his way down to the two men playing cards. One looked up at the doors, right through Nick, who froze on the spot. Then the airman reached under his bed and pulled out a packet of cigarettes and got one out for him and his fellow card player. They smoked and joked, unaware of Nick's 21st-century intrusion on their World War II ward.

As he watched them play rummy, Nick heard rain outside, drumming on the windows covered by shutters and blackout blinds. Because of the sound of heavy rain outside and the music, Nick didn't hear one of the doors open again So he was surprised as he turned to see a tall, thin doctor, with a pencil-thin waxed moustache approaching the only two men still awake in the ward. Nick rushed towards the doctor that the two airmen hadn't taken much notice of. If they had, they would have seen the trailing drops of blood the doctor left in his wake. The doctor moved through Nick.

Nick could see what the white-coated man held in his red hands behind his back. It was less of a scalpel and more of a bone-handled, surgeon's knife with a tapering blade down to a point at the end. His bloody, soaked hands were crossed behind his back, and in his left hand, he gripped a very familiar looking key.

"Hey, Doc, how's it going tonight?" the nearest card playing airmen asked, finally looking up as the doctor approached. The cigarette dropped from his lips onto the bed, as the French doctor rammed the blade deep into the blue eye of the young American airmen. The second airmen tried to get away, but with half a leg missing, and no crutches nearby, just got a slashed throat for his troubles.

"I don't need to see this," Nick hissed between gritted teeth.

It didn't stop the French doctor going from bed to bed, killing the American patients one-by-one as they screamed out helplessly. Glen Miller seemed to go on forever, only ending as the last airmen gurgled for air through the hole in his throat. Red covered the sheets, bandages, and screens, as a burly orderly in his fifties, ran into the ward and rugby tackled Dr Forque. The doctor hit the floor face on, sending his knife skittering across the floor, and the key flew under one of the beds.

As Nick bent down to see where the key had gone. Behind him, the doctor began screaming out the same word over and over again in his native tongue, "morbleu."

Then the music died, the lights went out. Nick found himself kneeling on the hard, polished ballroom floor all alone, in an empty room. The music from the era still circling in his mind, mixed with Dr Forque shouting, *"morbleu"* over and over. Nick knew it meant blue murder, translated into English. He hurried over to the doors and turned on the light switches. The side lamps and a huge chandelier in the central, round, ornate carving in the plasterwork of the ceiling flicked on. The ballroom was bathed in electric light, and Nick hurried back to the spot where he had seen the key fly under a bed. Of course, the bed was no longer there, and neither was there any sign of the key.

CHAPTER SEVENTEEN

The door reappeared on the night of the next full moon. Still his key could not open it, and by ten the next morning, it was gone again.

It had rained most of the week, making Nick even more sullen and down than he'd cared to admit. Lionel was still away filming, and Nick's chat up lines and invites to Crina had fallen on deaf Romanian ears. He wanted to get outside to the sweet spot in the garden and paint, but the rain delayed his plans. None of the dreary rooms in Forky's House gave him anywhere near enough natural light to paint in. He had a long-held belief that painting under electric light was an affront to art and nature.

Margo had managed to join the dots from one end of the Gates family tree to its current branches; matching those Micheldever had dug up for him. Sir Boris had two grown sons by his second marriage, and two teenage daughters by his third: the girls were nineteen and fifteen. His third wife was twenty years his junior, and at present still besotted with her husband, his power, and his limitless credit cards.

All avenues in the quest to find more keys were hitting dead ends. He'd searched the ballroom inch by inch, and even ripped up a few boards to search underneath, but came up with nothing but mouse droppings and an old thurpenny bit. His patience ran low, his frustration boiled over into anger. He took a sledgehammer and pickaxe to the wall down below, where the door would appear. The splintered wood panelling gave way to stone bricks. Stone bricks gave way to nothing but solid stone.

These went on and on, to fill the space inside the surrounding passages.

The next morning, when he came down to check, he could find no signs of his hard labour of the day before. Nick sat down on the cold stone floor next to his pickaxe and wept in frustration at what this house and the door was doing to him.

The end of June came around, and the sun returned to the sky and warmed his soul a little. Lionel rang him from Bulgaria to tell him he was off to Croatia the week after, as he'd secured a part in the latest series of *Game of Thrones*. Nick was delighted for him but missed the old thespian's company more than he let on. At least he could paint in the garden, taking in the flowers and gazebo. His picture matched the freshness and colour of the garden in full bloom. The week of rain had at least done it some good, unlike Nick. The scent of the rose garden often wafted through the open windows of the sitting room and library, almost painting a perfumery picture in his mind.

Crina had warmed a little to his odd ways. She still did not laugh at his jokes, though. One day he tripped over one leg of a stool in front of her, and she had burst out laughing as she wandered off to clean another dusty room. So Nick had played up on the slap-stick comedy when he was near her. This often left her smiling, but shaking her head at the same time at her foolish employer.

While at lunch in the pub he'd left his easel and latest painting of the house outside in the sunshine to dry. When he returned home to gather it up, he found that it had been added too, in a very crude manner. A short stick figure had been added to the foreground of the path down the garden and lurching in the shadows behind a tree was a black hooded figure. The hooded figure was just strokes of black paint, and the small stick-like figure seemingly painted by a child.

Nick looked around the sunny part of the garden but had to shield his eyes to stare into its darker recesses. He saw nothing usual but did spot the magnifying glass sitting on the centre bench in the gazebo. He was sure he'd put that away in the little tool shed in the corner of the grounds. He strode purposefully over to the gazebo to snatch it up. He looked left and right as he walked back to his picture and used the magnifying glass to examine the cuckoo figures on his painting. The black paint representing each figure was dry. The hooded figure, on closer inspection, seemed to be holding a drawn, downwards pointing knife in his blob of a hand.

He wondered if Crina had added the figures, but he was pretty sure in his mind that she hadn't. Grabbing the painting he strode over to a shady plot behind the shed, where two separate wooden slatted compost heaps were, and threw it on the farthest one along. He moved his easel and other painting accoutrements under the roof of the gazebo to leave them and the magnifying glass there.

That was the end of his artist period, for a couple of days.

Painting was the last thing on his mind today. Tonight, there would be a half-moon and the door that he hoped matched the key in his pocket would appear. He kept the red key with him constantly, even though it rubbed a little at the top of his thigh. The day wasn't overly hot, and there were raindrops carried in the north wind. So he put on his jacket and slipped the key in his inner pocket instead.

The morning wasn't too bad, but by the time Crina arrived to clean and make his lunch, he was pacing around like a tiger in a cage. She picked up on his pensive mood and kept out of his way. She cleared out one of the old servant's bedrooms in the back of the house, one floor up from him.

He couldn't settle at all. Books, computer games, thoughts of painting or even gardening crossed his mind, but he couldn't settle down to do anything for long. He even rang Micheldever twice, who didn't answer his calls. Nick left two scathing messages for the little man, which didn't improve his mood. He told Crina not to bother today with lunch and went out to the pub. He drank half of his pint of bitter before the clientele of the place wound him up with their daily repetitive prattle. So he got up and left before his paid food order arrived.

He found himself in the vast cemetery. Wandering the lanes and small overgrown, leafy green paths between the trees and gravestones. He found himself by the bench under the reaching angel, where he'd gotten this haunted quest from the tramp. He half expected the meths smelling bastard to stagger out and accost him any second, but he was pretty much alone. He sat down on the hard, slightly damp bench, and checked his phone. It was still only half-past one, and he had hours to waste until it got dark. He got up and wandered around the boundary. He could hardly see anything through the thick canopy of sycamore trees. There were trees and high old scrubs lining the cemetery wall.

After a while, he trudged over to Lionel's flat to water his plants and have a smoke or two. He waited there, watching *Cash in the Attic* on Lionel's television, for as long as he could stand it. He held out until half-two, knowing that Crina would have left by then. He didn't want to be around people today, not even his sexy Romanian cleaner.

The skies above the house were a white mass of cloud so any early moon would be hidden. He had a cola when he got home, before heading down to check far below. The wall was just a wall, and there was no magical portal there yet. Nick made the slow ascent back up to the house, and ate a packet of crisps, washed down with the remains of his can of Coke.

He did the only thing he could think of doing to keep him sane. He set an alarm on his mobile and went off to his bed. It took over an hour for him to drift off, even with his shutters closed. It seemed that he could pick up the whine of every individual car, van or motorbike, going past the house. He heard every creak of the old house and every tweeting bird on every branch around the garden like they were in the bedroom next door.

When he woke, it was dark. He fumbled around in the thick, soupy gloom to find his mobile phone, but it wasn't on the bedside cabinet. In fact, it was on the carpet just under the right-hand side of his four-poster bed, vibrating away to itself like a mad thing. Had he slept through the song to wake him up, and the phone rattled off the cabinet with the vibration? Or had spectral hands been at work in his bedroom tonight? Nick reached down under his bed, the top of his head resting on the floor, as he grabbed his humming phone off the carpet. He was about to check the time when the covers keeping him in bed gave way, and he fell out in a tumbled mess on the bedroom floor. Rubbing his neck and shoulder, he rolled into a sitting position, his back against the bed. He checked the time, it was just after nine at night.

Nick turned on his bedside lamp so he could pull on his jeans, socks and shoes. Checking that the key was still in his inner jacket pocket, he grabbed that off the back of a chair. He paced to the bedroom door and opened it. Weak light of dusk poured in through the doorway before he stopped and headed back to grab his torch off the dressing table. He jogged down the grand staircase, and into the sitting room, tugging on his jacket. He wanted to fire up his little spy cameras and laptop monitors before trudging downstairs. No point in walking all the way down and up again if the doorway wasn't there yet. The computer took ages to load, and then the camera programme even longer. He nearly didn't wait and was about to just head down there, when the four relay camera pictures flicked onto the screen.

He didn't bother with the other three, just one caught his full, undivided attention. The door was back.

Nick hurried out the room and ran off down the corridor towards the music room door. What he missed, though, was the half-formed figure of a boy running down the dark upper corridor, and the slower, juddery movements of the hooded figure that stalked after it.

Nick flew down the steps to the depths of the heart of the house. In fact, he would have flown down the fifth flight of steps if he hadn't grabbed hold of the bannister at the right moment. It made him slow a little until he was safely on the floor and running at full pelt down the inner corridor. He skidded into the wall, whacking his upper right arm, but ignored the pain. Because there, in front of him, in his torchlight, was the door.

Nick exhaled loudly. With only the camera above and his work tools for company, he slowly approached the door until he was standing right in front of it. He moved the torch from his left hand to his right so he could pull the key out his jacket pocket. He slowly put the key into the lock and then half-closed his eyes as he screwed up his face in anticipation of the worst happening.

Nick turned the key.

It moved with the ease of a hot knife through butter. The lock clicked several times as it turned, and then the sound spread out from the lock to cover the entire door. Every click and bang spawned another and another, like a ripple effect throughout the door and behind it. Louder and louder the mechanical movement grew, making Nick wince. He did not move, nor clap his hands to his ears. The workings of the opening door were brought up to a climatic crescendo and then ceased. Nick's ears rang for a few seconds and then ebbed away, leaving nothing but him and the doorway.

He reached out and slowly turned the black ringed handle. The door clicked open, and with a gentle push glided in on itself. There before his eyes was the totally red room that Tracey Sunderland had described to him.

Every detail she mentioned, and some she had forgotten, were all there inside, laid out in crimson. The bed, the desk, the tables, and chairs. The red candles with their red flames, and the red screen across the far corner. There were darker red drops on the red carpet, where poor Peter the caretaker had lost his hand. Because of the red colours of the room, the most striking thing about the place was the single brown door, thirteen feet dead ahead of him in the far wall.

Nick went to step inside and then stopped his foot in midair. The red room wasn't deserted he remembered, so he put his shoe back down on the stone floor of the outside corridor. He turned and bent down to grab the sledgehammer, which he placed head first at the bottom of the doorway to stop it closing behind him. Then, pocketing his torch, he picked up the pickaxe as a weapon, and slowly ventured inside the red room. As he did, he tried to take in all the room's surroundings. He wished he could take some photos with his camera phone, but dared not put down the pickaxe.

As he made it to the centre of the room, he could hear the whispering words coming from behind the screen. The words were quiet and repeating over and over in a hushed voice.

"*Absconditus-absconditusasconditusabsconditus.*"

Unlike Tracey and Peter before him, he knew it was Latin and what it meant: *hidden, secret, concealed from God.*

"Who the hell are you?" Nick called to the person, or thing, behind the screen.

The screen was suddenly knocked forwards, and the wrecked remains of a red-skinned man charged. He was dressed in blood-soaked shirt and breeches, Peter Podolski's half-eaten hand clamped between his blood stained teeth.

CHAPTER EIGHTEEN

The man known as Stephen to his doctor waited anxiously in his seat, while his medical records and test results were pored over.

"We did the full works as you requested, bloods, semen, urine, stool samples. Blood pressure and heart tests, full body and brain scans, and you know what, Stephen?" the doctor said, whipping off his reading glasses to look up at his patient.

"No, what?"

"You are one of the healthiest men of your age I know. You even put me to shame." The doctor smiled and held his glasses between the interlaced fingers of his cupped hands. "But to order these tests, you must have had some health concerns, or had a recent pain episode that scared you?"

"I just thought it was about time to test my health. I was thinking of maybe trying for a baby with my girlfriend and wanted to make sure I was in good condition," he lied.

"Well, I don't see why not," the doctor smiled. "Is there anything else I can help you with today?"

The number of a good shrink maybe? Stephen thought to himself but just smiled in reply to the doctor's question. "I don't think so."

"Then I wish you well with your endeavours," the doctor winked and stood to reach his hand across the desk.

"Thanks," Stephen replied and left the doctor's office with more questions than when he'd gone in.

He walked out of the office into the noon sunshine and wished for the cooler climes of his homeland. He didn't often get melancholy for his old home town, but the heat was nearly unbearable today. The only rolling green hills and swathes of heather he saw were on the labels of expensive bottles of imported whisky. He got into his parked car and cranked up the air-con. In his youth, he would have walked to the doctor's office as it would only have taken fifteen minutes, but nobody walked here for business, only for leisure. The cool air hardly had time to work its magic and cool him down before he was home again.

But he did not get out. He just sat inside his chilly red Porsche, staring through the closed iron gates at his home. He knew the dogs were inside, and that bloody walkie-talkie. He backed up his car and drove over to his girlfriend's house. The further away from his place he got, the cooler and less stressed he felt.

Maybe he would ask her if she wanted his child, maybe it wasn't such a lie after all. It could be that he heard his father's voice for a reason. Maybe to tell him he had a right to a life and to be a dad. Not just a retired assassin. Maybe there was a chance of redemption after all.

CHAPTER NINETEEN

Nick reacted on instinct.

He swung the pickaxe at the rushing red man. It speared into the man's side just under the ribcage. The man howled like a wounded animal and crashed into Nick butting him between his chin and neck. The momentum of the running man knocked them both off balance, and they went crashing to the crimson carpet, next to the side of the single bed. The jolt embedded the pickaxe deeper into the guts of the red man, making him grunt. Nick grabbed the side of the bed and managed to scramble onto it to free himself from his attacker.

He looked back down at the red man, as he tried to reach out for Nick. The bitten hand lost on the floor behind him. His teeth were red with blood as he strained against the pickaxe weighing him down. The man pulled at the pickaxe handle with all his strength. Lines like cords stretched over his forehead and then he coughed.

He coughed up blood. Red, to match the rest of the room's decor. The red man sank back to the carpet, defeated. His breathing coming in ragged gasps. His head turned to let his lifeblood dribble out from the corner of his mouth.

"Who are you?" Nick asked.

"I know you of old," the red man croaked, losing more blood in the coughs that followed.

"Really? Well, I don't have a clue who you are, mate, so you'd better introduce yourself."

"You have come for me at last, I see that now," the man gasped. "All I wanted was to live forever, but not like this. Not driven mad by loneliness, hunger and base desires. What I did was unholy, and to trick the Lord Almighty himself, but that was my folly, sir."

The thin. Red man's head fell back on the carpet and he vomited up more blood. Nick shoved himself off the bed, down on his knees beside the mortally wounded man.

"How did you try and trick him? what is your name?" Nick put a hand on the dying man's shoulder.

"I wanted life eternal, but not this Devil's Snare. I should not have signed away my soul for this. You…you…" The man's eyes were glazing over and his words getting softer.

Nick leant forwards into his red face and grabbed the lapels of his shirt to find they were wet with blood. "Give me your name?"

"I go to hell's damnation now," the red man said, not hearing Nick's words.

"Who the fuck are you, and why are you in this room?" Nick shouted into the man's face.

"I was once Peter…Pee-ter Gates. I am the…the second… guard-ian," the man's words trailed off to a whisper.

"What's through that other door?"

"Nothing," Peter Gates replied, before letting out a long rasping breath and then nothing.

"There must be something behind it. What are you guarding or hiding?" Nick shook the man's collar in frustration, but his head just lolled about on dead shoulders. "Fuck!"

Nick sat back on the bed and looked down at the corpse of Peter Gates. A man who, if he was the owner of Forky's House, should have been long dead and reduced to bare bones in his grave by now. Nick sat for five minutes to try and collect himself and his thoughts. He got up, as he had no clue how long the room would remain here. The last thing he needed was to be trapped inside like the poor dead wretch on the carpet. He checked the room thoroughly. The tables, desk, and chairs, but the place was devoid of anything useful.

At last, by his choice, he made for the other door. It was oak and plain looking, and a welcome respite from the rest of the red decor. It had a handle and lock on the side. The keyhole was shaped like an upright cross, and Nick wondered what manner of key could open it.

Then he looked back at the open door behind him, and at the key in the lock and he knew, Four Keys House. The house was built to cover the mysterious coloured rooms that appeared and disappeared with the phases of the moon. The rooms were built to make it even harder to get inside the next door, where all four keys were required to open it. He could picture them in his head, slotted together to make a larger key, the last key. The key to the door behind which, Peter Gates said, nothing lay behind.

The coloured rooms were the ones the Tramp was talking about. It was this room, beyond the final door that had him so fearful. Nick walked around Gates' corpse and to the other door and pulled out the key. He tried to place the red room key into the bottom slot, but it would not go. He tried the left side, but with the same results. He turned the key up and tried the upper lock this time, it did enter and stayed where it was, even if he let go. Nick pressed his ear against the wood and listened.

An image flashed into his mind. It was of his young son's last moments, his young hand reaching out for his helpless father. Just before the hooded monk pushed him onto the cold stone floor and stabbed him through the heart. The scream from his lips became a groan of loss as he pulled himself away from the door. Tears welled up and were pouring down his face as he stumbled back to stand over Gates' dead body. His tears fell on the corpse as he leant forward to retrieve the pickaxe stuck inside the man's guts.

He had to grit his teeth and wiggle it from side to side as his anger rose from his toes to the tips of the hairs on his head. Finally wrenching it free, he walked back over to the locked door and retrieved the red key. He pocketed it and then readied the pickaxe over his left shoulder. With a cry of loss and rage, he swung it at the locked wooden door with all his might.

Some sort of sonic boom happened just before the pickaxe hit the wood. It sent Nick flying backwards out of the red room. He let go of the pickaxe which crashed into a chair, taking off a leg. Nick flailing wildly, hit the wooden passageway wall outside the room hard, and fell to the cold stone floor unconscious.

The door to the red room slammed shut behind him.

Nick awoke in total darkness, groggy and confused. The back of his head was killing him, in fact, most of his body hurt somewhere. He slumped against a wall. His probing hands felt wood behind him and stone underneath him. He was glad that he could move all of his limbs, but not without some discomfort. He felt around him for his torch, but only found the head of the sledgehammer that had been wedged in the doorway to the red room. He patted his left trouser pocket and was relieved to find the key still there. Reaching into his jacket he pulled out his mobile phone. He knew the screen was cracked as soon as his left thumb brushed it. It wouldn't turn on, so he was isolated in the darkness.

Wood panels behind, and the stone floor beneath, meant he must be in the passageway outside the red room. He crawled forwards, reaching out with his hand. It touched only flat wooden panels. He felt a yard along left and right but couldn't locate the door to the hidden room. It had vanished. To a weird plane of existence, where time ran much more slowly than on Earth.

He pushed his right arm against the wall as he tried and failed to stand up. So he crawled, heading, he hoped, in the right direction for the stairs.

He wondered if only the time spent connected to the Earth when the door was here, registered as time passed. If the room only appeared for say eight hours once a month for two hundred years, the passage of time may only be about one year inside, for every century gone by outside.

Nick crawled around the passageway, and out into a cooler and wider area. He found the stairs and began to crawl slowly up them. Halfway through his long ascent he pulled himself up on the bannister and managed to keep standing. He slowly hobbled upstairs, cursing every step, as pain juddered through his core. At last, after it seemed an age, he was pressing through the secret corridor and into the gloomy, but not so dark, music room. He headed for the corridor door and stumbled out, just as Crina walked by. She screamed and jumped at his appearance, as she thought she had the house to herself. Nick fell into her arms. Just noticing it was daylight outside before he closed his eyes against her neck that smelt of soap.

Nick threatened Crina with the sack if she called an ambulance. She cursed him in her native tongue and helped him hobble upstairs to the bathroom with the reasonable working shower. Nick could hardly stand unaided, so Crina stripped him down to his boxers and manhandled him into the bath and under the flowing water. Even the moderate power of the water caused him to slip over twice. He bumped his head the second time and saw darkness creep into the edge of his vision.

Crina cursed him again in Romanian as she stripped off her t-shirt, jeans, socks, and trainers. Scraping back and tying her hair into a long brown ponytail with a rubber band off her wrist, she stepped into the bath to help hold her employer up. She tried to stay out of the spray, but Nick couldn't straighten his back up properly. This caused him to lean over and overbalance into her waiting arms, making her nearly as wet as him.

Nick's head rested on her thin shoulder, his eyes cast down her taut, pale body. Her petite sky blue bra covered her small bust, while her mismatched panties were white and soaked through, showing off her dark hair underneath. A drop of water wobbled on the end of his nose and then fell between the small swells of her breasts. He tracked the drop until it joined with the other water soaking into the thin cotton.

The warm water was easing the pain in his back and his other joints. It was also sending him into a tired stupor, where the edges of the world were soft, warm and fuzzy. That was until Crina grabbed him under the chin and pushed his head off her soft, but strong shoulder, back into the heavy dousing of the shower head. The water stung his eyes, but at least brought some of the melting edges of his vision back into sharp focus. The bathroom was steaming up as the water increased to hot. Nick blinked the water out of his eyes and looked down at the lovely Crina. Her toned, thin body, with a hint of hip, was plastered wet and looking luscious before his eyes.

He moved forward, his left hand on her wet shoulder, for a kiss.

His eyes closed shut as he passed through the heaviest downpour edge of the shower spray. So the tight wet slap was more of a shock to his system than it should have been. The stinging contact sent him sidewards into the opaque shower curtain. His right foot slipped, and his legs crumbled under him. He fell out of the shower, hitting his head on the polished wooden floor, and once more his world of hurt darkened to nothing.

He awoke in his own bed, to find a fully clothed Crina mopping his brow. Crina pulled back her hand as he woke. She was frowning at him. Nick pushed down with his palms onto the new mattress and moved himself up on his pillows into a better resting position. A covert feel under his covers confirmed the feeling he had of being completely naked under them.

"How are you feeling?" Crina asked, but Nick could detect little of any concern in her voice.

Nick raised his hand and jauntily touched the numerous bumps on his cranium. They were tender but small and the skin uncut. "I'll live," he replied.

"Good," she said, rising from the seat she had pulled across to sit upon. "You owe me thirty minute more this day, in wages."

"Where are you going?" he asked, as she skirted the large bed and made for the bedroom door.

"Home." She turned her head only to reply, and then continued on towards the door and grabbed the handle.

"Was I out long?" His eyes lingering on her lovely, rounded behind, framed in her blue jeans. He noticed she and he both seemed dry after the shower.

"Only ten minute," she said, opening the door. She went through, turned and grabbed the handle on the other side as she faced him again. "You should see a doctor, though. I have no more time for you today. I have life too outside this crappy house."

She closed the door hard and left him there, naked in his bed, nursing his bumps and bruises. He did notice a rare show of emotion, frustration and anger in her voice, as she left. Images of her in her wet underwear in his shower came to mind, and his hand slipped under the tenting covers of his bed.

Nick rested in bed all day and did not get out until his bladder got too full to hold back. He felt like his body was twisted in places, but nothing seemed broken or badly hurt. He dressed slowly, glad the key was still in his trouser pocket. He put on a clean shirt, and shoes, and gingerly made his way down the grand staircase.

The sunlight was beaming through as it was after five, catching the dust motes in the warming rays. He was halfway down the stairs, hanging onto the bannister when something caught his eye. The motes were not just idly swirling and floating, they were converging, to form a solid mass in the sunlight. Nick stopped and straightened as best his back would allow. The hairs on his neck and hands stiffened like an electric current was passing through each individual follicle.

A familiar figure began to form. A mosaic of dust, dead flesh, and the scabs of rat's droppings from the dusty floors. A man with a hooded face. A man Nick had poured more hatred towards than even his own father.

It was the man who murdered his son.

He could see the cruel, crooked nose under the hood. With a great effort of will, the man walked up along the angle of the sunlight to where Nick stood rooted to the spot. He did not move, not out of fear but more from pain and seething rage at this creature, that defied even death to taunt him. It slowly mimicked the semblance of walking as it menacingly took step after step towards Nick. It had no feet or shoes, only legs and covered knees showing how the murderer would have walked when he was alive. Nick stood his ground, unsure what to do, this man was long dead. How could this mote ghast hurt him now?

The hooded man raised an arm, and from its hand, a dagger hung. It appeared more solid and fully formed than the hooded man holding it. Could it do Nick damage from beyond the grave? He stood up straight, though it pained him, against the advancing thing of dust and hate. He showed no fear, he was defiant, as the hunched man raised the knife higher.

Then a warm sensation moved through Nick from behind, like one of those slow-burn heat pads. Through him, sending healing warmth to every inch of his injured frame. Nick looked down to see the faded form of a boy rush through him, and then through the knife wielding, hooded, dead man on the stairs. The boy's passing sent the motes and dust and the creature everywhere. Scattering his form back into the nothingness of whence he came. A cloud covered the sun in the late afternoon sky, and both figures melted away in an instant.

Nick was alone once more in the house.

The sun returned no more than five seconds later, but there were no dust particles caught in its rays and no sign of anyone else on the stair. Nick's throat felt dry, but his aches and pains had vanished. He made for the sitting room, grabbed his wallet and jacket. He went out and left the old house to its own devices for a while.

He made his way up the high street to the library, but it had closed, and Margo wasn't anywhere to be seen. A mobile phone shop was open two doors down, though, so he went and bought another phone, and swapped his old sim card into the new mobile. Then he trudged back in the evening sunlight to the pub and ordered a pint, and a steak and kidney pie.

"Thirsty are you?" asked the landlord.

"As fuck," Nick replied and took his beer over to his usual table.

Nick devoured his dinner with more gusto than normal, even polishing off all his peas, which he usually left. He ordered another pint. When the landlady came over to clear up his plate, he ordered a treacle sponge for pudding as well.

It gave him time to think. So much had happened to him in the last twenty hours. The red room, with Peter Gates inside. The other door that led to somewhere, and the ghost of his dead son coming to his aid on the stairs.

He got out his new mobile phone, but it needed charging. The pub had a pay phone, so Nick pulled some change from his pocket and rang Micheldever's number. It went straight to voicemail. Cursing, Nick went to his table and drained his

second pint. He ordered a third when the landlady brought his
pudding over five minutes later. Still he could not get the gritty
taste of sand from his mouth.

He rang Micheldever's home and mobile number at nine, once
his new mobile had been on charge for a couple of hours. He
drew an answer phone blank with both calls. He left his mobile
to charge, and then checked his laptop, which showed up
various parts of the house. Two weren't working, but the one
down deep was. It showed just a wall where the doorway he'd
entered yesterday had been. Nick was relieved to see it gone,
as he didn't fancy walking down all those steps again. He was
tired physically and emotionally, and half-full of ale. So took to
his bed early.

Nick woke up just before nine the next morning. He had wet
eyes. The constant dream about his desert-stranded son, more
poignant than ever before. His back twinged in protest as he got
out of bed, but should have hurt more after the whack it took
yesterday. The less tender bumps on his head were going down,
so he headed for the shower. That brought back vivid memories
of a half-naked Crina, and he was soon tossing off again like
some love-sick fourteen-year-old schoolboy. He dressed in a
sharp suit he'd bought online, and a pink shirt without a tie. The
shirt collar felt stiff on his neck, but he left the house anyway, as
he had places to go. He'd only just got to the gate and unlocked
it when a white delivery van pulled up and parked on the road
beside the house.

This brought a few honks from the heavy traffic behind
him, but the black driver just stuck two fingers up, and headed
over to Nick, holding a cardboard box. It was for Nick, so he
signed for it, not recalling that he'd ordered anything else online
lately. Maybe it was some old order that he'd forgotten about. He
trudged back into the dark confines of the front of the house
and placed the box on the dry fountain, which had been Billy
Ryan's last repose. He used the edge of the red door key in his
pocket to break the brown tape around the box and pulled the
top open. Inside were white polystyrene bits which he brushed

aside to reveal clear plastic underneath, with something round, wrapped inside.

Nick gasped and stepped away from the box in shock. This caused it to overbalance and topple sideways off the fountain. As it turned and fell the contents of the box, accompanied by a snowstorm of white packing, fell out. The polystyrene stayed pretty much where it fell, but the plastic wrapped thing rolled away three feet. It was only stopped by a fallen branch from the overhanging trees above.

Micheldever's severed head, with his open blank eyes, staring up at Nick.

Once over the shock of seeing the private detective's head, Nick stuffed it back in the box and went around the house to the back garden. He took it to the tool shed and examined the box, but there was no address where it was sent from. Laying down an old, plastic fertilizer bag on the workbench, Nick unwrapped the severed head. The neck wound was jagged and uneven. Micheldever had not been beheaded with a sharp sword or blade, rather it had been sawn off while the wretch was still alive.

The lips of the private detective had been sewn shut.

Nick grabbed a rusty, but still useable, Stanley knife from the edge of the bench, and began to cut the dark, thick cotton that fused the purple lips of the detective together. Once free, and grimacing hard, Nick used a wide, flat chisel to prise the dead man's jaw apart. Inside the mouth cavity, where his tongue should have been, was another of the missing keys, wrapped in a plastic bag, with a folded note inside. Nick withdrew it quickly and tore the bag apart. He caught the little-folded note as it dropped and brought the new key closer to his eyes. It was similar to the other key as far as he could make out. Except where the red key's paint had faded away with age, this still had most of its black paint covering the semi-circular handle.

"I have the black key now, but why?"

Nick fumbled the note open. It was typed on a lined notepaper, with a serrated top edge. It read as follows:

Leave my family in peace.

Here is the only key we have left.

It was not signed, but Nick knew which family had sent it. He smiled at the words written on the page. Micheldever had done his job well, to the point that the patriarch of the Gates family had feared for his daughter's safety enough to give up the key. He put the note in his pocket and then drew out the red key. As he brought the two together, he felt a heavy magnetic pull between them. He let the red key go from his left hand. It flew two inches, to attach itself to the side of the black key, to form an L-shape.

Nick smiled to himself, and with great effort pulled the two keys apart, and put them each in separate trouser pockets. He wondered how far Micheldever had gone to scare or scar the family into giving up the black key. How far across the line did he go, to get his head cut off? Nick used a nearby spade to bury the head behind the shed in the dark corner of the garden. Not a fitting resting place for someone who had helped him get another key, but probably no more than the low-life deserved.

At last, a little later than planned, Nick set off down the road, heading to the local library and its museum. He passed a newsagent close to the library. It had a rack of newspapers stacked outside on the pavement, on a plastic covered rack. One lurid headline jumped out at Nick: *London socialite blinded in horrific rape attack.*

Nick danced up the library steps and kissed a surprised Margo on the cheek in welcome.

"I don't have any new news for you, Nick, I'm afraid," she said, taking her glasses off her nose.

"I have another line of enquiry for you and an offer."

"Sounds intriguing, young man. Out with it now, before I get even closer to my grave than I was this morning."

"Could you find for me the last resting places of the following people; Nicholas Clovis, Peter Gates, and Dr Forque?" Nick slouched on the reception desk next to her, fiddling with a pen attached to a chain.

"Yes, I suppose I can, and what's the offer?" she asked with pursed lips, but a glimmer in her eyes.

"Coffee and bun, on me, at the place across the road."

"Make it tea and toast and you are on." She raised her long neck as she smiled.

Five minutes later they were sitting across the road, on metal seats, pulled up close to an aluminium round table, that looked like a knight's shield glaring at them in the harsh sunlight. There were three such filled tables outside, hugging the pavement close to the coffee house. Nick had a coffee and an iced bun, and Margo her tea and buttered toast as requested.

The museum assistant had a blue folder resting on an angle from her lap against the edge of the table. She was flicking through an inch thick raft of notes, papers, and maps. Nick watched her poke out her tongue and lick her right forefinger every few pages or so, as she flicked through more pages. She used the fingers of her left hand as a make-do bookmark.

"Ah, that's the ticket," she said, pulling an A4 lined page covered with notes written on the page in various ball-point pen colours. "I have most of the information right here."

Margo waved the page in question and then placed it on the outside of the folder to read. Nick raised his coffee to his lips and sipped some down as he waited for Margo.

"Peter Gates' final resting place was quite easy to find, as it caused a bit of stink back in the day. Gates was well known in certain circles as a diabolist. So the family did not want him buried in their family chapel on their own large estate. Large donations to the upkeep of a certain cemetery *we all know* next to the house were made, to ensure he had a right and proper Christian burial at least." Margo looked up at Nick, bringing her tea to her lips, only to find it too hot to sip yet.

"So, Peter is buried next door to me somewhere, how very convenient," Nick said, putting down his coffee in favour of his iced bun.

"Well, that's not the end of it, Nick. Feelings were running high for several years after. At times of the year, Peter's tomb had been found daubed with animal blood and, certain unholy types had been seen loitering around the tomb at the dead of night. So a local farmer and his hands took it upon themselves to go and destroy the tomb and scatter Peter's *evil bones* outside of the cemetery." Margo said *evil bones*, in a witchy voice, and wiggled the fingers of her hand as she spoke them.

"And did they?"

"They tried, but when they broke into the tomb, the coffin inside was empty."

"Oh, a mystery. Do we know what happened to Peter's corpse?" Nick asked as he tucked into his iced bun.

"Nope, I could not find anything more salacious after that." Giving up on the tea, Margo reached for her first slice of buttered white toast.

"Anything on Dr Forque or Clovis?" Nick asked, after polishing off his bun and licking the icing residue off the tops of his fingers.

"Hmmm," Margo said chewing one-half of her toast while waving her hand in circles as she swallowed. "Couldn't find anything on Clovis, but it was a long time ago. I'll dig some more on that. Dr Forque's body was cremated and sent back to his relatives in France in late nineteen forty-five."

"You've done well having all that info to hand, even before I asked?"

Margo raised her teacup and winked at Nick. "I always try and be ahead of the game, Nick."

Nick smiled, even after his grisly start to the day.

CHAPTER TWENTY

The first week of July began with a thunderstorm of epic ancient Norse mythical proportions. The Thames Barrier was raised, as a month's rain came overnight, and outlying parts of the river's banks were flooded. The Met Office, who said it would be a clear night, backslid as best they could.

The North-West corner of Forky's House leaked like a bitch on heat, right down into the ground floor drawing room. This was piled high with unused furniture, and as long as his sitting room was dry, the new owner of the house couldn't care less. He sat on his sofa, listening to the torrential downpour with a large full glass of Merlot in his hand. His eyes were fixed on the screen of his laptop, showing only one grainy, green image of the passageway wall below ground.

There was no moon tonight, which also heralded the coming of the doorway in the cellars. Nick wondered how the door could tell if there were no moon in the sky. The clouds and heavy rain would cover up its surface anyway. He liked the sound of thunder and lightning, as it made every human around the world feel small, weak and insignificant. He sipped his red wine and blinked, still the wall showed no door. When the door appeared, surely the black key would open it, but reveal what?

Nick wasn't entirely sure. Lionel had described the blue room, like-for-like the same as the red room, except of course the colour. Would the black room have an occupant like the red one? Would he have to kill that poor soul as well?

He had a new weapon now anyway, a sword taken from the wall in an upper passageway. If the black room had an occupant or guardian as he feared, he would need to be prepared for another attack. Putting down his wine, he stood up and stepped into the hallway.

The storm had hidden the sun today. No sun meant no sunlight through the green-tinged glass roof, no sun rays meant no dust motes. His son's murderer had not made an appearance in the last few days, but nor had the phantom image of his lost boy.

When he returned to the sitting-room he found that the door had appeared on his laptop screen. It was like a virgin bride on her wedding night, changing for bed while the husband was in the toilet. Smiling at the door's coyness at not appearing while being watched, Nick took out his new mobile phone. He laid it on the table next to his laptop and patted his jacket pockets. He had a box of matches, a lighter, and a mini Maglite. From the sofa, he picked up a huge, black rubber torch, and his sword. He slowly made his way from the music room, down into the dark depths. It grew increasingly warmer as he descended like there was some invisible furnace below. He began to regret wearing his jacket, as his armpits began to dampen, but he needed to carry as many ways of making light as he could. The storm raging over London was soon forgotten as he reached the last step and headed into the passageway beyond.

There it stood, large as life and twice as ominous. For interest's sake, he tried the red key first, but to no avail. It went into the lock, but would not turn. So he put it back in his pocket, before transferring the torch and sword into his other hand. His left one hand free to take out the black key and slide it into the lock. It turned with ease, and the tiny click of the lock started to spread out through the inside of the doorway. Clicks and whirs escalated quickly to become deafening ringing of metal hitting metal. Nick had his hands full, so could not cover his ears, so he decided instead to retreat around the passageway corner until the ringing noise of the opening working of the doorway had fully ceased.

When he returned, the passageway was silent again. His free hand turned the handle and pushed the door inwards. He stood at the threshold but could see nothing inside the black

room except stygian darkness. He raised the torch from the
floor and swept it across the room over the threshold. As far
as he could tell it was an exact match to the red room in every
detail but one, the colour. The carpet, tables, chairs, bed and
linen were all black. Black candles with black flames fluttered
in the draft from the open doorway. They gave out no light to
the surrounding table or desk where they were sat. The other,
brown, normal-looking door stood opposite and to one side a
black dressing screen. Moving the torch into his right hand, his
gripped the sword and took one tentative step into the black
room.

Even with the bright, multi-bulbed torch, it was hard to
define one piece of furniture from the walls or black carpet.
There was not a fleck of any other colour on the carpet, a feat all
proud home-owners would admire. No dust, no strands of hair
or spots of fluff, could be seen anywhere.

Nick took two hesitant steps in. His torch sent out a lance
of light into this black, mysterious room. Nick was almost a
hundred percent sure another person was hiding away behind
the screen. Peter Gates was the guardian of the red room.
It made sense that this room, and the other two, would have
lost souls of their own. Empty men, with empty souls, selling
themselves for the trick of immortality. Men who left behind
vacant graves or tombs, because they resided in these infernal
rooms instead. Did they power the magic that fluxed them in
and out of existence on the whims of the moon? Or were they
guardians, who gave their lives and afterlives to guard another
door? An even stranger and alluring door that needed all four
keys to open. But a door to where?

Another step closer and Nick thought he heard the slightest
movement behind the dressing screen. What type of man or
creature would he encounter this time? Peter Gates's time in the
red room had done nothing for his mental state. Would each
such unfortunate share the same madness?

"Who are you?"

The voice came from behind the black screen. A once strong
voice, that was now strained, like imps had fletched at the
person's vocal cords with razor blades. Nick, in spite of holding

the sword in his left hand, took an involuntary step backwards. He mentally cursed the subconscious cowardice of his feet.

"Come and find out," Nick replied. He frowned almost instantly at his words, hardly the uttering of legend.

"You may not find my countenance agreeable, I fear." The voice behind the screen was slightly stronger but had more rattles to it than a rat in a drainpipe.

"I've got a sturdy mind and stomach. But it's your room so you can do what you like. I just want to examine the door in front of me without being attacked. Unless of course, you want to tell me what's behind it?"

"Nothing lies beyond the door, and I should know, I'm the one who put it there," the voice said, with a hint of a cough or was it a cackle.

"So, who are you then?" Nick forced his legs and feet to shuffle a few more inches forwards, very much against their will for flight and survival.

"Your question, perhaps should be, who was I? Before I died."

"Okay, be like that then." Nick managed to smile to himself, in spite of where he was. "Do you know a Peter Gates?"

"I do not. Yet Gates was my late wife's maiden name, so perhaps some cousin of hers?"

"Then you must be, or should I say were, Nicholas Clovis in life." Nick's voice was strong and full of smugness.

"Then you have me at a disadvantage, sir." The renewed rasping strength of the voice did not force a mild retreat from Nick's feet again. No, it was the bony black fingers that grasped the edge of the screen nearest the other door. They were thin to the point that little flesh separated skin from bones. The nails were black and tapered into sharp points, which would make holding a pen a most painful experience. Black nails and a black hand in the cuff of a shirt that had been soaked in the inky veil of night for centuries. This was not the colour of the man's birth, something had stained the skin beyond any ethnic trait. The sins had seeped through Clovis's pores, turning him into something out of the darkness of nightmares. A bent arm came into view, followed by a shoulder.

Then a face, that even Nick, who had faced many earthly or ghostly nightmare, shuddered at. Clovis' hair, hung lank and spare down to the wide collar of his shirt. His face looked like it had been dipped in tar and set alight to smoulder and blacken unto this. His eyes had no white, only black pupils on black orbs. His mouth was parted, and something slivered in the orifice, like an adder hiding behind an ebony wall of teeth. As Peter Gates, his distant relative had been red cast like his room, so Nicholas Clovis took on the appearance of the black room and blended into his surroundings.

"Do you see me now, intruder, see what I've become?"

"I preferred you behind the screen."

"You mock me sir? I should tear you apart and feast on your innards." Clovis' voice rattled in anger.

"Sword." Nick raised his left hand, wiggled the sword in the air twice, and then pointed the tip at Clovis. "So there are four rooms, but all decked out in different colours. Each holds a guardian or some poor *schmuck* who gave his soul to the *darkside* for a crappy, eternal life, stuffed in a box room for hundreds of years. Am I on the money so far?"

"There are four colours, yes, to match the colours of the moon. But there is in truth only one room, set apart but together, in the same space, and also not here at all. It is hard even for I to explain, but did I hear you correctly when you say hundreds of years?"

"Yes, you died in seventeen-sixty-two." Nick's revulsion at the man standing before him had not banished the smug smile from his face.

"But...but by my count of days, I have been trapped in this room for less than two and one-half years." It was hard to tell what emotions Clovis was expressing through his face. Nick kept his torch beam resting on the chest of the man's black shirt, so his head merged into the surrounding darkness.

"More like two and a half centuries." This got the mental gears whirring around inside Nick's mind. Each facet of the room appeared only once a month each month, so only twelve, maybe thirteen visits to this plane of existence each year. Time did not go with the rooms when they left. Only when they were tethered again to the mortal world did it clock in for the inhabitants of the coloured rooms.

Nicholas Clovis seemed to deflate before Nick's eyes. Not that there was much more than skin and bones. The dark, sunken skin on his face made his eyes look like much larger orbs of nothingness. He staggered to the left of Nick and near collapsed on his bed.

"So you built this house, and this room, but for what purpose?" Nick asked, lowering his sword to the floor.

"To cheat death." Clovis's withered long fingers intertwined on his lap as he spoke. "To find a place where God and his angels could not follow and drag my soul off to Hell."

"Well, it kinda worked to a certain degree." Nick nodded as he stepped over the withered man. "Except, you are a prisoner in this room. I'm sure Hell or Heaven couldn't be any worse than this."

"This was just part of my plan. I left instructions to be used after my death, hidden in the library. I needed four souls to inhabit each of the four parts of the room. Then and only then could I use the keys to enter the next door."

"What is through that door then?" Nick flicked the torch from Clovis's shoes over to the brown wooden door and back.

"The wastelands of space and infinity. Nothing lies beyond that door at all, where no god or gods can enter. It is a place away from creation itself. A place where no entity, mortal or deity, can find you. It is a haven of your own mind, a place where utter nothing is king. A place to hide forever and find true immortality."

"Then seeing that you are still here trapped in this black room of yours, things did not go exactly to plan?"

"Sacrifices had to be made to ancient powers, just to get this far. The unborn sire cut from my wife's belly. Yet I was betrayed by my brother-in-law and the four wretches destined for each room, to power the great eternal engines to get me through that final door were set free." Clovis pointed a withered finger and sharp nail towards the brown door. "My four keys were taken from me, and I was thrown into this darkest of rooms. Locked away with little hope ever for escape and tortured by seeing the door to my soul's salvation right before my eyes. You are not the first visitor I have had. Others have used the black key now and again. Yet they only sought the power of old magic to give them wealth and mortal desires. None had the vision to set me free or to collect the four keys again. But you could do that, you could set me free. How many keys do you have in your possession? Say it is not just the black key, I beg thee." Clovis looked up at Nick through the beam of the torchlight.

"I have the red key as well as the black," Nick answered, but did not want to put down his sword to fetch them out for Clovis's black eyes to gaze upon. "An ancestor of your wife followed in your footsteps, and he was trapped in the red version of this place."

"Then you are halfway there, sir." Clovis tried something akin to a smile, but the slithering tongues behind his teeth made Nick's stomach churn a little at the sight.

"Halfway to nothing. The other two keys are missing, Clovis and I have no clues at all where they are. I don't suppose any of your other visitors had the other keys or knew where they were?"

"No, they mostly screamed once they took sight of me."

"Can't say I blame them really you have a very Un-PC look about you now. I kind of guess you weren't always this colour?" Nick was trying to be tactful, not a thing he usually excelled at.

"No, as soon as the door was shut and bolted behind me, I slowly took on this Moorish skin."

Nick stared at the vague outline of the brown door ahead. He wanted to try the fused keys in the lock, yet not in front of an audience. He would wait until the red room was back again, and that had one less soul inside now due to him. He had learnt a great deal from what Clovis had said. Yet he, like the other souls trapped inside the four-in-one room, could not get any further to solving the mystery of the brown door. Not without the remaining two missing keys. Keys he would not find in the room itself, that was clear. Billy Ryan had possession of one during the sixties and Dr Forque back in the forties. So they had existed, and something told him that they were still out there somewhere to be found. Nick turned and walked out of the black room, leaving Clovis sitting on his bed, his face in his hands.

"Where are you going? You can't just walk away and leave me here?"

"I have keys to find me-old-son, come with if you want."

Nick didn't look back but felt and heard the sound of Clovis's following footfalls behind him. He walked into the passageway and turned in time to see Nicholas Clovis run into some kind of invisible barrier at the threshold. Clovis snarled at him, his nails screeching as he tore at the unseen wall that kept him trapped inside the black room, even with the door wide open.

"Sorry, but you are dead I'm afraid. You can't come back into this realm, only forwards into the next. But more likely you'll be stuck in here for all time. Bye, then." Nick kicked the heavy door shut with the side of his foot. Clovis's screams of rage were silenced as soon as the lock clicked shut again. Nick tapped the two keys in their separate pockets, and headed away from the doorway, whistling to himself.

CHAPTER TWENTY-ONE

The cigar box sat unopened on the cover of his double bed.
The ex-assassin sat on the carpet, his back pressed against the wall between his bedroom door and the large window to his left. His dogs were scratching and whining on the other side of the closed door, wondering why they had been so neglected of late. The Scotsman had spent the past fortnight just coming into either feed the dogs or take them out for walks. He no longer wanted to stay that long in his place anymore, let alone sleep in his bedroom. Over the last few days, the close, warm flesh comfort of his girlfriend had made him doubt the voices he had heard. Spooning her, his face pressed up to her honey scented hair, was real, he wasn't quite sure what the walkie-talkie represented. Unless it was a failsafe place to keep him sane, the place where he kept all his murderous guilt.

He scratched at an itch on the side of his neck under a mole. Then he laid his wrists on his bent knees. It was cool inside the bedroom, but nearly forty degrees outside. The sweat on his polo shirt had turned into chilly droplets, which sometimes dripped in an uncomfortable way. He laughed and shook his head, one thing he'd never been in his life was a coward. He pushed himself up off the wall, walked the short distance to the bed, and flipped open the cigar box.

The walkie-talkie was sitting there on top, looking harmless enough.

So he picked it up. He tried to turn it on, but of course, it had no batteries inside, it hadn't had for years now.

A sudden burst of static, followed by a long, sharp whine, made him drop it on the bed in shock. It bounced once and turned over, as he took a pace back from the bottom of the bed.

"Your father isn't very happy that you have been ignoring him," said a clear voice in English.

"This is some trick isn't it, who are you, who is doing this to me?" the Scotsman hissed at the walkie-talkie on the bed as he took another involuntary step backwards. His sense of survival was legendary, his body was telling him to run, run far away and never come back.

"I'm your father."

"I don't bloody think so."

What angle was this mystery voice trying to pull?

"I'm your father's father," the very prim and proper English accent replied.

"Pardon me, but Grandpappy George was nay English." The very thought would have made the big man throw up his pints of *heavy* on the nearest doorstep. The Scotsman wondered where the *nay* had come from, he'd spent a great deal money to learn to hide his Scottish roots. Maybe the mention of his proud Scottish grandfather had brought it bubbling to the surface.

"I'm everyone's father, and I have a crusade for you, my son."

"A crusade, what are you talking about?"

"You are going to Hell's everlasting cauldron, where the Stick Demons will rip your eyes from their sockets on the hour, every hour. Harpies will strip your flesh inch by inch and take their time about it. Moon Dogs will tug at your eviscerated intestines like there were lengths of sausages. Spiked Devils will geld you and lay your ravaged groin to the flame, and all the while, the Fallen One himself will take turns in sodomising your parents. Have I got your attention now?"

The Scotsman gulped slightly as the saliva in his mouth went down the back of his throat and made him cough. "Who are you?"

"I am Elohim; 'Ilah, Yahweh, your Lord God Almighty and I have a quest beyond any trial of Abraham. A crusade to end all wars and all deaths." The voice grew in strength and power and seemed to be all around the Scotsman, and inside his head also.

"Prove it?" he yelled putting his hands over his ears trying to keep the deafening voice from cracking open his skull.

"The woman who you lay down with is carrying your child inside her belly, it will die before the sun sets tomorrow." The voice was gone from the room and his head now, shrunk back to a tinny voice coming from the walkie-talkie.

"What! Why are you telling me all this?" he yelled, walking around and around a spot on his bedroom carpet. The circles getting tighter and tighter until he was turning around on the spot, much like his befuddled mind.

"To prove to you my credentials. Your son is growing outside the womb, inside one of its mother's fallopian tubes, it will soon cease to exist, and join me here in my loving embrace, unless…"

"Unless what?" he demanded of the voice.

"Unless you agree to kill someone for me."

"If you're God why would you want me to kill someone?"

"Because I'm God, and I kill everyone in the end, if you think about."

The Scotsman staggered to the bedroom door and grasped the handle. He could not hear the dogs behind it anymore.

"You go check on your woman. I'll be waiting here for your reply when you return." The walkie-talkie hissed, and the green light on the top dimmed, and the Scotsman ran from his bedroom. The dogs were quivering under a low table together, but he ignored them and ran over to his change bowl. He grabbed his car keys and drove over to his girlfriend's house, which was only ten minutes away.

He had the access codes into her apartment block and a key to her door. He rushed in sweating profusely and out of breath. She was nowhere in the living area, and he rushed into the bedroom they had shared every night this week. The en-suite door was open, and she came padding out in a silky camisole set, holding something white and pen-like in her fingers. It had her whole attention. When she looked up and saw Stephen she shrieked in fright, dropping the object to the floor. It landed on the carpet between them, a white pregnancy tester, its little screen facing upwards with a thick blue line across it.

Both man and woman, parents, to be, began crying at the same moment, both for very different reasons.

CHAPTER TWENTY-TWO

It had been a frustrating few days since Nick had encountered Nicholas Clovis in his black room. Frustrating, as he had got no further in locating the two missing keys. He didn't even have a clue where to start looking for them either, all his avenues of enquiry seemed like dead ends. He spent the morning trawling the internet from antiques sites to eBay, trying to find any trace of them, but with no luck. The usual English summer of rain had turned up, and it had been bucketing it down for three days solid. The only bright light in the gloom was that Crina had informed him that Lionel was coming home from filming at the end of the week.

So his frustrations built up into mammoth masturbation sessions, where all the vilest of porn from the internet were his playground. He had got no further in wooing Crina, with flowers or chocolates or him lavishing all his wealth upon her.

She would smile and pat his shoulder and walk off shaking her head. "I cook and clean for you, nothing else," was her daily mantra.

With the lashing rain and bad light, he could not paint either. Nick sat brooding over his laptop, with a bottle of Vat 69 close to hand, and a sour face that could spoil fruit at twenty paces. He ate his lunch Crina prepared in glum silence. He didn't even try today to engage her conversation, such was his morose mood. He watched the Godfather Part III on his film screen, not for enjoyment, but to pick holes in it and lament for the greater first two parts of the trilogy.

Crina left him after lunch, with the VAT 69 halfway gone. She had wanted to talk to him about work today, and about having some time off, but his mood had been as dark as the rain clouds in the heavens above. So, she pulled up her hoodie and hurried home without asking. He ordered a kebab for delivery, even though the shop was just across the road. Ate the meaty strips with delight, and was in bed, in a near comatose sleep, by eight o'clock.

"Son!" Nick shot up in bed, gasping for air as the memories of his dreams faded away. His mouth felt a little dry, but he wasn't hung-over. He was glad of that fact as he flung open the shutters to find that the sun had returned to this part of London. Smiling now, he showered quickly, brushed his teeth, and gargled long with mouthwash. He had an apple and an orange for breakfast. He grabbed a bottle of mineral water and all his painting stuff and hurried out into the lush green vegetation of the rear gardens. His easel and canvas were soon set up by the gazebo, in the sunspot of Forky's House. He stood before the blank canvas and closed his eyes, letting the hot morning sun warm his face.

Nick smiled, then he laughed and then he began to sing Sinatra songs, as he started to paint.

He wasn't sure how long he'd been painting, but he had stopped for nothing more than a breather and a sip of water. The sun was in the mid position high above the roof of the house, and his skin felt tight, where he should have put on sun cream. He wiped his sweaty brow on the edge of his t-shirt and looked down at what he had painted.

It was the desert sand bowl from his dreams. The sun and the moon at opposing ends of the top of the painting. The rest was coloured in ochre, orange, red and purples and blues, to depict the place his mind went every night. In the middle ground of the painting were four figures on horseback. The riders and horses were each of one colour, starting with black, then white, red and finally blue.

"The four horsemen," he whispered to himself. Then grabbing his water bottle, he retreated to the shade of the gazebo and sat down and drank his fill. He put down the plastic bottle, letting the drips of water fall from his chin, and gazed at his picture. The only person missing in it was his dead son. He sat a long while until Crina came and brought him chicken sandwiches, with lettuce and mayo on top for lunch. She waited for a minute, wondering whether to speak to him about something, but in the end didn't. He just stared at the desert scene. He tossed away the mayo slick lettuce and ate his lunch, his eyes never wandering that far from his painting. The dry chicken and the heat of the day had made him thirsty for a cold beer he knew he had in his fridge. He trooped inside, glad of the shade of the garden closer to the house.

He saw Crina at the sink as he approached the kitchen. She moved away quickly from what she was doing as he trotted down some steps and rounded the dividing wall that used to keep the staff out of sight from garden party guests long ago.

Crina was hurrying back from the pantry area, wet hands and arms still soapy from where she was doing the washing up in one of two adjoining Belfast sinks. She looked flustered and was trying to blow up onto her forehead, to move some fallen hair out of her left eye.

"You okay?" he asked, moving closer to push back the stray hair for her.

"Fine. Thank you," she crisply replied, plunging her hands back into the hot washing up water.

Three plates sat in the wire dryer to dry, as he nodded and walked over to the large behemoth of a fridge he had bought. He pulled it open and took out a cold bottle of beer. It felt good in his warm left hand. He looked over at Crina again as he closed the fridge and went over to a drawer to fetch a bottle opener. She seemed on edge today, but her sharp, quick replies were usual for her. Nick opened his bottle, let the cap drop into the drawer, and let the opener follow after. He turned on the spot and used his backside to close the drawer and leaned against the kitchen cabinet. He took a big slug of beer as he watched her wash up. She seemed reticent to finish the task like she didn't like being watched by Nick.

"Do you want to go dancing?"

"I have washing ups to do."

"Not now. One night, we can even drag Lionel along too if

you feel like you need a chaperone." Nick pushed himself off
the cabinet and halved the distance between them. He stopped
only because of the aghast look on her face. It suddenly came to
him he might be coming across as some creepy letch of a boss
to her. "Well think it over, eh."

Crina's shoulders dropped an inch as her employer left the
kitchen and went back out into the garden drinking his beer.
The tension in her neck lifted, and she withdrew her hands
from the water. She dried them on a tea towel as she hurried
over to the pantry. To her surprise the room was empty. A small
half-sized window was propped open above an old table that
had been left there for years. It was an old table from a lady's
bedroom and stood out among the brick larders and the storage
racks in the room.

"Where are you?" she whispered into the gloomy confines
of the pantry. But there was no one there to reply to her.

Nick had polished off his beer by the time he had made it
back to the sunnier rear of the garden. He resisted the sudden
urge to lob the empty bottle over the wall into the cemetery,
knowing that the surrounding trees would probably thwart
his efforts. So he put it inside an empty, tall Greek urn of a
flower pot. With his free hand's thrust in his trouser pockets,
he returned to his painting. He had a thought of doing another,
maybe of some Roman orgy, defiantly not of the drab weary
garden before him.

"What the fuck!"

Nick had just rounded his painting to find that it had been
interfered with. In the forefront of his picture stood a stick
figure of a child, holding a three fingered hand with a taller
female. Both figures were smiling, nearly up to their dots for
eyes.

The sound of a small pot falling off a wall and breaking
snapped Nick's attention to his left. He saw movement, behind
the lines of box there, either someone bent low, or a child. He
gave chase.

Nick ran forwards and jumped over a dividing curve of
overgrown lavender bushes. His legs jumped through some of
the woodier bits, and the smell invaded his nose as his feet hit

the ground running. He dodged left and was on the same path now as the fleeing figure. He only saw the back heel of a shoe round a bend of tall laurels as he continued the chase. Nick had to go left and right before gaining on the runner. He saw that it was a small boy, with jet black hair. The boy went left again at the end of an arbour of intertwined pear trees.

Could this be the ghost that haunted the house? Was it the remains of the son that was murdered and had come back to the place where many planes seemed to converge? He lost the boy for a while as he pelted down the path. Nick looked this way and that, and then spotted the black mop of hair running down the steps to get hidden behind the wall by the large kitchen.

"Come back," Nick had meant to shout, but because of his exertions, it came out like a croaked whisper.

The kitchen door flew open.

Nick was around the wall again and down the steps after the ghost boy. This was it, surely Crina would see the young apparition too. There'd be proof that his son's soul was drawn to this place, from another person's eyes. He burst into the kitchen breathing hard to find Crina standing rigid as stone before him. Her left arm was behind her, guarding the little dark-haired boy that quivered behind her legs.

"You can see him?" Nick stopped dead, with a squeak of his shoes on the kitchen floor.

"Of course, I can see him, he is my son," Crina replied. She was shaking from head to foot but kept her chin up bravely towards her employer.

"Your son?"

"Yes. It's school holidays now, and I have no money for care or friends to leave him with. Please don't fire me, he is a good boy, a quiet boy and will cause you no trouble I promise."

"He drew on my painting," Nick replied in a deflated way. Had the boy been here before, had he mistaken this living child for his dead son? Surely not at night. This was her son, his son was still dead, still a ghost of a child.

The boy, timid and shaking like his mother, peeked out from behind her legs. He looked no more than five or six and had a round face with dark eyes and full lips as his mother.

"I am so sorry about your painting, but he loves to draw and paint himself," Crina explained, close to tears.

"What's your name, kid?" Nick knelt down and bent his body to get a better look at the boy. "And why did you draw on my painting?"

"He does not speak," his mother replied for him, a hard protective mother's edge to her voice. She feared for her job but would protect her silent child to the last. "He's called Wadim."

"Did you paint you and your mummy?" Nick eyes and voice were still directed at the pale, frightened child. He looked a little like his son, age, height and hair wise, but his features were wildly different.

"He is autistic, he has trouble communicating with me most of the time. The world is a frightening place for him, and he doesn't understand a lot of things. I pay for him to go to special school, a good school. I can't afford to lose this job, please, I'll do anything." Crina's tears came, and she hated herself for begging for her job, but she'd do anything for her little boy.

"Was that you and mummy in the picture, Wadim?" Nick asked the boy again. He took in what Crina was saying, but wanted to focus on the boy.

The boy nodded, smiled, and then wandered off to the kitchen table and sat down and stared off up into the ceiling like he was in a different world than Nick and his mother.

"What are you going to do?"

"Do?" Nick looked at her. "I'm not going to do anything. You can bring him here any day you like, just try and keep him away from my paintings in future." The house was huge, and the boy didn't speak, it wasn't going to bother him much. There was nothing wrong with being quiet, in fact, most people talked far too much crap for Nick's liking anyway.

"Really, you don't mind?" Crina pushed away her tears, and she smiled up at him, changing the whole dynamics of her face. It made her look the woman she should be, not the downtrodden foreign cleaner that others saw.

"No, he might bring a little life to this dead place," Nick smiled back at her.

"And you want...nothing in return?" Crina cast her eyes

down to her chest and wrung her hands together in front of the zip of her jeans she permanently wore.

"Maybe that dance one night, if you can find a babysitter." Nick smiled, raised his eyebrows, and turned and left mother and child to it.

Crina's smile broadened as she watched Nick return into the garden. She went into the pantry and pulled a colouring pad and pens from her backpack and put them on the table for her son. He grabbed her arm and squeezed it as she opened the pad in front of him and put down his colouring pencils. He did not turn to look at her, but she knew that was the best expression of love he normally gave, and it filled her heart with love and joy. He took a red pencil and began to colour in a teddy bear sat next to a bucket on a sandy beach.

Nick didn't have the heart to paint over Wadim's little addition to his painting. So he set it aside and started a new picture. He thought about the orgy picture but didn't want the boy to scribble on that and his mother to see it. He tried his best to capture the drab gardens, the grey windows at the back of the house, and the area of warmth and light around the courtyard and grass around him. After a while, he gave up, turned, and painted the sun cast gazebo instead, and the magnifying glass propped up on the bench reflecting the sun in the blue sky.

By the time he carried his quickly dried painting back into the house, Crina and her son had left for the day.

Forky's House felt emptier than ever to Nick.

He stowed his paintings in the ballroom and decided to take a walk outside in the real world. After the cool of the house and shaded gardens, stepping outside his gate was always a bit of shock to the system. From the loud, steady hum of the ever-present traffic, the smell of car fumes, and the reflective summer heat off the near-melting pavements. Nick decided to cross the busy road next to his gate and not across to the shops, pub and Lionel's flat like he normally did. He'd never really been on that side of the road before, so he pushed his hands into his trouser pockets, pulled out his cigarettes and lit one up. He passed rows of Georgian, three storey townhouses, each with steps leading down to basement flats, or solicitor's offices and the like. He came to another crossing and waited for the green man to show. Across the road was the tube station and next to it a little enclave shop he'd never taken any notice of before.

The shrill hasty beeping of the crossing woke him out of his thoughts, and he hurried across. He stubbed out his just started cigarette on the top of a bin. He went past the entrance to the tube to the tiny shop directly to one side: *J R Morgan Shoe Repairs and Keys Cut*. A man well beyond retirement years was standing behind a high counter, surrounded by shoelaces, heels, insoles, and *Blakeys*. Behind him was a piece of hardboard with many keys hooks and varies keys of all shapes and sizes dangling behind him.

"Help you, sir?" asked the old man behind the counter. Nick could not help look at his big bulbous red nose, forcing himself to answer and not count the thin red lines that covered it.

"Yes, I see you cut normal Yale, Chubb type keys, do you do...well, odd shaped old keys?"

"Well, I can try, sir, what you got there?"

Nick smiled at the man and reached down into his trouser pockets as he kept the keys on him at all times. He thought about just taking out one, but brought out both to show the proprietor. Nick held them up, but slightly out of reach from the old guy, who popped on a pair of thick black glasses from his breast pocket of his shirt and had a look.

"Well, they are different," the man said, moving a hand closer to Nicks. "May I?"

Nick eyed the man's face, but could not focus on anything but his veiny nose, so reluctantly handed them both over. The shopkeeper took them both in separate hands, but felt the magnetic tug between them at once, and let nature take its course. The two keys snapped together like paperclips to a magnet forming a L-shape.

"Well, that's a bit different. They look brass, but must have an iron core. Been left too close to a powerful magnet have they?" The shopkeeper pried them apart with some effort.

"I think so, as you can see two are missing. Is it possible to make copies?"

"I could make a basic copy, even with the magnetic core, but teeth parts would not match the locks they are meant to go in. The ends of these two are similar but very unique. You would end up with something that looked nice, but wouldn't open any lock these and another two put together would match."

"Have you ever seen anything like them before?"

"No, not like this in all me years. But these go back to a time when locksmiths and key markers were artists. Nowadays it's just Yales and Chubbs like you say." The old shopkeeper handed the keys back. "You could try scouring antique shops maybe, or junkyards?"

"I will, thanks for your time." Nick pocketed the keys and waved and left the tiny shop. He still wasn't in the mood to go back to the house, so walked on past the shops and the pub, and along the way to see if there were any local antique shops nearby. He found one not far from the library, but it had no keys to match Nicks. He walked back to the pub and popped in for a pint and a bacon sandwich. After a brief convivial chat with the landlord and lady, he sat down in his usual place. Using his new phone, he scanned key site, eBay, and other places, but after looking at what seemed thousands of old keys, found none to match the Forky's ones.

He gave up and rubbed at his eyes. Being out in the sun all day, and staring at the screen on his phone, had left them feeling tired. He drained his glass and said goodbye to the landlord who was on his own behind the bar now. He walked home past the door to Lionel's flat. He was glad the old bugger would be back in a couple of days. He'd missed his company, and normally Nick never found people that interesting to miss.

Back home he sat down and switched on his TV to watch the news, just as background noise. He thought about making a drink, but the long walk down to the kitchen put him off. He sat back on his sofa and within ten minutes had nodded off.

He woke four hours later, feeling terrible. He couldn't be bothered to drag himself upstairs, so kicked off his shoes and flung himself down on his camper bed and slept the rest of the night away there.

The next day was still warm, but white clouds covered most of the London sky. Tonight, would be another moon, a half one, of which he had no key to match the appearing door and room. He wasn't that bothered, or the least bit excited by it now. It was more of an annoyance to him that he had two rooms that he still could not get inside. Each room would have a lost soul guardian, like Peter Gates and Nicholas Clovis. Each trapped inside a different dimension of the same room, their souls used to power it and keep it on its moon cycle. Yet Nick had messed with it all by dispatching the red-skinned Gates on his first visit inside the four-dimensional room. Would each of the coloured rooms need a sacrifice inside, a soul to power the room or whatever lay behind the brown door? None of which really mattered at the moment as there were still two keys missing.

Nick spent the morning searching the large house for any signs of the missing keys. His search was fruitless once again. The keys could be literally anywhere, down a deep well, or under a rubbish tip, or in the silt on the bottom of the Thames for all he knew. He was putting more books back on a high shelf, when he heard the door go, and the sounds of two sets of feet on the hallway floor. He hopped off the chair he was using as a step ladder and hurried into the corridor to see Crina and Wadim approaching. The boy instantly hung back behind his mother's legs at the sight of Nick.

"Morning, Crina," Nick said to his housekeeper, and then looked down at Wadim and smiled. "Hello, Wadim, how are you today?"

The boy, of course, said nothing in reply but did poke his head and body around his mother, looking less worried.

"He's fine," Crina said, lovingly tussling the black mop of hair on her young son's head. The boy instantly neatened his hair, the moment his mother stopped touching it.

"You are free to explore and draw anywhere you like in the house, young man," Nick said bending down a little to nearer the boy's height. "I have a large library with books full of wonderful pictures if you want to have a look?"

Wadim just shook his head, eyed Nick with suspicion, and pointed to the Star Wars backpack over his shoulders.

"He just wants to stay around me and draw. Is that okay?" Crina stepped forward, moving her left hand towards her employer and then hastily bringing it down to her side again.

"That's fine, just wanted him *and you* to know you're both welcome here anytime you like," Nick straightened up, thumbing back to the library door. "I'd better get on, books won't stack themselves. Saying that, in this place, they probably would."

"Thank you for being okay with him being here."

"Not a problem, Crina, anything for you."

It was the earnest tone to his voice that surprised her, and it was all she could do to hide her embarrassed smile and lead her son away down the corridor. Nick's smile was wide and as broad as his cheek muscles would allow. He had seen the dimpled grin on her face and went about restoring the books to their shelves with increased vigour.

Nick ate his lunch with Crina and her son in the kitchen just so the boy could get used to his presence. He waved them off when Crina had finished her hours for the day and then was left alone in the house, with all its dark memories. Nick, remembering the Star Wars rucksack on Wadim's back, ordered all the DVDs he could find and a few of the toys. If he could get through to the boy and make him feel at home here, maybe Crina would feel more at home in his arms.

The afternoon seemed to drag on forever without them. Knowing that the door could appear at any time, he set up his laptop and the single picture fixed on the empty wall far below. He rang Margo to see if she had dug up any news, but she hadn't. He sent a picture of the keys to her just so she could be on the lookout for them also. She was always off to charity events, and Scouts bring-and-buy sales, so she said she would keep her eyes peeled for them.

Nick played music and then tried to watch television. Neither kept him amused for more than twenty minutes. He filled another shelf in the library to complete a further bookcase but didn't feel like starting another. So he smoked four cigarettes in a row, just wandering the house from room to room, trying to figure out any key hiding places he might have missed.

Smoking another cigarette in disappointment, he headed out into the garden to sit in the gazebo to catch whatever rays of sunshine the clouds deemed to let through. He leant back and crossed his arms, sucking at his teeth in thought. He thought his brain might explode if he thought any harder about where the missing keys could be. He couldn't come up with any new avenues of enquiry that hadn't been done or suggested before. Tomorrow, or the next day, he would find the locations of all the local scrap yards and antique shops and then scour them for keys. It was something to keep him busy, but he didn't hold out much hope for his search.

He gave up on the garden at six and went back inside to fetch a packet of gingernut biscuits, before heading back to the sitting room. The laptop picture still showed the door-less wall on screen, much to his annoyance.

"Bored, bored, bored," he said to the windows and walls.

He never used to be like this, caught in one place for so long, well not since his son died. Thoughts came to mind of his son's *bitch* of a mother, and that was never good for his peace of mind. So he got up, munching his fifth ginger nut, and vacated the room. He didn't dally in the hallway either and made a sharp left turn. He wandered at pace down the passage until he got to the library. He rested his left hand on the door handle, but tapped it thrice and moved on. He'd had enough of stacking books on shelves for one day. His wanderings took him round to the billiards room, and he went inside and turned on the lights. The place was a mess. A rigid cover was half drawn off the dusty green baize table in front of him. He whipped it off in one swift action, sending clouds of grey dust into the air under the many low lights above the table. A search of the pockets brought only five balls, two whites, one with a dot, a black, a red and a pink ball. Further searches around the stacked chairs and overturned tables brought up two usable cues of differing lengths and a blue ball. Using the plain cue ball, he set the rest up into a small triangle at the far end of the table. His first high-powered shot zipped past the triangle of balls into the cushion at the back of the table and back up again where it hit the other edge just under his arm and finally stopped in the centre of the table.

"That was pathetic," he whispered under his breath, as he moved around the side of the table to take his next shot. This time, his powerful shot cannoned into the triangle of coloured balls, sending them scattering every which way, but not into the hole. It wasn't until he slowed his shots down that he actually potted anything. Nick passed an hour doing this and found the clack of the balls hitting each other at high speeds was soothing to his ears. When he'd put the cue down on the table and exited the billiards room, night was, at last, starting to fall. He wandered onto the balcony outside, as it was near, and gazed up at the darkened, blue sky. A blue-tinged full moon was already out in the cloudless sky. He hurried inside and gathered up his torches.

Through the music room, and down and down he went, coming face-to-face with the last door of the cycle he was on. Neither key unlocked the door, so he pounded on it with his fist and shouted. "Is anyone in there?"

If anyone was, they did not reply, or couldn't hear him. He pressed his left ear to the door but could hear nothing from the other side. Knowing that if he stayed there any longer, frustration would give over to boiling, unhelpful anger, he went upstairs and straight to his bed.

Nick woke confused from his ever-present nocturnal nightmare. He had been in the blistering sand bowl again, but only the blue and white riders had been present. Then out of the corner of his right eye, he caught sight of two figures holding hands. When he turned, they would vanish in the heat haze. Only from the corner of his right eye could he glimpse them. Two figures in the near distance, a woman holding hands with a dark-haired boy.

Then he woke. Not sure if the boy had been his dead son or Wadim, or if the woman was Crina? His mobile vibrated on the bedside table. He picked it up and saw it was a text from Lionel saying: *Got an earlier flight home, be back at my place by 9, be there, and put the kettle on, there's a sweetie xxx.*

It was twenty-five to nine now, so Nick quickly showered and dressed. He was out of the house by five to nine and at Lionel's door, just as his black cab from Heathrow pulled up. The weather had turned for the worst again, and it was raining slightly, the clouds above full and kettle grey. Nick opened the door and helped his friend pull his luggage out as the smiling, tanned actor paid the cabbie. They had a quick embrace. Nick's nostrils flared up in revulsion at whatever aftershave Lionel had bathed himself in this morning. They each took a case, and bag upstairs and dumped them on the bed in his mother's old room. Nick gladly put the kettle on, as Lionel relaxed back into his comfy leather chair and let out a raucous fart.

When Nick came back into the small, busy living room with the tea and biscuits, Lionel began to recall his foreign acting experiences. Two hours later, plus two more teas, a shot of brandy and a whole packet of Chocolate Hobnobs, Nick was finally able to get a word in edgeways.

"So, did you know Crina had a little boy?"

"Oh, yes, cute little deaf and dumb kid as I recall," Lionel replied in his usual un-PC manner.

"He's autistic, Lionel." Even Nick raised his eyebrows at his thespian friend. "So, you didn't consider mentioning it to me?"

"Why? Does it matter?" Lionel put his hand on his knees and leant forwards. "You are not still trying to get inside her pussy-willow are you?"

"Yes...no, I dunno. But you should have mentioned it," Nick replied, both confused and irritated off at the same time.

"So, *you are* still trying to drink from her Venus trap then. It won't ever happen, dear boy." Lionel leant back and settled into his chair again.

"Why not? I'm quite a handsome, rich, charismatic type of a guy."

"Well, of course, you are, and I'd turn you into a pillow-biter any day of the week, but I don't think she'll let you inside those tight jeans of hers."

"Why not?"

"Just an old man's observations," Lionel replied with a twirl of his fingers.

Nick leant forwards on his chair, he could see from the twitches on his friend's face and the sudden avoidance of eye contact that he was hiding something. "You know something."

"One does not let slip idle gossip," Lionel replied with only a brief glance at his friend.

"Tell me please."

"Well, last Christmas I invited her and the boy around on Christmas Eve for eggnog and mince pies to say thank you for her sterling work during the year. She imbibed a few sherries, and I asked about the boy's father. Well, she went quiet for a few seconds and then told me the boy was born from hate and violence rather than from love. I stupidly pressed her on what she meant, not initially twigging her meaning. She told me she was kidnapped by some criminals that her father owed money too and they, each gang member, over twenty of them, raped her over a twenty-four-hour period before she was dumped naked at her father's door."

"Oh no," Nick said, putting his face in his hands.

"Yet that was not the worst of it. When he found out she was pregnant, her father threw her out for bringing shame on the family. She took all the savings she had and took a risk to leave home and come to England to have her child." Lionel wiped a tear from the lines in the corner of his left eye.

"Bastards."

"Yes, indeed. I've suffered the odd dodgy night out, and a few gay-bashings but nothing compared to what she had to endure, poor girl."

"Some wounds never heal," Nick almost whispered to himself.

"You're right, so go easy with her, but don't...don't treat her any differently because of this," Lionel implored him.

"I won't. I'll just have to be the perfect gentleman. For a change."

"Now that's an acting part I would pay to see," Lionel said with an amused rise of his dark eyebrows.

"I'd better let you settle in mate."

"Yes, I do feel a little weary from my recent travels."

Nick stuck his left palm out in a stopping motion. "No need

to get up, old man, I can let myself out."

"Good plan. But less of the *old* please, I'm in the prime of my life," the old actor called after him as Nick went onto the small landing. Smiling at his friend's words, he trotted down the stairs to the front door.

The next week slowly returned to the glorious warm summer again. Nick would eat his lunch with Wadim each day and compliment him on his drawings or doodles. The boy said nothing in reply, and mostly didn't even acknowledge that Nick was in the same room as him. Crina seemed to appreciate the effort, though. He twice caught her grinning to herself as she turned back to clean, cook or wash up for him.

On the third day, Nick looked up from his latest, and most difficult painting, and stretched his back out. As he did, he caught sight of a black mop of hair disappearing behind the tall rows of lavender not far to his left. Nick took down the picture he was working on and put it in the gazebo. He put a blank canvas on his easel and headed off to the house.

Nick used an upstairs working loo and took his time. He washed his paint dotted hands and then splashed water over his hot face and neck. He patted some of the water off his face with a towel but left the cooling drips on the back of his neck. He checked his emails and then slowly trotted down the servant's staircase and headed out into the garden again, via the open balcony.

He took the same path as he had to go into the house. Whistling an Elton John song, and making as much noise as he could, he approached the sunny end of the garden. The gazebo stood empty, and there was no one near the blank canvas. Nick forced himself not to try and peer through the wildflowers as he rounded his easel again.

A broad grin widened over his handsome face, and he looked down at the child's painting of a boy and his mother in stick form, holding hands. This was in the far right bottom corner of the blank canvas, daubed with heavy black strokes. Yet there was another figure on the canvas, on the far left, squeezed far too close to the edge. This was a taller figure, with a smiling face, dots for eyes, but done with bright red paint.

Nick's smile faltered a little. Did the red paint have any significance? Was it just a simple painting of a child with a reclusive mind, or did this have more sinister overtones? Was it just a random man, done in a random colour, or was it, Peter Gates?

CHAPTER TWENTY-THREE

He didn't go back until all the tests and scans were done. Their options were stark. Nature might run its usual course, and the pregnancy would abort itself, or she could take a pill to stop the egg growing, which could rupture the fallopian tube and kill the mother. No options were given for the child to be born, that, it seemed, was impossible. He convinced the mother of his unborn child to go home as he had one more expert to talk to. He'd just dropped her off at her place, and it took him thirty minutes to extricate himself from her sobbing embrace.

He nearly had two accidents coming home, as he pushed the accelerator pedal a bit too hard. He finally made it, through his electric gates, and parked up. He wasn't usually one for emotions, but he wasn't sure if his head would explode with tears or a wrathful anger. He went inside, every step felt like gravity increased tenfold. Only when he got through his front door, and his two happy, but hungry, dogs ran up to him, did his footfalls lighten. He knelt down and hugged them close, as they covered his cheeks with saliva. He made a fuss of them, fed them well, and changed their water bowls, before even thinking of entering his bedroom.

He was calmer now. More like his old self, yet that was what the voice wanted, the old him.

He pushed back his pets as he entered the bedroom. Then closed and locked the door behind him. The walkie-talkie lay on the bed next to the empty cigar box. Things had gone far enough, his mind was playing tricks on him. Ghosts of guilt belonging to the people he killed had finally shattered the wall that kept his haunted past at bay. Now he was paying for it and for all their dead souls. He picked up the walkie-talkie and went to his french windows, unlocked them and slid them open. He moved past the segmented long white drapes, and outside into the furnace of the afternoon. He strode to the balcony so he could launch the bloody thing over the side and down into the waves below.

"I really wouldn't do that if I were you," the walkie-talkie squawked into life.

"I just want rid of you and your deadly whispering," the assassin said to the hissing black oblong in his hand.

"Because then you will be responsible for another death. Your unborn son's death and I thought that wasn't you anymore."

"My child will die anyway." Tears of anger ran down the Scotsman's cheeks as he gripped the balcony to steady himself.

"Not if I can help it," the echoing voice replied in between the static noise.

"The doctors said either the bairn will die, or her." More of his Scottish voice coming to the fore now, the more emotional he got.

"I can save your child. I can save your firstborn."

"How?"

"Does that matter? If I save your child, will you take another life for me? One soul for another?"

The Scotsman stood, gripping the hot balcony rail until his tanned knuckles whitened. He drew back his arm to throw.

His arms moved forwards, past his head, but then he turned his body at the last second and did not release his grip. He slumped to the hard floor of his balcony and cradled the walkie-talkie in his lap.

"A life for a life," the low voice whispered from the black, hard plastic and rubber that covered the speaker. "An eye for an eye...an old life for a newborn?"

"Yes, I'll do it, but fucking save my son first, will you!"

"Wheels are already in motion, my son," the voice seemed distant, and the crackles of static rose sharply in volume.

"Who do I have to kill?"

But the voice didn't answer. The green light on top of the

walkie-talkie went dull, and the static fades on the slight warm coastal breeze.

Her tears had been overwhelming her since Steve left to feed his dogs. She'd had a bath and was curled up on her round, white leather sofa, with only a white matching dressing gown on. She'd only started dating Steve for his money. Then the sex was always rough and urgent, and better than the boys she'd fucked before. Somehow between dancing, laughing, and diamond necklaces, she had fallen in love with him. It had always been casual to suit each other, but now she was carrying his child. She wanted to be with him forever. But as her cool hand slipped under the folds of her dressing gown to touch her bare flat belly, she felt fear.

The modelling that had taken her out of her shitty hometown, to fly the world, to live on a diet of coke and champagne and toast, gave way to something else deep in her core. She realised she wanted to be a mother, wanted even a dull, drab life that she escaped from so long, but even that was going to be denied her.

Her baby was going to die no matter what. That was real life, and that's what she craved.

The doorbell of her flat chimed, and she got up, pulled the towelling belt of her gown tighter around her pregnant middle. *But for how long*, she thought. She kicked on her fluffy white slippers. She padded to the hall up to the door and opened it inwards, her mind on many other things.

She was shocked back to reality when she saw three nuns were standing on the landing outside her flat. One was tall and bulky, with a tanned, almost Samoan face. The middle nun had a pale, but pretty face, bordering on the angelic. The nun next her was dark of skin, with high round cheeks that made her eyes look like piggy brown dots in her face.

"Can I help you?"

"Are you, Alina Vascu?" the centre nun asked in a crisp Northern Irish accent.

"Yes," Alina said, more than a little confused. "Did the clinic send you?" She thought they might be some sort of religious counselling scheme run by a charitable wing of the clinic.

"No, our Lord and saviour sent us to help you get through this most difficult of times."

"I'm not really a believer, or in the mood right now," Alina said, and started to close her front door. She didn't mean to be rude, but she wasn't one for religion, nor had the energy to be pleasant, not today of all days.

Before she could shut the door, the silent Samoan nun shoulder barged the door, knocking Alina to the floor in shock.

"What are you doing? Get the fuck out of my house now, before I call the police!" Alina scrambled backwards as the large, black nun followed after the bulky Samoan one. Alina turned in fright and managed to get to her feet to flee when she was caught. The two large nuns grabbed and held her arms in their iron-like grips. They pushed her towards the nearest free wall space. The back of her head whacked against the picture hung there.

"Let me go, you fucking whores," she cried out, as she struggled hard, but she could not get free. The two nuns then kneed her on the outside thigh of each leg, sending numbing pains down them to her toes. The nuns then kicked her legs apart and stepped on her slippers with their heavy shoes to stop her moving.

The smaller, pretty nun came into view. Standing before Alina, with her arms folded and hands in the sleeves of her black habit.

"What do you want?" Alina was pinned to the wall now, and her tears began to roll again down her tired cheeks. "I have money, I'll fetch it for you."

"Hush now, we want no money or rewards on Earth. We are here to do our Lord and saviours bidding," the softly spoken nun said, taking a step closer to the shaking young woman.

"Please let me go," Alina begged.

"When we have finished his bidding." The pretty nun took her hands from out of her folds, but there was something wrong. The right hand was there, but the left hand was missing at the wrist. It ended with tapering, puckered skin over a nub of white bone. The nun moved closer and undid Alina's belt, and pulled her white dressing gown apart, showing her naked legs and hairless groin beneath.

"What are you doing, I'm pregnant, leave me alone," Alina sobbed as the nun moved close enough to put her cold right hand on her bare hip. It felt like an electric shock of fear throughout her shaking frame.

"I know, and we are going to fix that for you," the pretty nun said. Then lowered her maimed arm and pushed it between Alina's labia lips, seeking the entrance to her vagina.

"No, you can't," Alina barely got out a whisper.

"Deep breath now, child," the nun whispered and punched her left arm deep up inside the former model. Alina's scream was winded out of her, as pain like she never felt before erupted between her legs and she fainted dead away.

CHAPTER TWENTY-FOUR

Nick repeated the same experiment the very next day. He was halfway through his picture taking his time. He put this away, propped it up the wrong way around in the gazebo, and went inside for a cold can. He chatted briefly with Crina about cleaning products that she needed money for. Nick drank half of his Coke before, popping to the loo.

The respite from the burning sunshine was welcome.

When he returned outside he suddenly had to take an interest in a pear tree to his left on the way back, to give the mystery, small painter time to make his exit. Trying badly not to smile, he kept his gaze forwards at the gazebo, as a small dark shape hurried to a hiding place.

When he returned to the new canvas he'd placed on his easel, he saw that the black mother and child had been repeated on the bottom right. To the left stood the taller, red, smiling man, but he had been painted three inches closer to the black figures. Nick had no idea what the crude child's picture was representing. He set it aside gently and fetched the slower piece he was working on.

Nick white-washed the two canvases, as he only had one blank one left. Instead of moving his picture the next day, he set up his spare easel a little way to the left. He put his picture in the gazebo at lunchtime, leaving the dry whitewashed one out and ready to be used. He ate lunch and then trotted upstairs for one of his long breaks. He was hot and sweaty. So he sprayed himself with *Lynx* and put on a fresh t-shirt. This he hoped had given his garden graffiti artist time to sneak in and do his best *Banksy* effort, and sneak off again.

Nick wasn't disappointed. The whitewashed canvas had the usual black mother and child holding hands, yet the red, smiling figure was now holding hands with the boy. A rustle behind the lavender indicated that the artist was still in residence.

"Do you want to come and paint with me, Wadim?" Nick called out to the rows of fragrantly flowering bushes. This brought a rush of movement as the young boy ran off as fast as his crouching gait would allow. Nick smiled to himself and wondered if the red man was now friends with the boy and his mother and whether that was a good thing or not.

The plan was slowly working, so Nick made a subtle change to it the next day. He had his lunch outside with a cold beer. He had a bottle of water too in the shade of the gazebo, so he didn't need to make any trips inside. If he needed to pee, behind the sheds would do. He was sure Micheldever was getting used to it by now.

He set up the spare easel, and second whitewashed canvas a little closer to his own, and painted until movement to his left, and the rustle of the lavender told him his young painting comrade was close. All he had to do was wait and hope. Nick kept his eye on his nearly finished painting as best he could. He would look down to avoid the creeping, speechless boy, moving closer to his right.

Nick found it increasingly difficult not to crane his neck to look directly. His smile got wider as the boy rounded a low wall and stood watching him, and the vacant, tempting blank canvas. He smiled as the young boy, with his dark mop of unruly hair, much like his late sons, edged closer. He wanted to giggle but bit his lip as the silent boy made it to the far edge of the easel. Nick really had to then bit his bottom lip to suppress a laugh of victory, as Wadim picked up a long brush. Out of the corner of his left eye, he saw the boy had squeezed out some black paint directly onto his brush and began to paint the three figures again. Each adult was holding a hand with the boy, but all the figures were painted in black this time. Smiling away to himself, so the dimples in his left cheek showed, Nick licked his lips, and mixed up some new colours on his palette.

Wadim did a quick double take of Nick, picked up his own palette, and began to squeeze different coloured paints onto it, like the adult next to him. Every time Nick glanced to his left, the boy was mimicking his every move. Nick stepped back two paces to test this. He put the end of his long brush to his top lip and held his palette across his middle.

The young boy followed suit. Nick moved forwards again and made a slight adjustment to part of his painting. Wadim, who was caught out a little by the sudden movement, did the same.

"So what do you think, Wadim, is my painting any good?" Nick tried to keep his voice as casual as he could. He didn't want to startle the boy. He took a deep breath and turned to look at the young boy.

Wadim was looking from his painting to Nicks. He pointed at Nick's painting and gave a thumbs up. Then pointed to his own masterpiece, and lifted the palette and his brush, giving a double thumbs up and the ghost of a smile.

"Ah, so you think yours is the best, eh?" Nick turned a little to face the silent child.

Wadim nodded, looking at Nick's painting not at him, but the child was smiling broadly. "Everyone's a critic," Nick muttered.

Their brief, one-sided conversation ceased then, and they went back to their paintings. Nick working on the bottom edge of his painting, which was nearing completion. While Wadim added a line of grass behind the people, and then a slightly green-tinged, orange sun as high up on the canvas as he could reach, which was just above the middle.

Crina had searched the house from top to bottom but could not find her son. With her full lips pressed together in worry, she headed out into the garden to ask her employer if he had seen him. Her arms were crossed across her chest as she walked through the shady part of the garden. She went up the path, and round the pear trees, and stopped dead in her tracks in its mixture of curled leaves.

Her autistic son was standing next to her strange employer.

They were pointing at each other's easels and laughing. Wadim liked slapstick humour and was very fond of Laurel and Hardy, or TV programmes where people fell over a lot. He didn't get jokes, or sarcasm if you told him to pull his socks up that's what he would physically do. He never spoke and had no interest in making friends of any age. His hugs and kisses were rare treats to be cherished until the next time. Now, here he was laughing at Nick's painting, while he was taking the mickey out of the boy's painting. Both were laughing, both were interacting, both were making eye contact.

Crina was in two minds whether to retreat back to the house and not break the spell of this landmark moment for her son.

Nick looked up from his joke with the boy and saw her standing behind the pears trees. He waved her forwards urgently.

Crina tentatively made her way round, into the sunshine. The warm sun caressed the lines on her cheeks and the huge smile on her face. She walked around the easels, her arms still protectively across her chest, but with her heart soaring with joy. She walked past Nick and stood in between him and her son, who turned and beamed up at her. Even though she was smiling, she let out a sob of joy and felt a tear of happiness roll down her cheek. She swallowed hard, forcing down the emotional lump in her throat, and ruffled her son's hair. He pointed at his and Nick's paintings and she finally took notice of them.

Her son's painting was what he usually did, stick men and women, but this time he had added something new. It may just have been a line of green grass or the sun up in the sky, but they were new and exciting admissions to her mind. It was like he was becoming slightly more aware of his surroundings. The figures were interested too, it was him and her as usual, but the third, large adult figure was added.

"Who is that, *iubita mea?*" she asked, calling him *my beloved* in her native tongue.

Wadim just nonchalantly thumbed his right hand towards where Nick was standing. She looked up from bending over her child to the grinning Englishman. Then she took in his picture, it was of her, standing in an arbour of white and yellow flowers. The tiny flowers and green vines trailed down into her full, brown hair, as she stared out of the picture, looking more beautiful than she could possibly imagine in real life.

"Time for us to go now, Wadim," she said but giving a lasting look and smile to her employer. Then she bent down to kiss her son's round cheek to get him moving. The boy put down his paints and took her hand in his. His eyes were off to the left of his painting, and the joy had faded from his face a little. Then she stretched herself and kissed the surprised Nick on his cheek.

"Thank you," she said in a low husky voice.

"What for?"

"For painting time of course," she winked, and then led her son out of the garden, with no less than three glances back over her shoulder to Nick.

Nick stood rooted to the spot until they were out of sight. Then took both pictures inside the house and set them up on chairs in the ballroom. He went onto the internet and ordered twenty more canvases for next day delivery. At least one part of his life was making some progress. The search for the missing keys was going nowhere fast.

CHAPTER TWENTY-FIVE

One of the nurses at the clinic called it a minor miracle. The doctors, though, huffed and puffed their way through, just giving out medical terminology like it was confetti at a wedding.

The Scotsman had rushed over to find his girlfriend's door wide open. He ran inside to find her slumped unconscious against the living room wall. Her white dressing gown was parted, as were her legs, and there was a round pool of blood leaking from her vagina. He hurriedly wrapped her in a blanket and drove her to the clinic. Everyone thought she had miscarried, but scans and tests had brought a more shocking result. The baby was still viable, growing inside Alina's womb.

Alina did not wake up for another hour. When she did, she screamed the white, clean, private room, down. She raged about three nuns, one with no hand who had interfered with her. The doctors had to sedate her to calm her down.

The Scotsman stayed beside her bed. When she woke again, still agitated, he grabbed her and shook her, and told her the baby was alive, in her womb where it should be, and wasn't going to die. This seemed to calm her, though she had many nightmares the next long night.

By the time she came home, three days later, all memory of the nun intruders seemed to have faded from her mind. All she could do was make plans for the future together, and their unborn baby. They would move in together, but neither of their places seemed like child-friendly environments. Steve promised to start looking for a larger family home for them all, and the dogs. He had brought Mr Smith and Mr Wesson over after they got back from the clinic to guard her.

He had not felt so loved, and part of something greater, for so many years. He stayed with her as long as he dared, but he had to go home and face the music. Neither she nor the dogs wanted him to go. All three whined, in their own way, but he brushed it off with a fake smile, saying he needed to fetch a change of clothes.

His apartment seemed oddly unlike his home as he stepped inside. He would be glad to move to somewhere new, somewhere with a bit of soft colour, and have loved ones to come home to. This place was sterile, and bare, like his old life, and he yearned for something else, something he thought he'd never have, love and family. Just as he had cast off other old lives before this, he still had loose ends to clear up first. He had to burn the bridges behind him, and erect a Hadrian's Wall around the past, so he could move on.

He crossed the living room and pushed open the bedroom door. The cigar box and walkie-talkie were sitting innocently on the bed, waiting for his return. He strode forward and grabbed the walkie-talkie while his reserves of nerve held and held it to his ear.

"So, tell me, who do you want me to kill?"

CHAPTER TWENTY-SIX

The end of the month was nearly upon him. Tonight, there would be a half-moon again, the red moon.

The last few days, Nick had hardly thought about the quest for the missing keys at all. The thought of the mystery room reappearing again brought little excitement. At least he had the red key and would be able to get inside. He wondered if Peter Gates's dead soul would be inside.

He was sitting in the garden, waiting for Crina and Wadim to show up. He had got a little bored with painting now but had found something else to occupy him while he waited. He had found a nest of ants on the side of the gazebo, half buried under the wooden floor. The tell-tale signs of a small mound of fine grains of earth were pushed up against the side of the wooden structure. Red ants busied themselves running in and out of holes, and onto the hot paving stones in front of the gazebo.

Nick lay on his side, head on elbow watching these tiny insects scurry about their business. One scurried up the back of his arm, paused at the wrist, and had a little nip at him.

"You little shit."

When Wadim came tearing down the path, running with an awkward giraffe-like gait, Nick was sitting crossed-legged on the stone slabs at the side of the gazebo. The excited young boy ran around to see what his new friend was doing.

"Hello mate," Nick smiled up at him, and the boy smiled back.

Wadim looked down to see the ants nest. Lots of the tiny red insects were racing all around the fine mound of piled earth. Some were on the grass and dirt, while others were scurrying about on the flat stone. Wadim bent down on his knees, his behind nearly touching the paving stones, without overbalancing, as only children can. On the flat paving stones near Nick, were what the boy at first thought were bits of dirt. On closer inspection they were burnt and shrivelled up red ants.

Nick saw the young boy's brows knit in confusion.

"Here watch." Nick raised the magnifying glass from his lap about shoulder height, between him and the boy. The shadow of the magnifying glass appeared on the grey stone, the glass hardly visible. In the eye of the circle, was a round white dot about the size of a ten pence piece. Nick moved the magnifying glass down towards the stone, and the white dot shrunk to a more focused beam, just larger than a match head. A red ant came exploring by, and Nick shifted the angle of his arm and then refocused the intense ray of light over the insect's body. It only took two seconds for the red ant to turn up into itself, blacken and cease moving.

Wadim looked up from the fried ant to Nick with a wide open mouth and eyes full of boyish awe.

"Did you like that?" Nick asked the boy. "Would you like to see me do more?"

Wadim nodded his head like it might fall off, and Nick scanned the hot paving stones for another victim.

"More," the boy said.

"Okay, let me find my..." Nick looked up, the boy who didn't speak had spoken. "What did you just say, Wadim?"

"More," the boy uttered, and then reached excitedly for the magnifying glass with both hands, wanting desperately to try. Nick handed it over, and sat up a little, watching the boy. Wadim went to town on the ant colony like a vengeful deity, burning any ant that dared step one of its six legs onto the paving slabs.

"Can you say any other words, Wadim?"

The boy didn't answer. He sat crossed legged, with his tongue sticking out the side of his mouth, incinerating ant after ant-like it was a video game.

"Aren't you bored yet?" Nick was amazed at the concentration on the boy's face as he sort out new ant victims.

"Bored of what?" a female voice asked coming up them and to the left.

Nick looked around to see Crina appear over them, blocking the deadly rays of the sun, so even her child looked round in annoyance. Then she saw, and her motherly delight to see them getting on so well, turned to livid anger.

"What are you doing Wadim?" she asked, snatching the magnifying glass from her boy's hand. "Killing innocent ants, is that what you are teaching my son?"

"Look, I'm sorry, we got carried away," Nick answered, standing up. "But he was enjoying it, he even spoke to me."

"My son cannot speak." Crina seethed with anger. She grabbed her son and pulled him roughly to his feet. "Go inside, Wadim and stay out of trouble until I come find you."

Wadim struggled out of his mother's grip as he burst into a hysterical bout of crying. The magnifying glass fell from his grasp and hit the paving slabs below, shattering the glass inside. Wadim ran off as fast as his awkward running style would let him. His wails and crying slowly diminished as he got further away.

"Look I'm sorry about the ants, Crina, but forget about that, Wadim spoke to me," Nick said, grabbing her upper arms to try to get her to see the good part of this.

Crina eyes widened in fear, and she shoved Nick against his chest with her palms. The shock and speed of her attack sent him tumbling backwards to fall against the wooden side of the gazebo with a bump. He felt pain in his right palm, his lower back, and his head, but the only thing he was worried about was if he'd sat on any dead ants.

Nick struggled back up, looking at Crina. The anger on her face turning to fear of retribution, for attacking her employer.

Crina saw the blood on her employer's hand and raised her palms over her face and then up through her untied hair. "I'm so sorry, I did not mean to do that."

"It's okay...it's my fault for grabbing you and teaching your son bad habits." Nick pulled a handkerchief from his trouser pocket and wrapped it around his cut hand. He must have landed on some of the broken magnifying glass. "Only a minor wound. But your son did speak to me, well he said the word, *more*, anyway."

Crina did not speak. Tears rolled silently down her high, round cheeks.

"Look, let's put all this behind us, and focus on the only good part of this whole episode, your son spoke to me."

"Why?"

"Why what?" Nick stepped a foot closer to her, brushing down his dirty trousers with his hands. She retreated two steps to his one. "I would never hurt you, Crina."

"Why did he speak to you, a stranger man, and not *to me*?" There was real venom in the last two words of her sentence.

"I don't know, we were just boys being boys." Nick stood his ground and did not attempt again to close the gap between them. "Maybe he sees me as a father figure?"

"You would not make a good father." Crina was still simmering with anger and had got back some of her fight. She thought her job at Forky's House was gone, so she had no reason to hold back now.

"No, you are probably right there. I was the worst father a boy could have. I let my boy down in the worst possible way."

"You have a son?"

"Had a son. He was murdered, and I failed to stop it from happening. I lived, and he was stabbed to death right in front of my eyes. No, you are right I'm not good father material, nor am I much of a son myself. My father threw me out of his house years ago. But that was okay, I was young then, full of myself. I thought I could build a better home than him and have a son that would never stop loving me. But what is a house without a family, just another recluse for a hermit? I don't love, and I don't want love in return…because that just brings you pain. Pain I can understand, but a great empty hole of nothing inside you, where your son's love should be…I can't ever get over that." Nick raged, cried as his fist beat at his chest, tears running down his face, and dripping from his chin to the paving stones below.

Crina moved forwards, reaching out her fingers to place her palms on his wet cheeks. She spoke not a word but instead pressed her soft lips against his. After a second of shock, he reciprocated, their lips open, tongues tasting of salty tears, exploring each other's mouths.

Nick guided her in their passionate embrace up into the gazebo. He sat down and Crina straddled him as they kissed. She pulled her T-shirt over her head. He saw she was not wearing a bra. Her breasts were small, but the nipples were hard and dark, and Nick pulled her warm body closer and sucked one deep into his mouth. They quickly shed their clothes, and Crina eased down on his large erection, glad she was so wet to accommodate him inside her.

On the paving stones, two burned red ants twitched and moved inside the tearful salty globes that encapsulated them. They struggled like newborns out of their water eggs, alive again and back from the dead.

Wadim stood on the dressing table in the bedroom on the first floor. He could just about see the gazebo from his position. He used the bottom of his fist to clean the dirty glass. He could see his mother and Nick naked, and together in an embrace that mystified him. One minute they were angry and shouting, and the next kissing and more. He could not fathom the swift change in them, or what their naked embraces were for. But on one level he liked it, he liked that Nick and his mother were hugging so close.

"More," he whispered to the cobwebs and the cracks in the window pane. "More, more, MORE!"

Then a more important idea wormed its way into his mind. He got down and pulled open the dresser drawer to find an old lined pad and a pencil. He took them out and closed the drawer. Opening the pad on the dresser, he began to scribble and draw like a boy possessed. It was a drawing far beyond his years and limited art skills, but he did it anyway. He was hot and sweaty by the time he finished, and his *Scooby-Doo* t-shirt was sticking to the curve of his back. He had to wipe the sweat from his eyes before he could look at what he had done. He dropped the pencil from his grip, as the fleshy part between his thumb and forefinger were aching.

The pencil drawn picture showed the curved arches of the insides of a church. An altar and cross stood behind two figures that dominated the centre of the page. It was so precise and life-like that it seemed a grey and white snapshot of life caught on a camera rather than a drawing. On the steps before the altar was a boy about Wadim's age, with curly black hair like his. The boy was afraid, his arms raised in fear. A man in a dark cloak, with a hood, stood over the child. Only the long crooked nose of the monk-like figure could be seen under his cowl. His left hand was holding the boy down at the shoulder, while the right was plunging a dagger half a blade deep into the boy's heart.

In the bedroom, from the shadows between two large deep mahogany wardrobes, a small darker shape watched him.

Night had fallen at last. It did not take away the heat of the day, in fact, it felt more humid than ever before.

Crina lay naked under a single white sheet on the sofa-bed in the living room of the cramped flat she shared with her son. He had the only bedroom, and she had to make do with the sofa-bed every night. It was third-hand, and the metal springs stuck into her ribs if she went to sleep in the wrong position. It was after one in the morning, an hour and a half after she went to bed, after a long soak in the flat's small tub.

She couldn't sleep. All she did was replay the events of the day on a continuous loop in her mind. Most of the memories were confusing, some erotic feeling she'd never thought she'd feel again, after her rape. Her fingers had wandered down between her sweat covered legs. She was still sticky wet there, and she pleasured herself to the second orgasm of the day, also only the second one of her life. She had tried before, of course, but that had only brought vile images, like an iron spike through her forehead of her most darkest of days. She would recall every face of every man who had raped her, except the one with the balaclava that had sodomized her.

Yet tonight these images stayed back in her past, only images of Nick's face and body came to mind, and the sweet pleasures they had shared in the gazebo. She could almost recall the sun on her bare skin as they made love. It was something she could do again, over and over, as she had been in control.

Then her mind, aching for sleep, switched to Wadim. She felt guilty for shouting at him, he wasn't to know burning ants was a bad thing. Nick should have known, but he was as damaged as her in some ways. He'd tried being a grown-up father once, and she didn't blame him for escaping back to more childish ways, after seeing his son murdered.

Then there was Wadim's word: *more*. His first and only word. She had taken him out for McDonalds for tea after leaving Nick's house. He had waved his empty fries box and said, "More."

In fact, she kissed his forehead and bought him another entire meal so he could get another different Disney toy. It had been a day of many firsts, but, she hoped, not lasts.

Nick spun the red key round and round on his left forefinger as he trotted down the secret staircase, whistling a happy tune. He couldn't recall a better day for many a year. He'd made friends with a boy cut off from the world and had witnessed him speak his first ever word. Then in the gazebo with Crina was sublime. Maybe things were starting to go his way at last.

Now he had the red room to contend with again.

Nick wondered how long it would be before he got bored with the house. How long before the tediousness of searching for keys he may never find in a thousand years hit him. Nick was like most people, he could be patient and play the long game on things that interested him or have the attention span of a three-year-old on a shopping trip on things that didn't. How long before he just did his usual thing, his father hated him for and just give up?

Yet at the moment, even though the missing two keys frustrated him, the house had its interests. Those interests were moving from the dead to the living. From Lionel's endless stories to Crina's shy lovemaking, to her son, whose outer shell he had just cracked.

Nick clapped his hands together and pulled the key off his finger and rounded the bend in the last passageway. The door was there in his torchlight, and he suddenly wondered why he hadn't set up some temporary lights down here. Then the thought of laying cables, or with three hundred yards of extension cables, popped that idea from his brain. He reached forwards and unlocked the door and opened it inwards.

The red glow from the still lit candles showed that Peter Gates's twice-dead corpse lay in a pool of fresh blood on the red carpet. It was hard to tell where bloody clothes gave over to the blood pool, and then the carpet. Nick moved inside the red room and then took out the red key from its lock. Then he moved back outside and put the sledgehammer head on the other side of the open doorway, against the frame, to stop the door closing behind him. Nick walked up to the corpse and gave it a hefty kick with the end of his left trainer. The corpse moved no more than he expected it to. Using his flashlight to avoid blood puddles, Nick knelt down beside the cadaver. He wrinkled his nose before he began to rifle through Gates's pockets, on the off-chance he might hold one of the other keys.

He didn't, but it had to be checked to make sure.

Nick stood, making clicking sounds with his tongue as he looked around the room. He searched the place from top to bottom but found nothing of use or interest. He examined the brown door closely without touching it.

"What are you hiding?" he whispered and then wondered why he was speaking in a low voice.

A slight creak and then a squeal of ancient hinges alerted him to something amiss behind him. The red door was slowly closing of its own volition. Nick rushed back, leaping over the red body on the carpet. He was glad he put the sledgehammer inside the door frame as it gave him time to get his fingers in the gap and wrench the door open. He kicked the door so it juddered backwards and then he retreated to the safety of the passageway.

"Can't get me that easily. Lost your little soul and need a replacement, eh? Well, you can fuck right off." Nick reached his hand forwards to grab the ring and pull the door shut, then decided against it. He turned on his heels and headed off back out of the passageways. He took the stairs two at a time, and came back to the real world above, smiling. He had nobody to question in the red room, but he had learned a few things while he was briefly in there.

He grabbed his wallet, jacket and phone and left the dark

house. He bought a tray of chips from the kebab shop and took them up to Lionel's place. He still had the spare key to the actor's flat. Lionel was dozing in front of a detective drama on ITV.

"Wake up and get your glad rags on, I'm taking you out for a pint," Nick said, before popping a warm chip into his mouth.

"And what did I do to have the honour of your company so late in the evening?" Lionel grumbled from his chair, as he pushed himself into a standing position.

"Late? Geezer, it's only ten to ten, enough time for a couple of cheeky pints and mother's ruin chasers down the old battlecruiser," Nick said, going full-cockney.

"Are *we* auditioning for Eastenders now?" Lionel tutted, and raised his eyebrows.

"No. *We*, are just in a goodly mood for once, so put down your pipe Gandalf and kick off your slippers, its booze-time," Nick smiled and ate two chips at once.

"Heaven help me from a heterosexual in a happy mood," Lionel mumbled and shuffled off into his bedroom to find his shoes.

Nick laughed loudly and then threw some more chips down his neck.

Crina was surprised to find the man she had willingly slept with yesterday sitting on the steps of his large house. She still had her usual jeans on, but had put on a more feminine V-neck, pale blue blouse, and wore her hair down. Wadim, who had been pulling her along since they stepped off the bus, tugged loose from her grip to run over to give the surprised Nick a full-on hug.

"Well hello to you, Wadim," Nick said, after his initial surprise. He looked up at Crina, and her shocked face turned to joy. He smiled at her, and she smiled so brightly back at him, he laughed with joy. "Hey, how about a hug for your old mum, eh."

"Okay," Wadim replied with only the second word of his young life and rushed to hug his mother around the waist.

Crina had to fight back the tears of joy, as she pulled her son to her.

"I was thinking, we should blow this joint and have a nice family-type day out, what do you think, Wadim?"

"Okay," Wadim said and hugged his mother's waist even tighter.

"That okay with mother?" Nick sauntered up to Crina and planted a quick kiss on her full lips.

"Okay," Crina repeated her son's new word, and they headed off into town for a fun day out.

They took a boat trip down the Thames and a ride on one of the open-top tour buses. Crina had lived in London for years, but had never once *seen the sights*. They ate fast food, drank fizzy drinks and had a great time. It rained a little about three, so they took to wandering the streets near, but not in, Soho, drifting in and out of shops to avoid the intermittent rain. Wadim was always rushing ahead like a kid reborn, while Crina clung to Nick's right arm and shoulder. She supplied him with loving kisses all day, but only when her son's attention was elsewhere.

Their wanderings took them down a narrow lane, with a collection of old, new and vacant shops squashed into very close proximity. Nick was eyeing up a pub on the right side of the enclosed lane when Crina tugged him to the left side.

"Where is that boy?" she said, her hands turning this way and that amongst the people in front of her, where she had last seen the running back of her son.

They hurried forwards to find Wadim pressed up against a glass doorway to a shop. The entrance to the shop was out of view until you were right upon it. Nick had to step back to the other side of the lane to see the sign etched in gold on the dusty window of the shop. Crina bent down and gave her son a gentle telling off for leaving her side and gave him a stiff hug afterwards.

"*Gottschalk Antiques,*" Nick muttered, saying aloud what the sign depicted.

"More, more," Wadim said, pointing at the glass door of the small, gloomy antique shop.

"There's nothing interesting in there for you, no toys," Crina said to the side of her son's face. It was something she had gotten used to, not having an eye-to-eye, fully focused conversation with him.

"Oh, come on, mum," Nick said, creeping up behind her to tickle her under the armpits a little. "What's the harm in having a little look inside?"

Wadim looked at her and pointed past his lips inside the shop. "More."

"Outnumbered by boys now am I?" she tutted as she opened the door of the shop to let Wadim hurry inside. A bell rang as she followed her son in, and Nick followed, after patting the seat of her jeans impatiently. Crina turned around with a fake frown and slapped his hand away harder than he expected. She raised her eyebrows, and he gave an, *I'll promise to behave,* look.

Then they stopped and looked around the dusty old place. It looked like a film set from a *Peter Cushing* horror film. It was stacked to the rafters with old junk, bookcases filled with books, and other nick-knacks. The whole place had a creaking aspect about it. If the shop could be described as a colour, it would be brown.

An old man of indeterminate years leant against a set of glass display cabinets he used as a counter. He had a wild, mostly salt rather than pepper beard, that moved up to his skull to form a hairy ring. The forehead and the top of his pink head looked like they hadn't seen any hair in many a decade. He was short, with a black waistcoat over a crumpled white shirt, the sleeves of which were rolled up, and looked like they were held in place with bicycle clips.

"Anything I can help you with today?" he asked with a tired voice that seemed like it had got used to time wasters and how to spot them over the years. His voice was tinged with an accent, probably German, Nick mused, thinking back to the shop sign on the window.

"Just looking," Nick replied, almost like an automated response. Then his mind began to think, not just respond. "You haven't got any old keys lying about here do you?"

"Not unless they are part of a piece of furniture or lock, no," the man replied, and cast his eyes down on the catalogue they had interrupted him flicking through when they came in.

Nick sneered at the man when he wasn't looking and turned to take Crina's warm hand in his. They began to wander around the stacks of things, looking for where Wadim had ended up. They found him at the end of a corridor of old furniture, chairs, and desks. He was standing in front an old, tired looking, mahogany bureau, the upper flap had been pulled down to show some little drawers, and cubbyholes inside. A blue leather mat was fitted on the inside of the flap, for some Victorian gentle-person to write their correspondence on. Two drawers were pulled out either side of a larger long section of wood between them.

"What you up to, mate?" Nick asked as they got behind the boy.

Wadim had pulled open both little drawers and had a hand in each of the holes behind them

"You should not mess around with stuff that is not yours, Wadim," Crina hissed in a low voice, so the shopkeeper would not hear.

Wadim ignored them both and pushed his hands in deep, a blank look of concentration on his face. Crina moved her hand to pull his out, but before she could there was a click and a panel in between the two drawers fell suddenly open. Nick and Crina moved around behind Wadim as he reached into the low, dark hole, and brought out a foot long and two inches wide, box, covered in a purple baize, like they use on snooker tables. He pressed two invisible release buttons, and the purple lid flew open.

"What have you found there?" Crina said to her son.

Words that Nick hardly registered, for there inside the box was one of the missing keys. It was identical in every way to the two he already had but had a little line of white enamel on the handle end. Wadim smiled, turned and handed the box to Nick.

"How did you find that?" Crina asked her son. "I'm sure Nick is really interested in it, though."

Both man and boy ignored her. Nick had only eyes for the prize. He smiled down at the boy and tussled his dark mop of hair. He didn't know why he and this boy had met, but he now knew it was meant to be.

"I love it," Nick whispered and turned to head back to the shop owner to buy it off him at whatever price the man wanted.

Wadim followed after him, taking no notice of his mother. Crina closed her open mouth, not entirely sure what was going on here. Then she thought of how happy she was, and how her son was speaking a few words and put any worries back into the dark cages in the back of her mind.

Nick was mentally totting up how much cash he had in his wallet as he approached the counter. He had about four hundred and fifty quid left from the day out, that hadn't been too costly so far. How much would he offer? Two hundred to two fifty and hope for the best.

"Where did you find that?" the antique's dealer asked, with a rising interest. He even closed his catalogue and stood up straight, as much as his old back would allow. The till in Nick's mind was slowly going up in tens from his original thoughts, like a loud *ka-ching* in the frontal lobes of his brain.

"In one of those dressers back there." Nick thumbed back towards the corner hidden by stacked rows of old crap. "How much for it?"

The old man took the white key from the box and twiddled it around from side-to-side in the first two fingers and thumb of his right hand. Then closed his left eye and moved it closer to his right eyeball. Nick was sweating buckets. He just wanted to punch the old man and grab the bloody key out of his gnarled old fingers. He was never a patient man, but he couldn't really do that in front of the boy and Crina. The antique's dealer, who obviously must get little trade to string this out so much, weighed the key in the palm of his left hand.

"Cost ya," the man behind the counter finally stated.

"How much?" Nick said, restraining his anger behind his gritted teeth. His hand moved to his trouser pocket for his wallet, but he forced himself to not get it out, as that would be an obvious sign he wanted it badly.

"Hmm, twenty quid."

Nick had his wallet out and slapped a twenty-pound note on the table before the old man could utter. "Do you want a bag with that purchase?"

Nick lost a lot of interest in the day after that, and they took the tube home no more than half an hour later. He kissed Crina goodbye at the tube station, and Wadim lets him hug him. Nick saw that Crina wasn't too enamoured about the way the day was coming to an end.

"We'll do this again later in the week, maybe London Zoo this time," he offered her an olive branch of romantic hope. "It's been a while since I had to entertain a child." Nick's face was hot and tired, and he let his voice drop a little.

Crina looked at his pained face and thought of the son that Nick witnessed dying in front of his eyes. She hugged him close and kissed him beside his left ear. "I understand," she whispered.

"See you tomorrow then, at the house," Nick thumbed over the road to where the tall sycamores hid his domain.

"You will, both of us. Wave now, Wadim." Crina lifted the boy's nearest arm, but it was floppy and non-responsive.

"He's tired," Nick said, giving Crina a peck on the cheek.

"Yes, a busy day out, thank you, Nick, for everything," she replied.

"My pleasure and there is more fun to come," he said, retreating, and waving his hand in semi-salute. When he got to the next crossing, to get to his side of the road, Crina hadn't moved. She was trying to lead Wadim along by his hand, but he would not budge an inch. He seemed to be away-with-the-fairies, staring up at the branches of the corner sycamore tree in Nick's front garden.

Nick had to turn his attention to cross the road. Once across he walked to his house, his eyes still fixed on Crina and her son. She had to pick her son up in her arms to carry him home. Still, the boy's eyes were fixed on the corner of Forky's House. Nick waved, but only Wadim with his head in his mother's chestnut brown hair could see him.

Wadim raised his free right arm and waved.

Not at Nick, but the small boy with hair like his, sitting in the overhanging branches of the sycamore tree.

CHAPTER TWENTY-SEVEN

Nick stood in the wide hallway and fished out all three keys. He took them with him at all times, the only safe place being about his person. He fished the red and black keys from their separate pockets and stuck them together. Then he got his newly found purchase, fumbling and joined it with its fellows. The three joined keys made an equal T-shape as he lifted them up into the dusty sunlight. The sun's rays always seemed more alive this time in the late afternoon, almost early evening. In the mid-afternoon, it seemed to move the dust in a lazy manner, but nearer to the end of the day, the dust motes whizzed around like nobody's business.

Nick moved into the thick of the sunlight, onto the second step of the staircase. He turned the keys over and over just before his eyes. The black-and-white keys were on opposite sides to each other, with the red key in the middle, with only the blue key now missing. A sudden thought struck him, and he pulled the magnetic keys apart with a little effort.

He did not notice the dust motes zooming together to conjoin and start to form the head and body of a figure.

He was too engrossed in the mystery of the keys. He tried his hardest to put the black-and-white keys next to each other, but they resisted interlocking, like one, had a negative and the other a positive charge. The red key would not sit opposite the black or the white key. It seemed each had their place in the final configuration.

Nick only became aware of the hooded, crooked nose figure, when it grabbed the other end of the keys he was holding. He fell backwards onto the worn carpet of the stairs in shock. His son's killer floated above him, his mouth open in a mute scream of rage. His head and upper torso firm, while his lower half ended in his monk's robes. Nick pulled himself up a step, using his right elbow and hand. He clung on to the keys with all the might as the ghostly monk tried to rip the them from his grasp.

Nick grimaced and had to grab the semi-circular ends of the keys with both hands. His fingers were in the holes of the keys, pulling against the supernatural strength. Nick lifted his knees and dug his heels into the next step. Then pushed himself up not one, but two steps, sliding up on his behind. He felt his shirt come out of the back of his trousers as he tried to wrench the keys sideways to fool the attacking dust-ghost. One finger of the mote-made apparition left the sunlight and seemed to melt away in the part of the staircase not touched directly by the sun.

The monk's mouth formed a pained scream, stretching his mouth unnaturally wide. Nick tried to kick at the murderer, but his shoes passed through the lower part of the dust-ghost and then reformed again. Nick tried to push up but found he couldn't. The ghostly monk had reformed around his ankle, trapping it there, and he feared he would be dragged down the stairs at any moment. All he could do was throw himself over to the left and heave his side over into the shadowed part of the stairs, where no direct sunlight fell. The resistance on the keys vanished, and Nick rolled over to find that the monk was only half-left. A thing of the motes in the sunlight nothing more, he could not move beyond this form, unless he lost his physical manifestation and strength.

"Not this time."

A passing cloud then blocked out the sun, and the figure vanished like the dead entity that it was. Nick took a second to catch his breath, and then made a run for the living room. He was in the open doorway, looking back over his left shoulder when the sunlight returned. It was brighter now and reflected off the tiled flooring. The ghostly dust remnants of the monk could not be seen anywhere. Nick closed the living room door behind him and went to fix himself a whisky.

It took half an hour for Nick's rage to simmer down to near normal levels. He couldn't believe, even after death, he was being tormented by the man who had killed his son. He'd never seen the murdering monk's ghost form in the intervening years between his son's murder and now. It was Forky's House. The place was the epicentre where strange forces met, and other worlds and planes collided. It had a dormant power, which seemed to let memories of things, and people long dead, creep in at the cracks and corners. His whisky glass ended in shattered pieces in the back hearth of the unlit fireplace.

This destructive act seemed to put an end to his foul mood. He held the three joined keys up in front of his eyes and decided to laugh. The monk's moment had been long ago, his half-victory should remain in the past. Nick had new journeys to make, with Crina and Wadim at his side. Only the little matter of the last missing key thwarted him.

Lionel turned over in his bed, half awake. His bed covers failed to contain his long frame. They had come un-tucked again at the foot of his bed, exposing his size ten feet. With a *'humpft'* of displeasure, he sat up and tried to flick the sheets back over his cold feet. He was turned towards the window that overlooked the yard and garages behind the shops. The neon strips on the hands of his alarm clock showed it was only a little after four o'clock in the morning. It was still dark outside, and about as silent as this busy intersection of cosmopolitan London ever got. His attempts to grab the end of the sheets with his large toes failed, so he had to sit up and try and reach down the bed to rearrange them.

It was only then his that half-asleep eyes became aware of another source of dim light. It had a bluish tinge to it, like the moon was out. But the glow was not coming from his bedroom window, or from behind his drawn curtains. Nor was it coming from his door, which was always shut tight. No, this blue glow emanated from the faint figure of a man cast in the same colour and dressed in a nightmare of double denim blue.

"Hello, Lionel, my little *lover boy*," Billy Ryan said through blue-tinged lips.

Lionel Hawthorne screamed out into his tiny flat in a high falsetto.

Nick and Crina rolled around in the tangled mess of his sheets, both naked and covered in a sheen of sweat and other such post-coital emanations. Their love-making was filled with smiles, tender moments, and passion Crina never knew existed. She was happier now than at any other time in her life that she could recall. Her childhood had not been great, with an overbearingly religious father, who thought any independent thought from his daughter was a sin from Hell. Then after the gang-rape by men her father owed money too, when she needed him the most, he had thrown her into the street for bringing shame on the family.

Wadim was happy running about the house and connecting with the world around him more than at any other time in his short life. The violence of his conception could never again outweigh the joy of having a boy who loved and hugged her. She had Nick to thank for that, for setting something free in her child. She kissed Nick hard, with her soft lips, and pulled him on top of her again, and urged him inside her.

Wadim wandered the first-floor corridors of the large house. He was used to his mother being at work or doing other things while he was there, like cooking and cleaning. The house was larger than anything his mind had ever imagined before, and he wandered around just staring at things, taking them in. After a while, he found himself at the rear of the house, and he entered an old bedroom he liked to come and draw in. There was the dressing table in front of the window, which let in more light than most of the gloomy, and sometimes damp, rooms. There were spots of clean glass in the windows where he'd used the bottom of his fist to circle clean. So he would often end up here, with his pad and colouring pencils. He also liked the green vine-like wallpaper in this bedroom. It was old, stained and peeling in places, but green was his favourite colour.

He set down his pad on the dressing table. Then before he sat down, he took his colouring pencils out of his *Star Wars* pencil case. His first pencil was pink, and he placed that above the middle of the left-hand page of his colouring book. A green pencil followed, and this went to the near far right above the book. A light blue followed, and this went just off centre, closer to the green one. A black, red and lighter green followed, and one-by-one they were placed in the colour coded order that meant everything was right in the world to his brain's standards. Quickly the pencil case was emptied until all his pencils were lined up, like a paint chart rainbow. His normal pencil, rubber, and pencil sharpener stayed in the pencil case, as they did not fit into the pattern. He'd tried to make them fit before, but it only led to stress and rage-filled disappointment. It irked him that he could not find a solution to making them fit, but keeping them inside the pencil case had been his mother's idea, and it helped him get past that sticking point. He'd lost count of the pencils he'd just snapped in anger or the number of times the rubber and sharpener had found themselves in the kitchen bin at home.

Now what he couldn't see didn't bother him so much.

Anyway, it took time and joy from his drawing time. He placed the pencil case at the side of the desk. Stopped and eyed it and then flicked it onto the floor. *What he couldn't see didn't bother him as much*; rule applied.

But then he could see the pencil case peeking out behind one leg of the dressing table. He had to bend down to get it and take it over to the bed behind him. He placed it there, so it was truly out of sight, out of mind. Then he walked back to his chair, knowing he was ready to start his drawing.

Except he wasn't. Somehow one of his red pencils and one of his green ones had been swapped over in their colour coordinated positions. Wadim frowned and looked around the room. The bedroom door was closed, and it was devoid of anyone else but him. If anyone had come in and swapped them around, he would have seen them. Wadim grabbed them both, one in each hand, and swapped them back to their original and proper places. He took a yellow pencil and began to colour in the round sun on the picture of a playground in his colouring book. He bent down over his book to do this, his nose nearly touching the page. His tongue was sticking out of his mouth in concentration by the time he'd coloured in the sun.

When he looked up to put the yellow pencil back and exchange it for a green one to do the grass next, he was confronted by his beautifully lined up pencils standing up on their ends waiting for him. Wadim was scared, and pushed himself back away from the dressing table, retreating to the middle of the room by the end of the single bed. He had only looked away for an instant, now the pencils were balanced the other way up on their coloured nibs, ends pointing to the ceiling. Wadim edged towards the door. He glanced around the small room, with its green vine-like wallpaper, and wondered who could be doing such magic.

When he looked back to the dressing table, his questions were answered. Sitting on the chair, he had just vacated was the boy with the black hair like his, the one from the tree the other day. The boy had his back to him and was colouring with his green pencil. Wadim wanted to ask who he was, but his brain wouldn't let him take that risk. He wanted to know what the boy was doing here, using his pencils, and where had he come from.

Wadim had no friends at the special school he went to. He wanted friends, someone to play ball with him the playground, or *Star Wars* perhaps, but his body would freeze up, and he kept himself to himself. Wadim could go running and crying to his mother, but he wanted to see how the boy was doing with the colouring book: *his colouring book!*

Anger pushed away the fear, and he edged closer, keeping to the end of the bed at a safe parallel distance. He stepped forward again, letting his anger push back the fear from his body. The boy turned towards him now and smiled like an angel. "Do you want to be my friend, and draw together?"

Wadim nodded and moved closer to see how well the other boy had done. He expected to see green grass on the page, but somehow the green pencil had produced a sandy colour. It covered the bottom of the page, where the green grass should be.

Crina's affections had affected him so much that he had forgotten tonight was another key moon moment. It was the Seventh of

August, and there would be no moon tonight, and the black key
and the black room would come into play. He turned on his left
elbow and plumped his pillows. He leant over and sniffed the
pillow on the other side of his double bed. It still smelt of the
cheap, own-brand shampoo she used for her full-bodied, long
chestnut hair.

She had been gone an hour from his warm embrace, but he
still could not find the energy to get out of bed, even though
it seemed empty without her. The need for food and drink
forced him out. He showered and dressed first, and then went
downstairs to sate his rumbling stomach. He threw together
a chicken sandwich with cheese and onion crisps on top and
washed it down with a cold beer. A look out into the garden
showed it was raining very lightly. He opened the back kitchen
door and went outside, under the shelter of the balcony and
watched the rain. It wasn't cold, and the smell of the warm
precipitation made his nose stuff up a little.

He was in two minds whether to even bother to go visit
Nicholas Clovis in his black room tonight. He still had a fortnight
to wait until the white key would come into play, and that held
more interest for him, as it was at least a new room for him to
wonder at. Only the blue key remained out of his grasp, but he
didn't seem as worried about it anymore. Trips out to auctions
and antique shops with Crina and Wadim in tow had come
to nothing. It was because he was forcing the issue. The white
key had been found by fate, chance, or divine intervention. The
last key would come to him the same way, if not in the same
manner. All Nick had to do was wait, and in the meantime enjoy
the long, hot summer days with Crina and her son while he did.

After much thought, he did go down to open up the black
door and visit Clovis for the second time. Only to answer one
question that was nagging his mind.

The black tainted Clovis was equally pleased to have his
company, even though Nick kept to the doorway. He leaned on
the frame opposite the door, with his arms and legs crossed.

"You have returned I see," Clovis said, as he came skulking
from behind his black screen.

"Yes, because I have one question for you."

"Ask away, sir, your company is most welcome to such a lonely wretch as that I have become." Clovis extended his long thin arms, making him look even more emaciated.

"How did you make a room to trap a soul in it?" Nick pointed to the locked exit from the Black Room behind Nicholas Clovis's wretched form.

"It's a long morbid tale." Clovis nodded and crawled a little closer towards where Nick stood. "Each room must have a soul with some link to this house to power and channel the last great gateway, and the mysteries that lie beyond, that no man has ever witnessed. I used the darkest magic ever. Every room is a part of one room, ever power cycle of the moon needs a soul trapped in it. Like mine, sadly. Every colour, blends into one at the end and gives access to the door beyond."

"I kinda thought as much." Nick frowned and chewed his bottom lip.

"Have you collected all four keys then, pray tell?" Clovis asked, inching closer to the open doorway.

"I now have three of the set of four, but I have the luck of the devil, so I'm sure the last one will soon come into my possession."

"And then what will you do, will you risk entering the last door?"

"Well, I'll answer that with a riddle."

"A riddle, what game is this, sir?" Clovis stopped creeping closer to the doorway, his legs bent ready to strike.

"How do you keep an idiot in suspense?" Nick asked with a cheeky grin.

"I don't understand, what do you mean?" Clovis's long arms reached up for Nick, his nails seemed to grow and extend somehow as he did, like the black cast man was some kind of autumnal dusk shadow.

"I'll tell you next time," Nick laughed, and jumped back out of the threshold of the room, just before Clovis made a lunge at him. The wretched creature bounced backwards into the black room, with the door slamming shut loudly behind him. Nick didn't stop laughing until he climbed out of the secret entrance in the music room. He had all the information he needed now to conclude this investigation of Forky's House. All he needed was the last, blue, key.

CHAPTER TWENTY-EIGHT

His dreamscape was still the dusty, desert bowl of sand. But there was no sign of the four coloured riders this time. He raised his hands to shield his eyes, but the shimmering water-like illusion that was the horizon made his eyes water. He blinked as his eyes thought they saw two dots in the distant, shimmering heat haze. He blinked again, and he was rewarded with the sight of two small black figures walking towards him from converging angles.

He ran in a straight line towards them. Slowly the shimmering gave way to just hot sand, but the two small figures came into focus. One was his dead son and the other Wadim. As he closed to within fifteen feet of the dark-haired children, he noticed something odd about them. They left weird footprints in the sand behind them. His son's footfalls left behind burning images of where he had trod like his shoes were on fire. Wadim, on the other hand, left footprints that would instantly transform into trainer sized, one inch high sods of grass. Both walked towards him, smiling, and their arms raised up to embrace him.

He looked left to right, from one to the other, not knowing which embrace to covet first. The footprints of fire and grass now began to spread across the desert landscape, battling each other to take over this dream world. He looked down at the two boys, one framed by flames, and the other by a lawn of rising grass. Both reached for him, needing his comfort, and he screamed to the heavens as he did not know which one to choose.

Nick woke to a drumming sound in his head.

He was alone in his bed, and the morning light was bleeding

through the gaps in the age warped wood of the shutters. The drumming sound ceased, only to be replaced by the ringing of the door chime of his front door. Frowning, Nick jumped out of bed, tugged on a pair of jeans and yesterday's T-shirt. The ringing the doorbell now accompanied by the banging of a fist as Nick hurried down the grand staircase.

"Hold your horses," he cried towards the shut front door. The tiled floor went from warm to cold to a bristly welcome mat under the naked soles of his feet. He unlocked and opened the door as a huge yawn caught up with him.

Lionel was in an anxious looking state at the front step. His grey hair was a frizzy mess, and he looked like he had stubble on his chin, which was most unlike the clean-shaven thespian.

"Sorry about the early hour, but I need to talk to you, urgently." Lionel didn't wait to be asked, he just slipped sidewards through the door, making Nick shuffle back quickly.

"What time is it then?" Nick peeked outside as he closed the door, but the sun was up about 5 a.m. this time of the year so it did not help him guess the time.

"About a quarter to eight I think," Lionel replied, looking this way and that like he was a fox being hunted. "I need to speak with you urgently."

"Living room." Nick pointed and followed.

Nick sat down on his sofa and rubbed the sleep from his eyes. Lionel paced up and down around one of the armchairs.

"Will you sit down? You look like you have ants in your pants." Nick waved his hand towards the armchair in front of the grey-haired actor.

"Sorry," he said and did as Nick asked. Even though he was seated, he did not stop moving. His left knee jigged up and down, while he was twiddling his thumbs over and over.

"What the hell is wrong with you, man?" Nick finally asked, getting sick of his friends agitated, jerky movements.

Lionel looked Nick straight in the eyes, as he rubbed at his stubbled chin in an apprehensively "Suddenly I feel a bit of an old fool," he finally replied.

"Why's that?"

"Well, it all seems a little silly in the cold light of morning, but I've been having nightmares the past few nights."

"Welcome to my world," Nick muttered and rubbed his palms over his cheeks and back through his hair.

"What?"

"Nothing." Nick waved. "Go on, go on. What are these nightmares about?"

"Billy Ryan," Lionel said simply.

Nick sat up straight. "What about him?"

"I don't know if they are nightmares or what, but it's like his ghost has been visiting me for the past few nights. He's standing at the edge of my bed, leering at me, cast in a cold, blue light." Lionel's normally pale skin looked even further drained.

"What does he want?" The mention of blue light had piqued Nick's interest.

"To lure me back to that sick little sadomasochistic blue room of his I'm sure."

"But he can't. He's long dead, and anyway, the key to the blue room is missing."

"Ah, well, erm...when I said I didn't know where the key was...that was more of a little white lie." Lionel reached into the pocket of the jacket he was wearing and produced a very familiar looking key, with flecked blue paint at the end.

"You had the key all the time."

"Yes...sorry." Lionel nodded. "I didn't want anyone ever to go through what I did. My mother took it before the police got hold of it. I've kept it in her favourite cuckoo clock, hidden away ever since. I hope you aren't going to get all butch and mad with me?"

Nick hurried forwards and kissed Lionel full on the lips. "May I?" he asked, pulling back and pointing to the key in his stunned friend's hands.

"Well, I wasn't expecting that response...yes have it. Maybe it will take the nightmare visits away if I don't possess the bloody thing anymore." Lionel raised the key up before him like some Holy Grail, and Nick took it quickly from the man's trembling grasp.

"Now you don't have to worry about it, Lionel."

"Now I'm worried about you, Nick. That key and that room

are evil beyond the normal meaning of the word."

"I can take care of myself, my friend." Nick's eyes never left the last missing key as he spoke. He did not notice until the dull sunlight into the room changed, that his friend had got up and moved to the open living room doorway. "You going? I was just about to make tea."

"No, I must be getting back home," Lionel smiled thinly at him and went halfway through the doorway before turning back. "You will be careful won't you, Nick?"

"Looking after myself is what I'm good at," Nick smiled broadly at his friend.

"I don't doubt it for a second." Lionel turned, left the room and then the house.

Nick waited for the front door to close shut before running into the hallway. He stopped and took an alternative route through the music room and up the servants' staircase to get back to his room. He ran over to the fire and reached up inside to find the wooden box he had brought up from the lower levels. He lay the sooty box on the bedsheets and opened it: the three other keys lay inside. He took them out and put them together for the first time in *God knew* how many hundreds of years. They seemed to hum and vibrate in the palm of his hand. Four keys joined to make another master key.

There would be a half moon tonight, and a first chance to enter the blue room and try out the combined keys in the brown door. He hadn't even seen the white room or its occupant yet. He might never need to now.

Nick leaned back in his bed and placed his bare feet up on it and laughed. Maybe this haunted house ghost hunt was over, and he could move on with his life. Then he thought of Crina and Wadim and wondered what part they had to play in his future plans after Forky's House.

When Crina and Wadim arrived later that morning they found a note pinned to the bannister of the grand staircase:

PICNIC TIME MEET ME OUT BACK

Crina took her son's hand and led him out into the garden. When they got past the pear trees they saw that Nick had been busy. He had raided the local shops for food, sandwiches and snacks, which were laid out in bowls on a sheet placed on the oval lawn in front of the stone slabs and the gazebo. A filled ice bucket had a chilled bottle of champagne inside, and two long neck flutes lay next to it.

Nick was there in his best suit, and a pale yellow shirt, sitting on a cushion. He directed his stunned guests to similar cushions placed around the picnic blanket.

"Come one, come all," he said, beckoning them closer.

"What have we done to deserve all this?" Crina said, sitting down close to Nick on his left, while Wadim sat down with a bump awkwardly on his cushion around the food to the right.

"I'm just in an excellent mood, and I want to share it, that's all." Nick leaned forwards on one knee and planted a kiss on Crina's nearest cheek. "Champagne, madam?"

"Yes, please." Her smiling face turned to her son, who was also smiling back at her.

They drank too much, ate too much, and laughed until their jaws ached. Crina wanted to clear up after they had finished, but Nick wouldn't hear of it. She left two hours after the picnic. She could still feel the hardness of him inside her as she walked Wadim to the bus stop. It had been quick and intense, and Nick had whispered that he *loved her* afterwards. As she waited for the bus home, something she thought could never ever happen bloomed out from her chest and up into her mind. She loved him too.

Nick took the four corners of the blanket and pulled it up, breaking plates and shattering the food remnants inside. He tied it up at the ends and carried it over past the sheds to a dark corner of the garden. There behind a wild gooseberry bush he tossed the picnic things with a satisfying crash.

Nick wasn't one for washing and clearing up.

He sat in the warm gazebo and closed his eyes. He wasn't sure what he would find behind the brown door tonight, or what risks to his soul and body he might face. At least he'd given Crina and Wadim a fond farewell.

Nick was camped out in a fold-up chair down in the sub level corridors, just after dusk. He had two hand-cranked lanterns placed beside where the doorway would appear, plus two torches of his own. He sat and drank from a can of coke, not wanting to partake of any more alcohol today. He might need his wits about him when the Blue Room and its occupant appeared. The only things that nagged at his eager mind was that his guess about who may be in the white room may never be resolved. That bugged him a little, but not knowing what mysteries lay beyond the brown door intrigued him greater. He drank some more of his fizzy drink and waited impatiently. When his drink was gone, he lit up a cigarette, crossed his legs, and waited.

Nick had never seen the portal arrive before, and he didn't this time. He was bending down, stubbing out his third cigarette butt when it happened. When he looked up, he was a little taken aback to find it there waiting for him. He wasn't sure what he had expected, a flash-bang-whizz, or a plop, as two worlds collided, something monumental at least. But no, it just appeared, framed in silence, with no movement of the air in the passageway.

"Oh, well," he said, to the darkness and stood. He took the blue key from his jacket pocket, leaving the other three fixed together. He licked his lips and inserted the blue key into the lock. It turned, and the familiar chimes and clicks began until they shook the foundations of the house. Nick opened the door two inches and then took the key from the lock. He used the toe of his shoe to gently prod the door open. It moved away from him, slowly revealing the duplicated furniture of the other two rooms, except this time it was all in blue. Not dark dusky blue, but a lighter blue, a couple of notches above sky blue.

Nick fixed the blue key in place with its three siblings and then weighed the combined keys in the palm of his left hand. He waited, taking in the familiar sights of the room. It appeared empty. But appearances, in this house, were always deceptive. Then he heard it, a soft, rumbling voice coming from behind the blue screen. It was snatches of a song from the sixties that Nick had forgotten he knew.

"Rockabilly rock, rockabilly roll, this old rhythm is gonna steal your soul." The low, deep voice behind the blue screen sang lower and slower than the original recorded version. Nick gripped the keys in his left hand until they began to bite and hurt his skin. The pain raged up to his brain, and with a snarl, he ran into the blue room. He made a beeline for the blue screen, which he kicked hard, propelling it backwards into the person that hid behind it. There was a cry of shock as the screen fell and half concertinaed onto itself. It revealed a shortish man in blue denim, and a face to match his clothes and surroundings. Nick was on him before he could half scramble out from the screen that had collapsed on him. Nick grabbed the denim jacket by the collar and pulled him high enough to punch his fist into the blue, drawn back lips.

The short, blue man managed to only get out a grunt of pain, before Nick's fist hit him again. Again and again, the blows came down on the man's face, breaking his nose, teeth, and cutting his lips. The blood was royal blue, not red as Nick had hoped, but he kept on punching until his own hand began to send protests of pain up his arm. He opened his hand and let the bloodied Billy Ryan fall back into the wreckage of the screen.

He was still conscious, with one eye swelled up. His good, blue eye blinked rapidly as he looked up at Nick in shock and pain. Billy Ryan spat out two broken tooth shards and a lot of blue blood. His breathing came in wheezy whistles through the gaps in his teeth. He raised a hand to his damaged face, pleading for leniency. He got none, as Nick kicked out hard at his wavering arm, breaking it with a satisfying crack.

Sobbing with the pain, the former rocker just lay, as he could do little else, and gazed up at his attacker with his one good eye.

"Lionel Hawthorne sends his regards, *Billy.*" Nick mocked the wild man of rock from the sixties. He looked down at his fist, it was covered both with Billy's blue blood and his own red blood from cuts the musician's teeth did to his knuckles.

Nick transferred the combined keys to his other hand and flexed out the fingers of his damaged one. Leaving Billy Ryan to nurse his injuries, Nick moved up to the door, and without hesitation put the four keys into the lock of the brown door. He felt his body tense, and the keys turned four times in the lock with just the meagre clicks of any normal lock. There was no build-up of noise like the door to the four coloured rooms. The key would not move any further in the lock as he felt the locking mechanism open. He grabbed the handle and pulled the brown door inwards and saw what lay behind it.

Darkness.

No light or shadows or stars or constellations, just utter solid blackness. Nick reached his right-hand forwards and touched the abyss. His palm touched the surface of the void but could not push it any further. The oblong of nothingness framed in the doorway would not budge.

"What the hell is this," Nick said, slapping the solid matter with his hands in rising frustration. "Is this a trick?"

Billy Ryan mumbled out a rasping laugh from where he lay in the corner of the room.

"What the fuck are you laughing at you fucking rock dinosaur?"

"Dope get bore knickers in a twist mate," Billy managed to croak through his puffed up lips. "Ib's all your fault anyway."

"What do you mean?"

"I felt it," Billy said, in a stronger, more recognisable voice, as he pushed himself back to lean against the wall behind him. "The loss of power."

Nick stopped and frowned. He knew where this was going, and he knew that Ryan was right, it was his fault.

"You killed one of the other guardian's soul, somehow didn't you?" Billy Ryan spat blood and bits of teeth onto the screen that now lay across his legs.

Nick closed the brown door and locked it shut again. Then he strode from the blue room without another word or glance back at Ryan. He shut and locked the blue door entrance and went back upstairs to find a bottle of brandy and get himself ragingly drunk.

CHAPTER TWENTY-NINE

The walkie-talkie had been silent for days. He'd left his pregnant fiancée resting in bed at her place while he returned to his old house. The dogs were guarding her, and he'd hired a man to sit outside the apartment complex where she lived.

The Scotsman held the black walkie-talkie in his hand. Then he hefted it as far as he could over the balcony of his cliffside home, and into the sea below. It was gone with a tiny splash into the waves. He was pretty sure he had done the wrong thing in trying to get rid of it, but the silence from the small round holes in its speaker grille was driving him to distraction. He would sell both their places and maybe move somewhere else instead, maybe up a hill somewhere on a Greek island.

He was hot and parched so he went into his kitchen to see if he had any orange juice or failing that cold water. He was just over the kitchen threshold when his front door chimed. That was wrong. You had to buzz in at the entry gate to be let in before you could reach the doorbell. The retired assassin crept around to a low storage cupboard in his living room. He knelt down flat on the plush carpet and reached between the legs of the piece of white furniture. When his hand came back, he held a small, snub nose pistol with grey gaffer tape, which had fixed it under the bottom of the cupboard. It was one of his little pride and joy weapons, a seven round, one in the chamber, safety on, Walther PPK pistol. It was the preferred weapon of Ian Fleming's most famous British super-spy, and just a fun and handy thing to have around the house in case of emergencies. He clicked the safety off and moved towards his front door. The little monitor near the front doorway showed a nun was standing at his front door, and she was dripping wet. The Scotsman frowned and, hiding the pistol behind the front door, opened it to see what she wanted.

"This is private property, how did you get in here?" he asked, looking the nun up and down. She was young and pretty under her soaking wet habit, that clung to her body. He could see that his gate was slightly ajar, enough for a person to walk through, but that wasn't right. It was either closed, open or moving left or right. It should not be stuck like that unless it was broken.

"I think you dropped something," she simply said, taking his free hand and slapping the wet walkie-talkie into it. He looked down at it, shocked and bemused. There was no way the nun could have swum out, fetched it, and be back up at his place in less than a minute. He looked up, but she wasn't there. She was walking back out through the gap in his gate. He watched as she walked out of sight, and the gate slowly closed after her, like it had been waiting for her.

"Don't do that again, or your child and its mother will die in terrible agony," the walkie-talkie suddenly hissed to life in his hand. He jumped with the shock and dropped it to the floor, spinning around on the tiles. "The time is approaching, be ready to travel at a moment notice, Donald."

"Where am I going?" he said in a low scared voice.

"To London, to kill someone who has outlived their usefulness."

"To kill who?"

But the walkie-talkie fell silent again.

CHAPTER THIRTY

It took Crina and Wadim twenty minutes to find him the next morning. The music room was the only place he would not let her clean, so as a last resort she tried there. She opened the door with her son beside her. An oblong arc of expanding natural light opened out the dark room. She spotted his shoes first, down on the floor as he sat with his knees raised, and his back against the mural covered north wall. She instinctively pushed Wadim back with her hand, and she moved two steps into the shadowy music room. She was fearful that he had done himself some self-harm, the morbid side of her mind pushing to the fore. Things had been going so right with him, Wadim and her life for once, she was sure something terrible lurked around the corner for them all.

Nick's head was bowed, covered with shadows. His limp wrists rested down on his raised knees. He had the air of a broken man.

"Are you okay?"

When he didn't answer, or move, her anxiety rose within her. She turned back to hush Wadim out the room, as he had taken two tiny steps inside. She returned her gaze to Nick, who had raised his head. The light from the door as she moved caught his eyes, and they had a reflective glow for a second, like cats' eyes. Then she could hear the hitch in his chest and realised he had been crying. She rushed over to him, as he pushed himself up the wall to meet her in an emotional embrace. His arms encircled her, and his sobbing face went into her neck. She stiffened, due to old mental scarring, but then she slowly put her hands on the back of his head and let him cry it all out. She knew she loved him at that very moment, and her heart was his forever.

The day after his emotional episode Nick invited Lionel around for lunch. They ate a picnic outside in the sunshine with Wadim and Crina. His mood had returned to his normal happy-go-lucky state. Nick smiled warmly at Crina as she passed a bowl of salad, their fingers touching ever so slightly. She hadn't asked him what had been wrong yesterday and he loved her for that. They shared a secret smile before Nick passed the bowl onto Lionel.

"Do you have something a little less healthy, and a tad more meaty?" Lionel raised his eyebrows as he eyed some cooked chicken drumsticks.

"You do like your meat, eh, Lionel." Nick winked at the older man.

"Oh, very droll I'm sure." Lionel put down the salad bowl and grabbed some chicken satays on a plastic tray.

"So, how have you been sleeping the last couple of nights?" Nick ventured as he added some cold meats to his plate.

"Sadly, alone."

"No bad dreams?" Nick pressed.

"No…all gone now." Lionel leaned back on his arm and put a satay in his mouth.

"Good." Nick nodded and turned to wink at Wadim, who was licking the butter off the top of a slice of French bread.

"I am a bit worried that you might be stealing my cleaner away from me." Lionel gave a knowing smile from Crina to Nick. Crina blushed and bent her head over her plate, so her chestnut hair covered her face.

"Even if I do, I promise to come round and clean your flat myself," Nick said, popping a cherry tomato into his mouth.

"I'll hold you to that, young man," Lionel replied and laughed gently.

"Thank you for just being there for me yesterday," Nick said, coming up to encircle Crina's waist with his arms as she did the washing up. Lionel was playing hide-and-seek in the garden with Wadim, who was really coming out of his shell. Nick kissed her neck and nuzzled closer. She closed her eyes for a second and drank in his embrace.

"Will you tell me why you were so upset?" Crina pulled off her rubber gloves and turned in his arms to face him.

"I... I was just thinking of my son. It was years ago, but sometimes these things sucker-punch you from nowhere." Nick pressed his lips together, ran his fingers through her hair, and kissed her on her full lips.

"I think—no—I know, that I love you, Nick," she replied, after their breathless kiss.

"I know," he said and kissed her again.

The next few days were full of steely, grey skies, and bursts of torrential rain. It didn't dull Nick's mood when he had Crina and Wadim around him. Each day the time they left got later and later. Nick didn't mind at all, he enjoyed both their company in different ways.

Tonight though was the full moon. It might not be visible in the cloud-covered sky, but that didn't affect the portal to the white room arriving just after ten p.m.

The rain was still pounding down as he descended into the darkness. Nick wondered if they ever had floods in the passageways buried so deep under the house. He also wondered how much it would cost to have a lift fitted, to save his aching legs on the walk back up.

"Keeps me fit, I suppose," he said to the darkness, as he made his way off the last step, and headed over to the passageways. The doorway was there, waiting for him. He took out the white key and turned it in the lock for the first time and waited for the mysterious workings behind the door to begin. He clicked his fingers as the noise rose, he was getting used to it now. He pushed the door open and had to rein in his eyes a little at the glare of the all-white room. It looked like some hellish hospital room, every piece of furniture in the place was white. Sitting on the bed was a tall, thin man, with a long white coat on. He was just sitting there, staring at his freakishly white hands.

"Doctor Forque I presume," Nick said and walked into the eye-wincingly white room.

Nick lay alone in his bed his mind racing. It has been two hours since he'd left the frustrations of the white room behind, but he was too wired to sleep. The good doctor had refused to reply to Nick's questions in English or French. He just stared at his hands, that looked like they had been dipped in white paint and said not a word the whole time Nick was in there.

The brown door opened up again, but he was still faced with the same impenetrable blackness as before. He knew it was his own fault. All he could do was sit, brood, and wait for the red room to come round at the end of the month. That's where all his problems lay.

CHAPTER THIRTY-ONE

After sorting out Lionel's nightmare problem, Nick managed to cajole him into babysitting Wadim at his place for the day. He wore his best suit, shirt, and tie, while Crina wore a pretty red, cross-over, revealing top, like a mini-dress over her cleanest pair of blue jeans. She had on a pair of black flats. They were old, and in need of chucking out, but they were the only shoes she owned.

They took a taxi into town and parked by an exclusive boutique shop in the heart of Knightsbridge. He paid the taxi driver money to keep him circling around every five minutes as there were red lines outside the posh shop. Nick confidently stepped past the hesitant Crina and pressed the buzzer to be let in.

"It's Mr Hobbs," he said into the buzzer's speaker.

"Come right in, Mr Hobbs, we've been expecting you," said a nasally voice from the inside of the shop. A buzzer sounded, and Nick pushed the door open, then turned and held out his hand to Crina to follow. She looked warily at him and the shop front. She had been expecting a night at the pub or curry house, not some expensive clothes boutique. She took his hand, and he gently led her inside, to a shop with so few shelves and dresses on display, it didn't look like it was open for business.

A skeletal looking woman with a pinched nose and high blonde hair tottered over to them on her thin legs, and three-inch stiletto heels. The only plump thing about her was the collagen injections in her puffy, top lip. It gave her face a disapproving air like she had a sherbet lemon stuffed in her mouth.

"Can I help you?" she looked at Nick, but her eyes were scanning Crina up and down.

"Yes." Nick turned to his lovely companion. "This is Crina, she needs a stunning dress, shoes, handbag, the works. Money's no object."

"Hmmm, I'm sure we can find something for madam." The shop assistant's words said one thing, but her face said something far more on the negative side.

"And a glass or two of champagne while we wait too, please. Come on, chop-chop, times-a-wasting." Nick clapped his hands together so loudly that it made the emaciated shop assistant flinch. She hurried off to get a tape measure, while Nick led Crina over to an ornate sofa by the window, and near the changing rooms. The boutique was playing *Adele* on a loop, and by the end of an hour there, Nick wanted to strangle the singer, or the shop assistant with his bare hands for not changing it.

At last, the dressing room curtains were pulled open after many false starts. Crina stood there, wobbling on her red-soled high heels, looking even more beautiful than Nick could ever imagine. She wore a stunning scarlet dress, cut down to the waist in a plunging V-line. The bottom of the dress was ankle length but slit in two places to reveal her shapely legs. She held a matching clutch bag to her middle like her life depended on it.

"What do you think?" she asked, her full lips covered with sparkly red lip-gloss that showed off her perfect mouth.

"I think we have a sale," Nick said to the shop assistant.

"You sure I look okay?"

"Woman, you look perfect." Nick stood and held her bare arms to kiss her cheek.

The cabbie couldn't resist a wolf-whistle as Crina and Nick got back into the cab. "Where to next then?" he asked, looking in his rear-view mirror at Crina.

"The Rib Room for lunch," Nick said, looking into Crina's dazzling eyes. He put the bag full of Crina's old clothes on the floor of the cab and took her nearest hand in his. The cabbie pulled into the traffic for the short drive to the restaurant. They had more champagne, and Crina was glad when her main meal arrived, as she was getting light headed.

"Why are people staring at me, am I using the wrong fork?" she whispered, leaning over the table at Nick.

Nick smiled at the sight of her cleavage on view as he looked around at the other tables nearby. "No," he whispered back, "it's because you are the most attractive lady in the room."

Crina smiled confidently but still kept her voice low. "I do feel so nice in this beautiful dress, but why are you doing all this for me?"

"Because I want you and Wadim to move in with me, that's why," he replied, and took a small blue ring box out of his jacket pocket and placed it on the table just in front of her plate. Crina's sparkling eyes shone even more with tears. Her shaking hands reached over and opened the little blue box with an audible gulp. Inside was a white gold ring, with a set of three large diamonds on top.

Lionel was exhausted. He lay on the sofa to catch his breath after chasing after Wadim all day and fell fast asleep. The boy was kneeling by the coffee table, happily doing one of his drawings. The living room door suddenly clicked, and slowly opened, with a slight, drawn-out squeal from the hinges. The hallway outside, though, was empty. The sun was shining through the windows above, in a clear afternoon sky, only interrupted by the early rise of the moon.

Wadim jumped to his feet and took a glance at the prone actor. Seeing he was fast asleep, Wadim walked over to the door to peer into the hallway and ground floor corridor. The hallway was empty, so the boy looked down the long corridor. It was like a long dark train tunnel, with light from the windows over the balcony at the far end of the house shining like a safety beacon. The door to the room with the drawings on the walls was open, and Wadim just caught sight of his small friend going inside. He rushed off after the boy who looked a little like him and shared his love of drawing. The other dark-haired boy about his age didn't speak a word, Wadim could understand that.

The doorway to the music room was open. The lights clicked on, making Wadim blink at the sudden light in the dark room.

In the north wall, there was something different. There

had been a little, fat naked boy made of stone in an inner bit of the wall, but now he was facing Wadim like a secret door had opened up behind him. The other silent boy stood at the secret entrance. He was holding a lantern up to the side of his face, and Wadim could see he was smiling kindly at him. Then he was gone, and the light from his lantern faded from the music room.

Wadim hesitated for a moment, he wasn't supposed to run off anywhere his mother drummed into him. Yet this was still inside the house, so with a shrug, he entered the music room, and turned on the lights. He rushed over to the secret entrance and saw that it led into a little passageway, to a much larger, darker room beyond. Another lit lantern sat just inside the dark passage. Beyond it, he could see the bobbing light of his friend's lantern as he moved further away from Wadim.

He didn't want to lose sight of his only friend, so rushed forwards and grabbed the other lantern from the floor. He came out of the other side of the passageway to be surprised that the large room beyond was a wide staircase, with no other exits, that just led down into the well of darkness below. His friend was halfway down the first set of steps, so Wadim hurried after him. He could see that he was carrying a wooden box under his right arm, while his left held the lantern level with his pale face.

No matter how fast Wadim hurried, the other boy kept the same pace, so he was always ten feet further down the steps than he. Wadim tried to increase his pace with loping, awkward strides, but the other boy always seemed to increase his pace at the same time, without the need to look backwards. As the staircase went on and on, Wadim gave up trying, and his steps became weary and slow. Just as he thought he would have to sit down and rest his aching legs the last turn of the staircase came into sight. A square, flat area was visible, and a single arched passageway led off to the right.

Wadim's friend, his footstep as silent as his mouth, was soon striding through the arch in the wall. The loss of the other lantern brought the brooding darkness closer around Wadim. He struggled on down the last of the steps and was very glad to be walking on a flat surface again. He felt hot from his climb down the stairs, and it seemed much warmer down below the house. He hurried under the arch, his head bobbing left and right as he sped after his friend. The entrance led directly to a passageway that split into two, both going in the same direction. Wadim could see one way was pitch black, while one had the faint glow from the other lantern. Wadim followed the light, hoping his friend would stop soon as he was breathing heavily.

It took four turns for the passageway to come to a dead end. He turned the last corner to find his friend kneeling on the floor before an arched doorway, with stone surround, that looked out of place with the panelled walls. The box was in front of the kneeling boy, the lantern to the right of it. The lid was open. Wadim moved forwards and peered down inside the box. In some silky material sat four keys that all looked the same. His friend pointed at one key and then up to the lock in the doorway. Wadim was excited to see the white key he had found was in there, but the boy was pointing to another key. This one seemed more worn than the others, and all the paint on its handle had been chipped off.

The silent boy pointed to the other key again. Wadim knelt down and picked the key up from inside the velvet lining of the box. He did not linger close to the boy, as he had a dank smell about him. Wadim didn't worry, as he had to be coaxed into the bath at the best of times. He moved over to the doorway, put the key in the lock, and turned it. A tiny click sounded out from the lock and was answered by two more, and then four, that grew louder and louder. Wadim clapped his hands over his sensitive ears as the noise grew. He began to cry as the wall of echoing noise cross-wired his brain and caused him pain.

His back hit the wall behind, and just when he thought he could stand no more, it stopped. There was only silence in the dark passageway deep under Forky's House. He moved his hands from his ears an inch and waited for the sound to return, but it didn't. He looked at his friend who was standing by the door. The loud noise that terrified Wadim had not bothered his friend at all. Maybe he was deaf? He had children in the school he attended that could not hear or speak.

The boy smiled again and pointed to the door handle. Wadim slowly lowered his hands from his ears and wiped the tears from his cheeks. He sniffed, moved over and pulled the handle open, and pushed the door in. He was a little embarrassed to cry in front of his new friend, and he felt the usual red anger rise within him. He used it this time to fight his fears. Wadim picked up the box of keys and held them under his left arm. He walked inside to find a red room, with red carpets, everything in the room was the same colour. He took the red key from the lock and placed it next to the others in the box.

Even the candles and flames were bright red. Then he saw something lying on the ground, like an old discarded red coat. He took a step towards it and lifted the lantern high so he could see what it was.

Wadim didn't notice the door to the red room being pushed nearly shut behind him by the dark-haired boy. Nor did he notice him grab a candlestick from the desk behind him, as Wadim finally saw it was a dead, red skinned man, lying on the carpet.

CHAPTER THIRTY-TWO

They could have stayed out longer, but Crina was eager to get back to the house and tell Wadim their exciting news. Her excitement rubbed off on Nick, as they took the same taxi home, at great expense to his wallet. The full moon was already above the tube station across the road, looking pale red against the blue sky.

The front door closing woke Lionel from his late afternoon slumber. He had barely made it to a yawning, sitting position, when the newly engaged couple came giggling through the open living room doorway.

"Oh, hello, you two," Lionel said, rubbing at his eyes before stretching his arms out above his head. "I must have had a quick forty winks."

"Where's Wadim?" Crina asked, putting down her new purse, and the bag of old clothes on the coffee table. She still looked like a film star, but her lipstick had been kissed off.

"Oh, he was here a second ago, I swear." Lionel looked at the red colouring pencil laying on top of the drawing pad on the coffee table where he'd last seen the boy.

"Wadim," Crina called his name as she went around the back of the sofa to see if he was playing quietly there as he often did. He wasn't there or anywhere in the living room. Crina pulled up the skirt part of her dress and hurried in the hallway.

"Jesus, Lionel, you had one job," Nick said, running his fingers through his hair.

"I'm an actor, not special needs carer I must remind you," Lionel said in a gruff voice as he got up. He followed after Nick into the hallway as Crina cried out her son's name again.

"Where is he?" Crina turned to the two men in the hallway, her joy turned into fear for her missing child.

"I'll check the garden, out back," Lionel suggested, as it gave him an excuse to get away from Crina's withering looks of concern.

"Crina, you look upstairs, and I'll take this floor." Nick grabbed her and gave a quick reassuring kiss. "He won't have gone far."

But Crina was already pulling away from him as he kissed her, holding her dress, she kicked off her new heels, and ran up the grand staircase. The sun motes were dancing in the hallway as Nick rushed through the light to the ballroom doors. He flung them open, but the large room was as empty as it ever was. When he turned to hurry to search another room he was stopped in his tracks by the hooded remnant of a monk before him. He had more substantial form than at any other time since his death but was trapped by sunlight from the windows above. Nick stayed where he was, out of the sun covered hallway. He could duck right down the corridor if he needed too, but the hook-nosed monk had him transfixed with hatred.

"Where's the boy?"

The monk did not reply. His sullen mouth opened wide with silent laughter. The monk raised a reconstituted arm and pointed a half-formed finger at the staircase. Then he slowly lowered it to the floor.

"WADIM!" Nick bellowed loudly at the monk who murdered his son in cold blood.

The sun went behind a cloud, and the monk fell apart into floating nothingness again. Nick ran to the bottom of the steps to find Crina running barefoot down them.

"I heard you shout have you found him?" she asked, breathing hard.

"No, but I know a place he might be." Nick took her hand as she reached the bottom step. "Come on, follow me." They ran around the staircase to the western corridor. When they reached the music room, the light was still on, and the secret entrance to the hidden staircase was open. Nick brought out his mobile phone, turned on the torch app, and hurried inside. He dragged the concerned Crina after him.

"What is this place where are we going?"

"It's a secret place under the stairs. There's a room at the bottom, and I think he might be there." Nick on and began to descend into the pressing darkness.

"And you think Wadim found his way down there somehow?"

"Yes, but I'm hoping that he hasn't."

Crina could hear the worry in his voice. "Is it dangerous then?"

"Just hurry, we have no time for questions we have to find our little boy."

Crina shut up and hurried on down the never-ending stairs in the black abyss. Nick took her arm and led her across the square stairwell to the two passages beyond. They rounded the last corner, heavily out of breath.

Light from a torch on the floor pointed like a lightsaber at the door in the wall ahead. Nick was relieved to see that the door wasn't closed shut as he first thought it might be. It stood an inch ajar. He hurried to get in front of Crina and gave the door a push to open it. He halted on the threshold, waiting for the door to swing fully open before venturing inside. The brown door was wide open, but only showed a solid black void beyond.

"Wadim!" Crina cried out from beside him.

Nick turned and could see the little boy was sitting on the edge of the bed. His legs were apart, and his arms were down in between them. He kept his head bowed like he had exhausted himself through prayer.

Crina moved into the room, but Nick grabbed her arm. "Wait, it might not be safe."

"He's my son," she turned and shouted into his face.

"Mama."

Both Nick and Crina stopped breathing and looked down at the small boy sitting on the edge of the bed. He looked up at them both. A little boy lost expression on his tiny features.

"Mama help me," he said again.

Crina, using inner mother's strength to get to her only child, shrugged off Nick's grip, and ran into the red room towards her son. Nick moved a step forward as he saw the little boy move to embrace his mother. Her red dress swished as she fell onto her bare knees into his loving embrace.

Nick stopped dead in his tracks.

Crina opened her mouth wide and let out such an elongated gasp of air that surely none would remain in her lungs. Then Nick saw the cause of the endless breath. The sword he had brought into the room on a couple of occasions was protruding from the middle of Crina's back. Red blood covered the blade and ran down to drip on the red dress that Nick had bought her today. Their engagement day. The boy pulled the sword from his mother and took tiny steps backwards from her. Nick rushed over to catch her as she fell sidewards onto the carpet. He cradled her on his bent knees, pulling her into his lap. Her mouth was opening and closing like a fish out of water. Her eyes were wide and filled with questions. She tried to speak, but only blood came from her throat, not words.

"Crina," he whispered, pushing a strand of her hair from her face. Her eyes bulged as she gasped for breaths that would not come. Then all the pain and clenched muscle tension of her body let go, and she went slack in his arms. He bent down and shuffled back so he could kiss her brow. Nick laid his dead fiancée's head gently on the carpet and then looked up at her son.

The red room had suddenly changed. There was more than just the scarlet glare of the red flamed candles. Flickering, silvery, ever-shifting light, glimmered and reflected off every wall and red surface.

The reason for the change in ambience was blindingly obvious.

The open brown door now shone with a light so bright and ever-changing, was flowing out from the *whatever* that lay beyond its portal. It rolled and danced. Glinting with every shade of the rainbow, but the whites, silvers, and gold rays shone the brightest. Nick watched as tendrils of the multidimensional light curled out over the edges of the door. It truly was a door to another realm.

Wadim stood facing him at the threshold of the doorway. He was a near black silhouette against the storm of bright light screaming around his body. Yet Nick could see that his right eye was blue like his mothers, while his left one had a black pupil surrounded by a glowing orange sclera. The boy dropped his matricidal weapon on the carpet and edged back closer to the dazzling light.

"Wait," Nick cried out, raising his left arm, his fingers stretching for the boy he couldn't reach.

The boy had stepped too close to the tendrils of glimmering lights. They wrapped themselves around his arms and legs, with strong caresses, and lifted him from the floor.

"Father!" the boy managed to cry out before the light pulled his body beyond this world into another. The wisps of light took the door with them and pulled it closed with a shuddering bang. The ever-increasing concussion wave hit Nick, sending him and Crina's body flying out of the red room to crash into the wall behind. The force of the hit, both winded him and turned his world black. Something hit the bridge of his nose hard with a sound of breaking cartilage. He fell sidewards onto his dead fiancée and felt no more pain for a long while.

CHAPTER THIRTY-THREE

Lionel found them an hour later. He tried to phone for an ambulance, but could not get a signal so deep underground. He had to shake his friend back into consciousness. Crina's dead body lay crumpled up half under him. Lionel knelt on the floor and wept, before handing over his pocket handkerchief so his friend could mop up the blood from under his broken nose. The door to the red room had vanished from the wall.

They cried together over her broken corpse. Lionel wanted to go back up and fetch the police, but Nick told him what had transpired, and slowly persuaded him not to. What could they do? Crina had been murdered by her own son, who was now, who-knows-where? The police would not believe them about magical rooms that appeared out of nowhere, with dead souls inside.

Lionel led the way with his torch. Nick's nose had stopped bleeding, but the front of his shirt was a mess. He reached down to pick up his dead beloved when he felt something between her arm and armpit. It was the connected four keys. He had pocketed them before Lionel looked round. He hefted Crina's light, limp body up into his arms, and stood up. He wavered for a second, and then followed the old actor out of the passages deep below the house.

They buried her behind the sheds, a reverent distance away from the head of Micheldever, already under the earth there. Lionel found a packet of Forget-Me-Not seeds in a tin in the shed and sprinkled them over the re-laid earth. Only then did they surrender to their shared grief, and their tears fell on the earth of her unmarked grave. They stayed there, comforting each other until dawn came breaking up the edges of the dark blue sky. Only then did they trudge back inside Forky's House and sat in silent loss.

CHAPTER THIRTY-FOUR

It took much longer than he anticipated for the call to come. He'd had his fake ID and Irish passport ready for over two weeks. Alina was still having regular nightmares about nuns and losing the baby. She begged him not to go. He kissed her on the lips and then had to use all his strength to pull apart her interlocking arms around his neck. He left her sobbing on the hallway of her apartment. Only by switching to his old cold killer side could he propel his legs through the threshold of her home. His body had felt like he was moving through a sea of treacle rather than air.

With a heavy heart, he got into the cab he had ordered, which took him to the airport. He flew to Germany as Stephen Carlisle. Then, using cash, paid for a single flight to Heathrow as Michael Flanagan. He posted his first fake passport at the airport back to his home address. He had no luggage. He went in only the clothes he wore. He carried the walkie-talkie in the deep inner pocket of his jacket, with a wallet full of pounds, dollars and euros.

The flight from Frankfurt touched down at eleven a.m., and he took the Piccadilly line tube into London. He headed, as instructed by the walkie-talkie, from the tube station, and across the road. He found the sniper rifle wrapped in an old, green cloth fishing rod bag. He checked the clip. He had six rounds to do the job. The Scotsman hunkered down behind a tree and took out a mobile phone he'd been sent through the post. It was pay-as-you-go and had no contacts or information on it. There was only one email with an image on it, and the briefest of instructions.

He sat with his back to the two twisted trees in the undergrowth and waited. The sound of a large jet passed overhead in the congested London skies. He felt sadness in the pit of his stomach. Not because he was leaving his wife-to-be and unborn child behind in another country. No, he felt sad because the sniper rifle felt so good in his hands again.

There was no one about, so he looked at the photo on the mobile phone. It was a picture of one Nicholas Hobbs.

CHAPTER THIRTY-FIVE

Nick had not left Forky's House for over a month until this morning. Lionel had come over every day and brought his food. Nick hardly spoke to him, and he dreaded his humanitarian visits. The old actor felt guilty for giving Nick the blue key, without which none of this tragedy would have played out. Crina would still be alive and Wadim with her. He was guilty about falling asleep and letting Wadim wander off. Lionel hated the deep hollow darkness that had spread around Nick's eyes since she had died. Yet he trudged over, all the same, his trips getting later and later, as the days had turned into weeks.

Using his mother's spare kitchen key, he let himself in. He'd bought sandwiches from the newsagents for them to share. Maybe today he could coax Nick out into the September sunshine. The hallway was empty, and so was the living room, so Lionel checked Nick's bedroom. The shutters were still closed, but the bed was empty. He checked the bathroom, the library, and the kitchen. He went out into the fresh September air and made for the gazebo. It and Crina's grave were Nick-free. Lionel walked the lengths of the east and west corridors on both floors but got no reward

He took a torch and went through the secret door in the music room to the passageways deep below. They were devoid of life too. Lionel did not stay down there long. He was puffed out by the time he made it back to the ground floor.

Nick had left the house.

CHAPTER THIRTY-SIX

Nick, in fact, wasn't that far away. He was sitting alone on a bench in the huge cemetery next door. The angel behind him seemed to be silently mocking his mood.

A small, old, Asian man, with wispy grey shoestrings of a moustache, sat down next to him. The man brought out a Tupperware full of sandwiches from an orange plastic bag. He opened the opaque lid and offered one of the triangle-cut sandwiches inside to Nick.

"So you've crawled out of your pit at last," the man said, in a crisp English accent.

"Very funny," Nick said, looking down at the dirt under his long nails.

"I hear you've lost another bride and child. Once is bad enough, twice is very careless." The Asian man drew back his Tupperware box and picked up a sandwich. He began to nibble at one end as Nick sneered, but did not reply. "Give you your due, though, this one was a real cracker, not like that first bitch you sired a son with."

"God, you are so bloody humorous," Nick shook his head and stared at the ground.

"I try my best. But you give me hours of entertainment. It's funny that you keep making the same mistakes over and over. I keep thinking one day he will learn and then I *might* let you back into my house. But no, you keep disappointing me."

"Oh, but I found the little room that you could not see into, I was good enough for that. I have seen the light through a portal unknown to you, to another place you can't even imagine. I do your dirty work and get no reward but your everlasting scorn."

Nick had risen to the bait once more.

"Yes, you found out the secrets of Four Keys House, and solved the puzzle, but you still lost the game, and you will always lose the game until you learn."

"Learn *what*?" Nick spat back, turning his head to face the other man on the bench.

"When you learn the puzzle isn't worth solving if the cost is too high," the Asian man replied. "It is in your nature, but even if you saved the mother and her child, you still would have destroyed them in the end. That is your flaw."

"So you are saying I can never win, never be happy." Nick picked at his dirty fingernails and cast his gaze to the ground.

"You could never have them, and the life you want." The man shook his head. "No."

"You wouldn't or *couldn't* allow it?"

"You could not have them."

"And why's that?" Nick sat and turned to look at the other man on the bench.

"Because you have to die for their sins, not the other way around."

"So it comes back to the same old story, you punishing me for the sins of the past."

"And of the present and the future."

"Is this our eternal struggle then? I have sons and the chance of life, and you take them away?" Nick was trembling from head to foot as his rage simmered.

"You must learn your place." The Asian man grew angry. "I am the father."

"I see...it's all about hubris now." Nick slapped the top of his knees hard. "One rule for you, and a trillion rules for everyone else. I had a son, but your worshippers murdered him. I have the chance to have a son again, and his soul is lost forever." Nick stood and walked three steps over the dried dirt path. He stopped and turned to face the bench again, tears in his eyes.

"You forget yourself and your place," the Asian man bellowed loudly. He put aside his sandwiches and stood, growing in stature.

Nick stared at the parched, cracked earth and spat on it.

"Oh, I know my place alright."

"You forget sacrifice is our creed." The other man opened his arms wide and lowered his voice. "Remember I lost a son once too."

"You let your own worshippers crucify him. You were always an unbending, proud fool." Nick raised his hand in the air, and then let it drop to his side. "I will be your undoing."

The Asian man laughed at Nick. Then a shot rang out across the deserted cemetery, and one man fell dead.

CHAPTER THIRTY-SEVEN

Donald ran out from his cover, over to the two men. One lay on the floor with a hole in his head, the other stood over him.

"Is it done now? Can I go home to my family?"

"Yes," Nick replied, standing over the dead body. He had a blank expression on his face. His father was dead. He had dreamed and plotted for this moment, but now he wasn't sure how he felt. Somewhere distant thunder rumbled, and slate grey clouds obscured the sun.

"Who was he?" Donald asked, looking at the bullet wound in the side of the man's head. No blood was flowing from the wound at all.

"He was my father, and your Lord Almighty," Nick simply replied before kicking the arm of the corpse to make sure.

"You're not making any sense," Donald said, not taking his eyes off the penetrating wound in the man's head. It seemed to him that there was a strange flickering glow from inside.

"You shall be forever exalted among the heathens my friend," Nick said and patted the man on the shoulder.

"What sort of rounds were those?" Donald ignored the other man. The man from the mobile picture. Which had the simple instructions typed underneath: *when this man raises and lowers his left arm, shoot the other person with him.*

"They were filled with the unworldly matter from a place far from my father's creation."

Donald shook his head. The younger man wasn't making any sense. He should leave, but his eyes were fixed on the flickering light coming from the wound. Soon it crept out from the hole in the Asian man's head and flowed out to cover and consume the body in its ever-changing coloured light. The thunder overhead rumbled closer and louder, and a great darkness was cast upon the Earth.

Donald staggered back from the corpse as it crumbled away into nothing before his eyes. Not even leaving a layer of dust to signify a man had died on that spot. "What the hell is going on?"

Nick laughed. "Hell is empty, and all the devils are here Donald," Nick spoke, but Donald's father's voice came out.

"What?" Donald staggered back another step, as the sky became as dark as an apocalyptic eclipse.

"I kinda tricked you into killing God. Now you have triggered the end of the world. But the funny thing is, that you poor mortals were under the impression that you had free will and a world that was yours. What you didn't grasp was this was my backyard, this was my Hell." Nick turned on his heel with a smile and began to walk back up the path to the entrance to the cemetery next to Forky's House.

Donald looked from the dusty ground to the retreating back of the man who had ordered the greatest kill in the history of mankind. He hefted the sniper rifle and aimed at Nick's retreating back. There came an awful rumble as the ground shook beneath his feet. Then the earth cracked, and Donald fell into the abyss and was consumed by fire. Nick turned and left the cemetery and made for his house.

Out of the heavens, fire rained down upon the earth, taking the pub out a with an ear-splitting explosion. The shops and the library went next, killing Margo and destroying Lionel's flat.

Nick walked on at his own pace, alone.

In the great hall of Gates's country estate, they stood in the cellar, robed in purple. Father stood next to his blind daughter and raised his hands to the ceiling in praise to his satanic deity. They who had built the house long ago, and given up so much in his service, died in the fire like everyone else.

Nick jogged up the steps of the house and was mildly surprised when the door opened. A scared Lionel peeked out at the darkness, and the fiery hell raining down on London.

"What's going on?" he quivered, holding onto the doorframe as the world quaked around them.

"The end of the world, my friend," Nick said, patting him on the shoulder, and he walked past into the dark house. He did not stop but continued on along the corridor to the music room.

"What can we do?" Lionel asked, hurrying after him.

"Not much." Nick shrugged before he opened the music room door. "Stay in the house, Lionel. It will be the last thing to go, and you might have time to get drunk before the end."

"They end of what?"

"Goodbye, my friend, it was nice knowing you." Nick kissed the old actor on the lips and left him standing in the hallway.

He entered the music room alone, heading for the secret passageway. The candles that lined the walls of the stairs flicked into life as he passed illuminating his way down into the depths of the house. The stairs were silent, and all sounds of destruction outside the house were unheard here. Nick walked, hands in pockets, calmly around the passageways to the waiting door before him. He pushed the door, and it opened without having to be unlocked.

The secret room was different now. It was split into four quarters. All the furniture was in the exact same places, but each fourth of the room was coloured: black, white, blue and red. The guardian souls stood in each section cast in the colours. Nick walked past them all towards the brown door in front of him. He took his hands from his trouser pockets. In his left palm were the four keys fused together to make the great key to unlock the door to another realm of existence.

"Nick," he heard her whisper.

He closed his eyes and put the key in the lock, trying to ignore her.

"Nick," she said it louder this time.

He exhaled and turned to see the red-skinned Crina in the slashed red dress he had bought her. "Don't worry, I'll save our son."

"But he's *my* son," she pleaded. Her arms were cast wide, and blood red tears fell from her eyes.

Nick turned and reached out to gently grab her hair and kiss her forehead. "*Our* son," he said again.

Images flashed into her mind of that room, of her worse day back in Romania, where she paid her father's debt with her flesh. She was on the rubbish-strewn floor again, lying in their filth, on a dirty mattress. Her torn clothes scattered amongst the discarded cigarettes butts they had used to burn her most tender parts. The group of leering men all cast in dark shadows apart from one. The man in the balaclava. He stepped forward into the light from the naked bulb above his head. Then did something that he didn't do on that day, he took off his mask. Underneath it was Nick's smiling face.

Crina fell to the floor of the red carpet. Misery, like a ten-ton weight keeping her used body down.

Nick turned the key and opened the door. He was instantly bathed in every shade of light possible. He took one last look at the mother of his second child and stepped through into the worlds beyond.

CHAPTER THIRTY-EIGHT

Forgotten images swirled in his brain and darkness was replaced with intense eye frying light. Forgotten images of him in a dark tavern in a drunken stupor, while Nicholas Clovis explained his vile plans to Nick's unhearing ears. Then flashes of playing dice with someone in a desert and then the howling of a jackal and the birth of his son, the Anti-Christ. Then the pain as the monk's blade stabbed his firstborn in the heart ending his life before it had really begun.

Then he felt like every atom of his being exploded.

Darkness.

Blinding light and then existence again.

Nick was worried at first that he'd gone blind. But slowly shapes came into view. He turned around, but the door was not there anymore. There would be no going back from this. White light faded into yellow, and he could see sand under his shoes.

He gazed around at his new universe and saw it was full of sand. Everywhere as far as the eye could see. The only colour in the desert was him, and a set of fresh footprints ahead of him. Footprints in the sand, where vibrant green grass grew. They led up to the rise of a sand dune and then disappeared from sight. Nick followed the footsteps. Increasing his pace to as much of a run that the shifting sand would allow. He soon crested the top of the dune, not realising he was leaving his own dirt covered footprints behind him.

The dust bowl from his every nightmare stood before him. But down from where the grassy footprints led was an oasis in the featureless sand-covered land. Trees, new and fresh, grew around a patch of grass next to a small pond of the clearest blue water Nick had ever seen. He ran down the side of the sand dune, falling twice in his haste to get to the oasis. The sand in his mouth turned to water as he ran along the floor of the bowl towards the lush greenery before him.

He ran towards the pond, where a little boy stood naked up to the waist. He turned to face his approaching father with one blue eye, from his new human mother and the orange tinted one from his original jackal mother.

ABOUT THE AUTHOR

Peter Mark May is the author of six horror novels (*Demon, Kumiho, Inheritance* [P. M. May], *Hedge End, AZ: Anno Zombie,* and *Something More Than Night*) and one novella (Dark Waters). He's had short stories published in genre Canadian & US magazines and UK & US anthologies of horror such as *Creature Feature, Watch,* the British Fantasy Society's 40th Anniversary anthology *Full Fathom Forty, Alt-Zombie, Fogbound From 5, Nightfalls, Demons & Devilry, Miseria's Chorale, The Bestiarum Vocabulum, Phobophobias, Kneeling in the Silver Light* and *Demonology* and *Tales From the Lake Volume 5.*

Website: http://petermarkmay.weebly.com/

Curious about other Crossroad Press books?
Stop by our site:
http://store.crossroadpress.com
We offer quality writing
in digital, audio, and print formats.

Enter the code FIRSTBOOK
to get 20% off your first order from our store!
Stop by today!

www.ingramcontent.com/pod-product-compliance
Lightning Source LLC
Chambersburg PA
CBHW060421180626
46817CB00007B/2602